"What, have you been warned against me?" he asked with a smile. "Didn't think I'd been in Bath long enough for that."

"I saw you at Sidney Gardens earlier today with your aunt. I don't mean to be uncivil, but Aunt Gussie said you have the reputation of being a...a reckless adventurer. It's also said you are..."

"A fortune hunter?" he supplied, seeming not at all offended. "Or have you heard the other version, the one in which I'm in Bath trying to turn my aunt up sweet, so she'll settle funds on me? You mustn't feel uncomfortable, repeating the rumors, Miss Lattimar. After all, I've been warned against you, too."

She stiffened, a feeling almost of...betrayal escaping. So her skepticism had been warranted. He hadn't helped her out of kindness, just on a whim, too devil-may-care to worry about the consequences. "I wonder, then, that you bothered to rescue me," she said, unable to keep the anger from her voice.

He halted, forcing her to look up at him. "I should think you, of all people, would understand. I dislike seeing someone branded for something only rumor alleges—me, or anyone else. A sentiment I suspect you share. I shall judge you as I find you, not for who your mother was. Everyone in Bath ought to do the same."

Author Note

Nothing in modern experience can help us fully appreciate how important having an unsullied reputation was for an unmarried Regency lady. Readers of Jane Austen may remember the despair felt by Lizzie in *Pride and Prejudice* after her sister Lydia runs away with Wickham. If a daughter shows herself immoral, society will believe the others in her family must be also.

Prudence Lattimar finds herself in a similar situation. Known as the child of one of her mother's lovers, Pru is considered disreputable before she even takes a step into society. All she wants is to marry a kind man who will settle with her in the countryside and give her the "normal" family she has always craved.

When a fresh scandal makes a debut in London impossible, Pru is taken to Bath. But not only does scandal follow her—the one man she meets who values her for herself is a reckless adventurer intending only a short stay in England.

Lieutenant Johnnie Trethwell finds Prudence to be the most unusual—and beautiful—girl he's met in his many travels, and her unfair treatment by society rouses his fighting spirit. However, friendship with an adventurer won't help her redeem her reputation—and he knows he can't give Pru the settled English home and family she craves.

But sometimes, falling in love makes you realize that what you truly need is completely different from what you thought you wanted.

I hope you'll enjoy Pru and Johnnie's journey!

JULIA JUSTISS

A Most Unsuitable Match

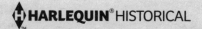

H HARLEQUIN® HISTORICAL

Recycling programs
for this product may
not exist in your area.

ISBN-13: 978-1-335-52293-1

A Most Unsuitable Match

Copyright © 2018 by Janet Justiss

Printed in U.S.A.

Julia Justiss wrote her first ideas for Nancy Drew stories in her third-grade notebook and has been writing ever since. After publishing poetry in college, she turned to novels. Her Regency historicals have won or placed in contests by the Romance Writers of America, *RT Book Reviews*, National Readers' Choice and Daphne du Maurier. She lives with her husband in Texas. For news and contests, visit juliajustiss.com.

Visit the Author Profile page
at Harlequin.com for more titles.

To Eve and Lenora

Words aren't adequate to express my gratitude for your love and support since the accident—especially when finding time to write becomes so difficult. Every time I've been about to give up in despair, you've pulled me back from the edge. I love you guys!

Prologue

London—late March 1833

'She's done it again,' Gregory Lattimar, oldest son and heir of Lord Vraux, said as he ushered his twin sisters, Temperance and Prudence, into the small salon of their Brook Street town house, where their aunt, Lady Stoneway, awaited them.

The vague foreboding she'd felt when her brother pulled Pru from happy contemplation of the latest fashions in *Godfrey's Lady's Magazine* intensified into outright alarm. 'What's happened, Gregory? Whatever it is, surely we won't have to delay our Season yet again!'

That pronouncement was met with a groan from her aunt, who came over to give Prudence a hug. 'I'm so sorry, my dear! I thought for sure we'd be able to launch you girls this spring!'

'So it's no Season for us, eh?' Temperance asked, crossing her arms as she regarded her brother grimly. 'What's the latest event to besmirch our reputations?'

'Your brother heard about it over breakfast at the

Club and summoned me for a strategy session straight away.'

'A strategy session about *what*?' Temperance cried.

'Easy, Temper,' Gregory said, putting a hand on her arm. 'I'm about to tell you.'

Though, as usual, she suppressed the emotions her more volatile twin was expressing, Pru could hardly refrain from raising her own voice. 'What happened, Gregory?'

'Farnham. Well, not being officially out, you won't have met him, but he's recently down from Oxford and followed the usual convention of appearing enamoured of our mother. He and another young admirer, Lord Hallsworthy, have been snarling at each other around her like two dogs over a choice bone. Apparently last night, with both of them well in their cups, Farnham claimed Hallsworthy had insulted Mama's virtue and challenged him to a duel. Which Hallsworthy accepted, the two of them dispensing with the usual protocol and going off at once to Hounslow Heath.'

'At night?' Temperance said incredulously. 'Besides, I thought duelling was illegal—and out of fashion.'

'There was a full moon and it is,' Gregory said. 'I don't know what got into them. The upshot was, before anyone realised what was going on, Farnham put a ball into Hallsworthy. The friends who caught up with them took Hallsworthy to a surgeon, but he isn't doing well. Farnham has fled to the Continent and, by now, the news of the duel, and over whom it was fought, is all over London.'

'Well, I say "bravo, Mama!" if she's still bewitching young men at her age,' Temperance said defiantly.

'If she only would consider how much her actions

reflect upon us!' Pru cried, beset by the familiar mix of admiration and resentment for her dazzling mother.

'To be fair, it's not her fault, Pru,' Aunt Gussie said. 'Paying court to London's longest-reigning Beauty has been a rite of passage for young men coming down from university since the Season your mama debuted. You know she does nothing to encourage them. Quite the opposite.'

'Which only intensifies their rivalry,' Gregory observed with a sigh.

'Mama *has* been trying to shield us, Pru,' Temperance added. 'Though she's certainly had offers, she hasn't taken any new lovers these last five years.' At her aunt's gasp, she snapped, 'Oh, please, Aunt Gussie, there are no innocent maidens *here*. Not after what we've seen going on in this house.'

Though her sister didn't blush, Pru felt her own cheeks heat at the reminder. They'd barely been out of leading strings when, even relegated to the nursery, they'd started noticing the parade of handsome men paying calls on their mother. They were hardly in their teens when they'd pieced together the whispers among the staff and come to understand exactly why.

'The Vraux Miscellany,' society called them. Knowing that only Gregory was truly the son of her legal father, while her brother Christopher and she and Temperance were acknowledged to be the offspring of other men.

Keenly as she felt this latest scandal, which might well delay once again her chance to find the love and family she yearned for, fairness compelled her to agree with her sister. 'I know Mama has been trying to live less…flamboyantly, just as she promised us. For all the good that's done,' she added bleakly.

'It's not her fault society conveniently forgives a *man* the errors of his past—but never a woman,' Temperance retorted.

'I haven't always agreed with her…wandering tendencies,' Aunt Gussie admitted, 'but married to my brother, I could certainly sympathise. He'd already begun to show passion only for the beautiful objects he collected before I made my come-out. I remember one morning in the breakfast room, I tripped over his latest acquisition, some sort of ceremonial sword. He rushed over when I cried out—it gave me a nasty cut! And completely ignored *me*, all his concern for whether the *sword* had been damaged!'

'If only he hadn't chosen *Mama* to add to his collections,' Temperance muttered.

'Well, that's past lamenting,' Gregory said briskly. 'We need to decide what we shall do now, which is why I asked Aunt Gussie to join us. Do you think the hubbub will die down soon enough for the girls to have their Season this year?'

Aunt Gussie shook her head. 'I received two notes from acquaintances before I'd even arisen from bed this morning, wanting to know what was truth, what rumour. With the Season beginning in just two weeks, Hallsworthy so badly injured he may hover on the cusp between life and death for some time, and Farnworth having quit England, it's likely to remain the *on dit* for months.'

'We could just brazen it out,' Temperance said. 'Really, Aunt Gussie, do you truly think we will ever escape being tainted by Mama's reputation? Since we are her blonde, blue-eyed images, we must naturally possess the same reckless, passionate character. As far as society is concerned, we're the "Scandal Sisters", and always will be.'

'I know it's unfair, child,' Aunt Augusta said, patting Temperance's arm. 'I understand your bitterness, but there's no need—yet—to give up on the goal of seeing both of you well settled—eventually. It's what your mama desires, as much as I do! Not this Season, alas. But soon.'

'That's what you've been saying for the last four years,' Pru said, trying to stave off her desolation over this new delay. 'First, you ended up having to assist at your daughter's lying-in the year we turned eighteen, then you were ill yourself the next year, then Aunt Sophia died, and last year, Christopher married Ellie. An absolute darling, whom I love dearly, but trying to overcome the infamy of your mother's reputation right after your brother marries a notorious former courtesan is clearly impossible. If we have to wait much longer, we will be too old for *any* man to wish to marry us!'

'You should rather pity the girls who did debut and marry,' Temperance told her flippantly. 'Stuck home now with a husband to please and a babe on the way.'

'Perhaps *you* would!' Prudence flung back, raw disappointment goading her out of her customary restraint. 'But having a husband who cares for me and a normal household filled with our children is all *I've* ever wished for.'

Looking contrite, Temperance gave her a hug. 'No female under Heaven is sweeter, lovelier or more deserving of a happy family. I'm sorry for speaking slightingly of your hopes. Forgive me?'

Feeling guilty—for she knew if she didn't keep such a tight control over herself, her reactions might be just as explosive as her sister's, Prudence said gruffly, 'I'm no angel. I know you were teasing. Forgive *me*, for being so tetchy.'

'If squelching the rumours is impossible, what should we do, Aunt Gussie?' Gregory asked.

'I think it would be best if I took the girls out of London for a while.'

'Not to Entremer!' Temperance cried. 'With nothing but empty moors and coal mines for miles, I'd expire of boredom in a month!'

'I should know, I was raised there,' Aunt Gussie said with a shudder. 'No, I propose taking you somewhere much more pleasant. Granted, with the Season beginning, it will be thinner of company than I'd like, but my dear friend Helena lauds its excellent shopping and the lending libraries. There will be subscription dances and musicales, as well as the activities around the Pump Room—'

'You mean *Bath*?' Temperance interrupted, looking aghast. 'Activities, yes—like assisting septuagenarians to sip the vile waters! That's almost as bad as Northumberland!'

'The city may not be as fashionable as it once was, but anything would be better than rusticating in the country,' Gregory pointed out.

'It's not as large a stage as London, to be sure. But for a lady more interested in a congenial partner than in snagging wealth and a title, it might do. At the very least, you girls would be able to mingle in society and perhaps meet some amiable gentlemen, without whispers of this affair following you everywhere. You'll gain some town bronze and if you find no one to your liking, there's still next year in London.'

'Sounds like an excellent idea,' Gregory said. 'And one that seems more likely to get my spinster sisters off my hands than inviting the censure of the *ton* this Season, as our intemperate Temper proposes.'

'But most of the *ton* hostesses know we were supposed to be presented this year,' Temperance argued. 'I don't want them to think I'm a coward—or that I'm ashamed of Mama! It's not *her* bad behaviour that precipitated this.'

'Do you want to make it *worse* for your mother?' Aunt Gussie asked sharply. 'Then, by all means, confront society and aggravate a scandal not of her making into such infamy that you can never be respectably settled!'

When Temperance looked away, her defiant words subsiding in a dull flush, she continued more gently, 'Your mama would be the first to urge you to be prudent.'

'Dear Aunt Gussie, always offering sound counsel to keep me from doing something rash,' Temperance said with a laugh, her anger disappearing as quickly as it had arisen. 'Very well, I may not attempt to breach the hostile walls of the *ton* this Season. But neither do I intend to languish in Bath. I'll stay in London— *discreetly* showing my support for Mama. Since I have no intention of ever marrying, what difference does it make to me? In the interim, if I promise to send him any treasures I uncover, perhaps I can persuade Papa to release some of the blunt he's put away for the dowry I won't need and let me go adventuring in Europe.'

'But you, darling Sis,' she said, turning back to Prudence, '*should* go to Bath. And I hope with all my heart you will find there what you are seeking.'

'You are adamant about remaining in London?' Aunt Gussie asked Temperance.

'Much as I will miss Pru, yes, I am.'

'I'd prefer if you could get Temper out of my hair, too, until this fracas dies down,' Gregory said to Aunt Gussie, ignoring the face Temperance made at him. 'But if you can at least take Prudence out of harm's way, I'll appreciate it. So the two of you will pack up and leave for Bath as soon as possible?'

'We will. And hope to find her that agreeable gentleman,' Lady Stoneway said, with a fond look at Pru.

The very possibility helping her crushed hopes revive, Prudence said, 'That would be wonderful!'

'Be careful what you wish for, dear Sis,' Temperance warned.

With the family conference ended and their aunt returning to her own home, Prudence and Temperance walked arm in arm back up to their chamber. 'Are you sure I can't coax you to come with us? We've never been apart! I shall feel so lost without you,' Pru said, the reality of being without her twin beginning to sink in with dismaying clarity.

She soothed herself with the thought that, painful as their parting would be, at the end of a sojourn in Bath might be new love and support—from a husband. And unlike the twin, who despite her protests to the contrary, must some day marry and leave her, *he* would love and support her for ever.

'I shall miss your cautious voice warning me against taking some impulsive and usually rash action,' Temper was saying, smiling at her. 'I do think it's a good idea for Aunt Gussie to take you away, though. Leave London, where, after this latest contretemps, we're bound to be pointed out and stared at wherever we go.'

Prudence groaned, the truth of that statement bringing a surge of the resentment and prickly discomfort she always felt when going out into public view. 'Thank you for the reminder. I shall avoid the modiste and finish obtaining any necessary gowns in Bath. It was bad enough last week.'

Temperance laughed caustically. 'Ah, yes, last week, at Madame Emilie's. When that whey-faced little heiress kept staring at us?'

'Very subtle, wasn't she?' Pru said, sarcasm lacing her voice. 'She could hardly wait for us to disappear behind the curtains for our fitting before asking in a horrified "whisper" that could be heard by every shopper in the establishment, "so *those* are the Scandal Sisters"!'

'If I hadn't been clad only in my chemise at that moment, I would have popped out, bowed like an opera dancer taking an encore and cried, *"Voila, c'est nous!"*'

'Whereas I would rather have left by the back door.'

'Only to sneak into the chit's bedchamber that night and strangle her in her sleep?' Temper suggested with a grin.

Pru laughed. 'The notion does appeal. Oh, Temper, I wish I could face it with humour, like you do. But it just *grates* on me like nails on a slate and all I want is to be *rid* of it! The scandal, the notoriety, the whispers behind the hands whenever we walk into a room. Oh, to become Mrs Somebody Else, wife of a well-respected man and resident of some small estate far,

far from London! Where I can stroll through a nearby village whose residents have never heard of "the Scandal Sisters", able to hold my head high and be talked about only for my…my lovely babies and my garden!'

'With a husband who dotes on you, who never tires of hugging you and kissing you and cuddling you on his knee…instead of a father who barely tolerates a handshake.'

Both girls sighed, wordlessly sharing the same bitter memory of years of trying and failing to win the affection of a man who preferred keeping them—and, to be fair, everyone else, including his wife—at a distance. Though Temper persisted in approaching Papa, Pru had given up the attempt.

'I don't expect to find the kind of radiant joy Christopher has with his Ellie,' Pru said softly. 'All I long for is a quiet gentleman who has affection for me, as a woman and his wife, not a…a relic of infamy and scandal. Who wants to create a family that treats each member with tenderness.'

'A family like we've never had,' Temper said wryly.

That observation needing no response, Pru continued, 'To a man like that, I could give all my love and devotion.'

'Then he would be the luckiest man in England!' Opening the chamber door, she waved Pru into the room. 'I shall pray that you discover in Bath the eminently respectable country gentlemen you long for. That he'll ask you to marry him, settle on his remote estate and give you a flock of beautiful children for me to spoil. Now, we'd better look through your wardrobe and see how many more gowns you'll need to commission in Bath so you can dazzle this paragon.'

Chapter One

Three weeks later, Lieutenant Lord John Trethwell, youngest son of the late Marquess of Barkley and recently returned from the 2nd (Queen's Royal) Regiment of Foot in India, limped beside his great-aunt, Lady Woodlings, down a path in Bath's Sidney Gardens. 'Ah,' he said after drawing in a deep breath, 'Bath in the spring!'

'It *is* lovely,' his aunt said as he helped her to a seat on a convenient bench. 'Though it doesn't offer quite the fleshly amusements a jaded adventurer like you might prefer,' she added, punctuating her reproof with a whack of her cane against his knee.

Surprised into a grunt, he rubbed the affected leg. 'How unsporting, to strike an injured man.'

For a moment, his aunt looked concerned. 'I didn't mean to—'

'Just teasing, Aunt Pen,' he reassured her. 'No harm done. But you malign me, assuming I mock the beauty of April in Bath. After blistering tropical heat, and jungle fevers, and pursuit by hostile natives, it is a soothing balm to return to the cool, tranquil beauty of England.'

His aunt studied his face, probably searching for the lines of pain he tried to conceal. '*Are* you recovering, Johnnie? You still have that dashed limp.'

'I'll be rid of it in good time,' he replied, hoping he spoke the truth.

'As you're going to be rid of the army? You know I hope to coax you into remaining in England, don't you?'

Johnnie shrugged, ignoring her last comment to reply, 'I'm done with the army, for sure. After seven years, I've had enough of restrictive rules not to my liking and kowtowing to some jumped-up Cit whose father paid to have him made a Company official.'

'Jumped-up Cits, eh?' His aunt chuckled. 'Blood will tell and yours is the bluest! Much as you've tried to distance yourself from your family! Not that I blame you. Idiots, most of them.'

'I never set out to distance myself,' he corrected, grinning. 'But with all his building projects, trying to make Barkley's Hundred the equal of Blenheim, Papa had virtually bankrupted the estate even before Robert inherited. With dowries for the girls—'

'And the profligate habits of your other three brothers.'

'There was left little enough for the youngest son. I didn't want to be a further drain on Robert's slender resources—then or now. Once I leave the army, I must have another way to earn my bread.'

'You know the best way to do it.'

'You'd have me to find a rich woman to marry. '

'Marrying a rich woman has been the alternative of choice for well-born but indigent younger sons for centuries—and a much safer alternative than trekking off to barter for treasure in foreign lands, as you propose to do! You might not possess a title, but your breeding can't be faulted.'

'The breeding you just disparaged?' he pointed out.

'Nothing wrong with the blood,' she flashed back. 'Just with several recent possessors of it.'

Declining to point out the lack of logic in that statement, he said, 'I happen to believe setting up a trading operation is a better route to wealth than sacrificing myself on the altar of some India nabob hoping to marry his daughter into the aristocracy. Or confirming the whispers already swirling around Bath that I'm a fortune hunter, intent on seducing a rich lady of quality. The "parson's mousetrap", they call marriage. Whereas I'd describe being tied to just one woman as more like…fitting myself for a garrotte,' he teased.

'A garrotte, indeed!' she scolded, whacking him on the arm. 'Those who disparage marrying money never seem to object when someone in their own family manages it. Since you claim to be unable to tolerate wedding an heiress, I suppose you think if you dance attendance on *me*, I'll leave you *my* fortune to invest in that trading empire?' she asked tartly.

Johnnie merely chuckled. 'If I were totty-headed enough to entertain that hope, I'd better be prepared to wait a long time! I expect you'll outlive us all. Besides, I would think your own sons stood in line before me in that regard.'

'They inherited wealth enough from Woodlings not to need mine.'

'Your grandchildren, then.'

'Both *my* boys had sense enough to marry girls with large dowries. Their brats won't need my money either.'

'In any event, I visit you—as you well know—because you're the most interesting relative I possess. You may leave that fortune to your dog, for all I care.'

'Hmmph!' his aunt said, looking pleased at his response. 'It would serve you right if I left it to some improving school for the instruction of indigent girls.'

As she spoke, the periphery of his gaze caught on a flutter of movement. Turning in that direction, he realised what he'd seen was the ripple of pale fabric against the green verge beyond the path.

Two ladies walked towards them down the central alley. He'd just begun to turn back towards his aunt when his gaze, scanning lazily upwards, landed on the faces of the ladies and stopped dead.

A bolt of pure physical attraction immobilised him, spiking his pulse, suspending breath. He'd bedazzled dark-eyed *maharanis*, beguiled matrons famed as the Diamond of their cantonment, but he didn't think he'd ever beheld a woman more breathtakingly beautiful than the one now approaching them.

Realising, if the walkers continued straight ahead rather than taking the nearby cross-path, they would soon draw too near for him to make any discreet enquiries, he bent to whisper in his aunt's ear. 'Good L—Heavens, Aunt! Who is that divine creature?'

Lady Woodlings peered down the path before straightening with a snort. 'Precisely the sort of female you need to avoid!'

Surprised by her vehemence, he gave the girl another quick glance. 'Avoid—why? I know fashions have changed since I've been away, but she doesn't look like a high flyer to me.'

'She might as well be,' Lady Woodlings retorted scornfully.

'Aunt Pen, I'm only a simple male,' Johnnie said with some exasperation. 'A clearer explanation, please.'

Sadly for a body eager to have the seductive Beauty pass more closely, but fortunately for his compulsion to find out more about her, the lady and her older companion did in fact turn on to the cross-path and proceed away from him. In partial compensation, though, he was able to stare openly at her enticingly rounded figure as she glided away, the gold curls beneath her elaborate bonnet shining brightly in the afternoon sunshine.

'Very well, Aunt Pen,' he said, once he was sure they were out of earshot. 'Who is she and why must I avoid her?'

'One of the Scandal Sisters. The twin daughters of infamous Lady Vraux.'

No more enlightened by that information, he said, 'Meaning, she was embroiled in some scandal in London? Remember, Aunt, I left university straight for the army and haven't been near the city in years.'

With considerable relish, his aunt launched into the tale of a beautiful but immoral, high-born lady who, after presenting her long-suffering husband with a son and heir, proceeded to scandalise the *ton* by blatantly flouting her many lovers, one of whom sired her second son, another giving her twin daughters. 'Why the devil Lord Vraux allowed her to name the chits Prudence and Temperance, I can't imagine! As if transgressing moral boundaries weren't enough—she must mock them, too.'

'So the daughter has shown herself as profligate as her mother?' he probed.

'Not yet. She's not even out, officially, though she must be approaching the age where most young ladies would be at their last prayers! The *on dit* was the girls were to be presented in London this Season—but then, a few weeks ago, two imbeciles just down from Oxford fought a duel over their mother. Of course, a presentation in the face of that would have been impossible. I'm surprised her aunt—that was her father's sister, Lady Stoneway, walking with her—dares to let the creature show her face, even in Bath! Though one must pity the poor woman, trying to find husbands for such a pair. It won't be easy, their fat dowries notwithstanding!'

'But you know nothing to the detriment of the daughter?'

'How could I, when she's not out yet?'

'Precisely my point, Aunt,' Johnnie said drily.

'Never you mind, she'll embroil herself in some scandal soon enough. As I've been saying, blood will tell. And you may get that look out of your eye, Johnnie Trethwell!'

'What look, Aunt?'

'The look of a hound who's just scented a fox! Why is it that, whenever one tries to warn some rascal with more energy than sense to steer clear of danger, he's immediately compelled to charge after it?'

'Probably because he's a rascal,' Johnnie replied with a grin. 'Come along now, Aunt Pen. Introduce me.'

His aunt drew back, a horrified expression on her face. 'I will never! I know I've been urging you to marry an heiress, but the poor looby who marries *that* girl? He may be able to spend her money, but he'll never stop worrying over who he'll find in her bed.'

'A pity. I shall have to contrive some other way to make her acquaintance.'

'Mark my words, John Stewart William Trethwell,' his aunt said indignantly. 'Take up with that creature and you'll never see a penny of *my* money!'

Johnnie leaned down to kiss his aunt's hand. 'There's nothing for it, then,' he said as he straightened. 'You'll have to leave it to the dog.'

With a hint of a limp, he set off down the pathway, determined to wangle an introduction to the divine Miss Lattimar.

Keeping a discreet distance, he trailed the young lady and her aunt as they left the gardens and proceeded towards the Pump Room. Once there, he was able to station himself across the room from her, where he could observe her without his scrutiny being obvious.

Her beauty certainly did not pale upon closer examination. Eyes of the deepest cerulean blue set in an oval face graced with flawless porcelain skin, full, apricot lips, those glorious golden curls and a figure that approached the voluptuous… He'd never seen a lady so breathtaking. But having seen—and possessed—a great number of ladies, as he observed her behaviour, his scepticism about the validity of his great-aunt's claims about her character increased.

It wasn't just the ethereal beauty of her face, which brought to mind the image of angels singing in heavenly chorus. There was a sweet gentleness and deference in her manner towards the lady who'd been identified as her aunt—and a wary caution when they were approached by anyone else. The blush that tinged her cheeks and the slight stiffness in her manner when a gentleman stopped to greet them—even the old retired soldiers there to take the waters—was so at variance to the sort of flagrantly seductive behaviour of which her mother was accused, he couldn't believe she was cut from the same cloth.

Unless she were the best actress in the history of the English stage, he concluded that she was exactly what she appeared to be: a beautiful, well-bred, pretty-behaved virgin.

Not, to be frank, the type of female with whom he had previously had any desire to further an acquaintance. But something about the unfairness of having this woman, who in his observation was exactly the lady she purported to be, accused and convicted virtually sight unseen of being a wanton, even by someone normally as non-judgemental as his great-aunt, roused his fighting spirit. And when a crony of his aunt's, one of the old *beldames* who ruled Bath society, gave her an obvious snub when her chaperon attempted to call the lady over, he found himself on his feet before he knew what he intended.

Limping quickly over, he seized the *beldame*'s hand before she could walk away. 'Lady Arbuthnot, what a pleasure to see you again and looking so fine!' he said, bowing. 'That's a charming bonnet!'

Pinking with pleasure, the lady replied, 'I'd heard you were visiting Lady Woodlings, Lieutenant Trethwell! Welcome back to England. What a relief it must be to be home again! I do hope you are making a good recovery from your injury.'

'How could I not, back in the salubrious climate and genteel company of my home country? Speaking of that—' Leaving a hand on her arm, he subtly steered her around. 'Would you do the honour of introducing me to these charming ladies?'

Too late, the woman realised that Johnnie had manoeuvred her into facing the women she'd just attempted to cut. The charm of the smile he fixed on her at odds with the tension in his gut, he waited to see whether the embarrassment of making a scene by refusing his request would outweigh her righteous indignation at having to acknowledge a girl of whom she disapproved.

Deciding to throw his last weapon into the fray, he said *sotto voce*, 'If you could do so at once, ma'am? Standing's not good for my bad leg.'

Apparently, that was enough to tip the balance. 'I suppose I can't refuse the request of one of his Majesty's brave soldiers,' she said with ill grace. 'Lady Stoneway, a pleasure to see you in Bath. May I present to you Lieutenant Lord John Trethwell, the great-nephew of my good friend Lady Woodlings and brother to the new Marquess of Barkley?'

The Beauty was even more beautiful at close range, Johnnie thought, everything masculine in him leaping to the alert. Though *she* stood serenely unmoved while the introductions were made, the flush on Lady Stoneway's cheek and that lady's tremulous smile showed at least her aunt recognised the significance of his intervention. 'Delighted to make the acquaintance of one of our brave soldiers, Lady Arbuthnot,' she replied. 'As is my niece, Miss Lattimar. Aren't you, my dear?'

He'd thought her shy, but the Beauty who dipped

him a graceful curtsy was quietly self-contained, he thought, rather than nervous or uncertain. 'Almost past her last prayers,' his aunt had described her. Though a female possessing such youthful beauty could never be considered a spinster, she was no blushing ingénue, even if she hadn't been formally presented. And small wonder she was self-possessed, if ever since she'd budded into womanhood, she'd been facing down innuendo that equated her to her infamous mother.

'A pleasure to meet you, Lieutenant.'

Her voice was as lovely as her face. He'd intended only to force Lady Arbuthnot to recognise her and then remove himself—not having, despite his aunt's urging, any interest in trying to entice a wealthy young female to wed him. But he found he simply couldn't walk away.

Instead, he held out his hand. 'With your permission, Lady Stoneway, may I make a turn about the room with your niece?' And before her chaperon had a chance to reply, he clapped a hand on Miss Lattimar's arm and bore her off.

Chapter Two

Not sure whether to be amused or indignant, Prudence obliquely studied her escort from the corner of her eye as she walked beside him. 'Was that an introduction, or a kidnapping?'

'You really couldn't refuse to stroll with me. Not after the signal service I just performed.'

He had her there. Truly, she wasn't sure what to make of him.

The image of a pirate had flashed through her mind when she'd first observed him in Sidney Gardens, leaning his tall, raw-boned frame down to murmur in his aunt's ear, dark golden hair curling over the collar of his regimentals. And the gaze he'd given her! Admiration and interest shining in grey-green eyes with a look so penetrating, it seemed he was trying to see right into her soul.

She felt another stir of…something, in the pit of her stomach, just recalling it.

Viewed up close, his lean, tanned face was even more compelling, with its high cheekbones, thin, blunt mouth, purposeful nose and arresting eyes. His regimentals hung rather loosely on him, as if he'd been ill. A fact his slight limp and Aunt Gussie had confirmed, when her aunt, alas, had steered them on to a side path back at the Sidney Gardens, warning Pru she should avoid this youngest son of a notoriously rakehell family.

Rakehell or not, he'd boldly coerced that disapproving matron into recognising her. A move that, had it failed, would have embarrassed him as much as her. Was he compassionate, clever—or just reckless, indifferent whether the gamble would work or not? Uncaring, if it failed, that he had brought humiliating and unwelcome attention to her?

But it *had* worked and would give a definite push to her campaign for acceptance.

'In fairness, I do owe you thanks,' she acknowledged at last. 'Lady Stoneway's credit and that of her friend Mrs Marsden are sufficient that most of Bath society deigns to receive me, but there have been… recalcitrants, Lady Arbuthnot chief among them.' She laughed. 'Now that you've so cleverly manoeuvred her into recognising me, I can breathe a sigh of relief. Although, ungrateful as it may seem, I'm afraid I can't afford to show my thanks by associating with you once this stroll is concluded.'

'What, have you been warned against me?' he asked with a smile. 'Didn't think I'd been in Bath long enough for that.'

'I saw you at Sidney Gardens earlier today with your aunt. I don't mean to be uncivil, but Aunt Gussie said you have the reputation of being a…a reckless adventurer. And with it presumed that you're about to leave the army, it's also said you are…' She hesitated, her own experience with rumour and innuendo making her loath to repeat further ill of him without knowing the truth.

'A fortune hunter?' he supplied, seeming not at all offended. 'Or have you heard the other version, the one in which I'm in Bath trying to turn my aunt up sweet, so she'll settle funds on me? You mustn't feel uncomfortable, repeating the rumours, Miss Lattimar. After all, I've been warned against you, too.'

She stiffened, a feeling almost of…betrayal escaping. So her scepticism had been warranted. He hadn't helped her out of kindness, just on a whim, too devilmay-care to worry about the consequences. 'I wonder then that you bothered to rescue me,' she said, unable to keep the anger from her voice.

He halted, forcing her to look up at him. 'I should think you, of all people, would understand. I dislike seeing someone branded for something only rumour alleges—me, or anyone else. A sentiment I suspect you share. I shall judge you as I find you, not for who your mother was. Everyone in Bath ought to do the same.'

So he *had* acted out of compassion. Anger faded, replaced by chagrin that such a gesture had been necessary—and that she'd initially judged him more harshly than he had her. Following on that was something else more unexpected—a deep sense of…kinship at his empathy. As if they understood each other.

She had no business feeling either chagrin or connection for a penniless soldier of dubious reputation. Calling on years of practice, she suppressed the volatile emotions before they could show on her face.

She'd be wise to escape the company of a man who had, in the space of a few moments, called up feelings strong enough to compromise the tranquil façade she must present to the world. And whose escort would do nothing to further her aim of attracting an eminently respectable man to marry.

Once she was sure her voice wouldn't tremble, she said, 'Much as I honour you for those sentiments, you must realise that with *my* reputation, I can't afford to be seen on easy terms with a man usually regarded as a careless adventurer.' She gave him a deprecating smile. 'The fortune-hunter part is less of a problem, since it's widely believed that only my large dowry would ever induce a man to risk marrying me.'

'Then he would be a very great fool.'

Surprised, she lifted her gaze back up to those grey-green eyes—and was mesmerised. Something flashed between them, some wordless connection accompanied by an attraction as fiery as it was unexpected. Her stomach swooped, her breathing grew unsteady and she could almost feel his arm burning her fingertips through the layers of her gloves and his sleeve. A sudden, inexplicable desire filled her to move closer, feel his arms around her, his lips…

With a start, she looked away, ending the fraught moment. Merciful heavens, what had come over her? *This man is even more dangerous than I thought.*

Jerking her hand free, she said, 'I had best return to my aunt.'

He caught up to her in a step. 'At least, let me walk with you. Otherwise, it will be said that you found my conversation so improper, you felt it necessary to abandon me in the middle of the Pump Room. Which will do *my* reputation no good.'

'Very well,' she said, not looking at him—and very

careful not to take his arm. 'But as I already told you, I won't be able to walk with you again.'

'Do you always do what propriety dictates?' he asked.

She looked at him then. 'I haven't a choice,' she said bleakly.

'We always have a choice, Miss Lattimar. I'll say "goodbye", not "farewell",' he murmured as they reached her aunt. 'Lady Stoneway, Miss Lattimar, a pleasure,' he said more loudly, bowing as he turned her over to her chaperon.

And then left them. She couldn't help watching as, his soldier's bearing erect despite his injury, he limped away across the room.

Her aunt's fan tapping at her wrist recalled her attention. 'That was handsomely done,' she said, inclining her head towards the departing soldier. 'I hope you thanked him as you walked with him, because you mustn't do so again. It would do your chances no good for you to become more closely acquainted.' Aunt Gussie sighed. 'A shame, for he is a handsome devil, isn't he?'

'Is he a womaniser? Or is his reputation just rumour?' *As mine is.*

'His reputation is more that of an adventurer. He went out to join the army in India right after university. Not that he had much choice, with the family already done up and no source of income for him here in England. Got himself wounded in some clash with the natives. His oldest brother inherited while he was away—a mountain of debt. With three other brothers who never met a lightskirt they didn't try to seduce, a horse they wouldn't wager on, or a Captain Sharp they didn't try—and fail—to best in a game of chance, it's no wonder he stayed away. Or is considering wedding himself to a fortune, if he's decided his wandering days are done. His pedigree is elevated enough that, despite his lack of funds, he might very well accomplish that—though he hasn't thus far shown any interest in doing so.'

'Has *he* never met a lightskirt he didn't try to seduce, a horse he wouldn't wager on, or a Captain Sharp he didn't want to best?'

'Whether he's as profligate as his brothers, no one knows. As I said, he's been away from England practically since he was a schoolboy. Another rumour claims that he has no wish to marry and is hanging about Lady Woodlings's skirts instead, hoping she'll leave *her* money to him. That one may be more credible, given the tittle-tattle about him cutting a swathe through the faster matrons at the cantonments in India. There are even rumours of a Eurasian paramour—a *maharani*, if I recall correctly.'

With her upbringing, Pru was hardly scandalised. Instead, she realised ruefully, she felt a little *envious*, that a man could go anywhere in the world and do anything he wanted. While she had to watch every word she said and every action she took.

His reputation as an adventurer might make him unsuitable husband material for *her*—but it certainly enhanced his fascination.

'People love to gossip about the strange and foreign.'

Aunt Gussie chuckled. 'When they aren't gossiping about the present and familiar! In any event, I doubt he's lived as a saint—not a man adventurous enough to leave hearth and kin at such an early age with scarcely a penny to his name and make his way in a continent halfway around the world.'

What would it be like to have such adventures? Pru wondered. To boldly go wherever the whim took you, pit your wits and courage against whatever obstacles you encountered?

Something she would never discover, she thought wistfully. She'd count herself fortunate to land a respectable husband and settle in a quiet, conventional village.

Suppressing the envy as she did every other disturbing emotion, she said, 'With his birth and that handsome countenance, I doubt it would take him long to charm some susceptible lady of fortune into marrying him. Charming his aunt, I'm not so sure.'

'I'm sure of neither, despite that handsome face. He'd do better to cozen up to a rich widow. Although, with his lineage, he'd be considered a good catch by most society families, the highest sticklers might not favour having a man with an adventurer's reputation marry their daughter.' Her aunt gave her a look. 'A young lady of...*fragile* reputation should never let an adventurer approach her at all.'

'You needn't preach, Aunt Gussie. I understand my limitations quite well.' Even if she had to squelch a ridiculous little pang of loss at the idea of never speaking again to the intriguing Lieutenant Trethwell. Never being able to coax him to tell her about his adventures in lands she and Temper had only read about in travel journals and memoirs—what a Hindustani village really looked like, what it was like to hunt a tiger, what sort of jewels a *maharani* wore.

Even if her fortune interested him, she couldn't redeem her reputation by marrying a man almost as infamous as she was. Those few heated glances, that unexpected rush of attraction, were all she'd ever have of him.

What they wanted for their futures was completely different.

She tried to picture him in civilian dress in some small country manor, talking about crops and dandling a baby on his knee, and laughed out loud.

Impossible!

As was any foolish desire for more of his company. She needed to keep her mind fixed on her goal: to marry a man with a reputation impeccable enough to rehabilitate her own, live with him and raise their children in a quiet village, creating a warm, happy family far away from the gossip and casual cruelty of society. She should lose no time scouring Bath for such a man—and then charming him into marrying her.

Feeling somehow dispirited, despite that firm conviction, she said, 'Shall we return to the Circus, Aunt Gussie?'

'Perhaps we shall. I am feeling a bit weary after all our walking.'

But as she took her aunt's arm to lead her to reclaim their cloaks, Lady Stoneway suddenly halted. 'Not quite yet, my dear! There's someone over there I should very much like you to meet.'

The tone of her aunt's voice could only mean the 'someone' was an eligible young man. A spurt of excitement pulling her from her melancholy, hoping the brisk walk in the gardens that had put roses in her cheeks hadn't disordered her curls too much, Pru clutched her aunt's arm more tightly and allowed herself to be led to the opposite side of the floor.

'Lady Wentworth, Mrs Dalwoody! How nice to see you both!'

The two ladies turned…their movement then copied by the tall man who stood beside them and Pru caught her breath.

She needed no introduction to know that this swoonworthy gentleman was as wealthy and nobly born as he was handsome. He wore his exquisitely tailored clothing with the unconscious sense of superiority found only in those with old money and important connections.

Or at least, he *appeared* wealthy. The distinguished family name, she could count on. The two society matrons her aunt had just called out would never have allowed a *nouveau-riche* Cit with social aspirations in their midst. And no man of lesser breeding would emanate such an aura of self-confidence, as if both accustomed to and taking for granted the notice he attracted.

For in truth, she realised, hers weren't the only eyes focused on him. He was the object of the interested gaze of every female in the vicinity—and most of the gentlemen.

'Lady Stoneway, I'd heard you were visiting Bath,' Lady Wentworth said warmly, giving her aunt—a friend of long-standing, Pru knew—a hug. 'With your charming niece, too!'

'Augusta, how good to see you again,' Mrs Dalwoody said. 'And, my dear, how lovely you've grown! Already budding fair to become a Beauty last time I met you, though I'm sure you don't remember. You couldn't have been more than fourteen, that summer I visited dear Augusta at Chemberton Park.'

With an amused smile, the young man cleared his throat. 'Please, ladies, in your enthusiasm for greeting one another, you've quite left me out! Won't you introduce me to these charming newcomers?'

'How impolite of me!' Lady Wentworth exclaimed. 'Lady Stoneway, Miss Lattimar, may I present Lord Halden Fitzroy-Price, youngest son of my good friend, the Duchess of Maidstone? Newly come down from university, and waiting to be appointed to an ecclesiastical post!'

He made them a bow as impeccably tailored as his coat—which was cut in the latest style, tightly nipped in at the waist with flaring tails. 'Ladies, honoured to make your acquaintance.'

The glance he gave them was politely brief—until, to Pru's gratification, it returned to linger on her. 'Miss Lattimar, Mrs Dalwoody is quite right. You are an Incomparable! Why have I not encountered you in London? I believe my friends must have been deliberately keeping you from me, to hoard this treasure for themselves!'

Pru knew her cheeks must be pinking at his gallantry, but she replied calmly, 'You must not think so slightingly of your friends, Lord Halden. I've not yet been presented in London.'

'Ah, that explains it, for I should never have forgotten so enchanting a face. Won't you stroll with me, so we might repair Fortune's lapse?'

Still a little dazed by his magnificence, at her aunt's encouraging nod, Pru placed her hand on his sleeve. 'You are newly come from university, you said. Which one?'

'Cambridge. I'm not the most downy of scholars,' he acknowledged with a deprecating glance designed to be disarming, 'but I did well enough that, as Lady Wentworth said, my cousin, the Earl of Riding, has promised me one of the livings in his gift.'

'Younger sons must make their own way,' she acknowledged, firmly yanking her thoughts away from another more scandalous and all-too-attractive younger son who'd been making his own way in the world. 'You had no taste for the army, I take it.'

He grimaced. 'With the wars ended, there'd be no way to distinguish oneself by bravery, and who would want to be posted in some colonial backwater, enduring the heat of India, or the storms and humidity of the Indies? No, I fear I'm just a solid Englishman, perfectly content to never leave these shores.'

She curbed the impulse to reply that she would love to explore beyond England's shores. And squelched the whisper of scepticism that said he was telling her what he thought she'd prefer to hear.

Why wouldn't he? He'd probably been raised from his nurse's knee to make himself agreeable in company.

Instead, she smiled and said, 'Why would a true Englishman want to be anywhere else?'

'My sentiments exactly.'

'A political career didn't interest you, either?'

He wrinkled his nose in distaste. 'Pandering to a lot of rabble in a clutch of grubby villages to win yourself a seat in Parliament? Decidedly not. And as for the government—well, a career in the diplomatic service is likely to land you at some point in the heat of India or the humidity and storms of the tropics! I'll keep my feet firmly planted in English soil. What about you? Testing your wings in the placid pool of Bath before venturing into the treacherous waters of London?'

'Something like that.' Knowing there could never be any successful union without complete honesty, she added, 'If you know anything of my…family situation, you would know that being in Bath is…more suitable now.'

He frowned and her heart sank. Rather than honestly acknowledging her circumstances, if he truly was unaware of them, had she blundered into making him suspicious that she was not as blameless a young maiden as she appeared before they'd hardly begun to get acquainted?

Then his face cleared and he smiled. 'I suppose we all have skeletons in the cupboard. Let's speak of something more pleasant. I take it from the ladies' greetings that you are only recently arrived. Has your aunt subscribed you to the balls at the Assembly Rooms? Quite refined, although of course nothing to rival London.'

'I believe she has.'

'Excellent. I shall count upon the pleasure of leading you into a dance at the next cotillion ball, then.'

The sound of boisterous voices ahead drew their attention. They both looked over to see a group of soldiers entering, one of whom, scanning the room, spotted them and gave a wave. 'Fitzroy-Price, old fellow,' he cried, leading the group over. 'Just knew there had to be someone among all these octogenarians with red blood in his veins.'

'And the prettiest girl in the room on his arm,' one of his companions observed.

'Well, don't just stand there!' the first one said. 'Introduce us!'

'I'm not sure your chaperon would thank me for making these rascals known to you,' Lord Halden said, looking uncertainly at the newcomers. But after several raised their voices, protesting his unfairness, he capitulated. 'Miss Lattimar, may I present Lieutenant Lord Chalmondy Dawson, a friend from childhood, and Lieutenants Trevor Broadmere and Austen Truro, whom I know from university. One could hardly find a more capital group of fellows—for rousting about. But how do you come to be here?'

While Dawson explained the unit containing the former college mates had set up an encampment to conduct training exercises west of the city, and had come into town in search of some jollity, Pru's eye was caught by a moving flash of scarlet as another soldier entered the Pump Room. He, too, looked around and then beckoned for a uniformed man already in the room to come join him.

Lieutenant Johnnie Trethwell.

After a short exchange, the newcomer plucked Trethwell by the sleeve and led him towards their group.

Pru drew in a sharp breath. Would Trethwell greet her by name—revealing she was already acquainted with just the sort of experienced adventurer society would assume a girl of scandalous reputation would seek out, reinforcing the image she was trying so hard to dispel?

While she waited, almost dizzy with anxiety, looking away as the two men approached, another soldier called out to the approaching men, greetings and genial insults being exchanged after the newcomers arrived.

Even though she'd been deliberately ignoring him, the wave of awareness Trethwell generated when he grew near telegraphed his presence.

While she struggled with that, Trethwell's companion said, 'Lord Halden! Heard you'd landed here after bouncing out of Cambridge. *Persona non grata* with the *pater* in London now, are you?' he added with a laugh—which her escort acknowledged with a thin smile.

'Lieutenant Markingham, Miss Lattimar,' Lord Halden said. 'Always did have an acid tongue. And…' He paused, his eyes scanning the Lieutenant.

'You're not acquainted with Trethwell?' Markingham asked.

'Trethwell?' Lord Halden repeated—while the adventurer, whose amused expression, after a glance at her face, faded to a mask of politeness, stood by silently. 'Sounds familiar. Ah, yes! Isn't that the family name of the Marquess of Barkley?'

'It is,' Trethwell replied.

'Then I was at Cambridge with your brother, James. Lord Halden Fitzroy-Price,' he said, according the soldier the slightest of bows. 'You are the scapegrace youngest brother who ended up in the army, I take it?'

Did Pru see or only imagine the flicker of anger in Trethwell's eyes before his lips quirked in amusement? 'At your service,' he drawled, returning a much more elaborate bow.

'I sincerely hope not,' Lord Halden said. 'Miss Lattimar, if I may escort you back to your aunt? I fear she would consider these rowdy comrades less than suitable companions for an innocent young lady.'

Ignoring the boos and laughter his dismissive comment created, the Duke's son clasped her arm and led her off.

'Sorry to be so presumptuous, Miss Lattimar,' he said. 'Most of that group were questionable enough. But your aunt would likely chastise me soundly were she to learn that I'd had the bad judgement to introduce you to a Trethwell. With the Lieutenant's eldest brother holding so elevated a title, the family is still received, even though rumour says their estate is mortgaged to the hilt. But the younger brothers are penniless rakes to a man, with the Lieutenant reputed to be the most infamous of the lot.'

On the one hand, as a member of an infamous family herself, Pru could sympathise with the anger she glimpsed beneath Trethwell's mocking tone and exaggerated bow. She knew all too well what it was like to be tarred with the same brush for a relative's transgressions. On the other, she could hardly fault Lord Halden for trying to protect her reputation.

Would he be so concerned, once he learned about her circumstances? Or would he conclude that she no longer deserved such consideration?

She hoped he would end up being as fair as Lieutenant Trethwell. She didn't yet know enough about Lord Halden's character to accurately judge whether or not they would suit. But if he should decide to pursue her, she couldn't fail to recognise that he didn't just fulfil, but wildly exceeded, every requirement on her list.

He wasn't only a respectable gentleman, but one of high degree, from an ancient family.

He wasn't going to pursue a career in the rough and tumble of politics, which would require residing for months in the gossip hotbed of London, or interested in the army, which would take him from home for months or years at a time. No, he, like many a younger son, appeared to be destined for the church.

Waiting to receive an appointment, probably in some charming village far removed from the stench and bustle of the capital. Where as part of his living, he'd receive a fine manor house, doubtless with a large garden and enough income from grand and lesser tithes to employ a small staff of servants and live a comfortable life.

What more effective way to polish a tarnished reputation to gleaming brightness than to become a clergyman's wife? Making rounds of the parish, calling on the sick, taking care of the lost and needy, and performing other good works?

Of course, it was a very large leap from a simple introduction and a man's far-too-common admiration for her pretty face to mutual esteem, love and marriage.

But he *had* liked her pretty face. She intended to use that attraction to lure him into getting to know her better.

A vicar's wife, respected, honoured and beloved by the community, she thought again, a glow warming her heart. For the first time since hearing of her mother's latest scandal, Pru began to hope she might free herself from the shackles of her past after all.

Chapter Three

Two days later, Prudence Lattimar strolled with her aunt through Sidney Gardens in the pleasant morning sunshine. Though a few of the highest sticklers refused to receive her, Lady Stoneway and her friend Mrs Marsden had done their work well. By now, she'd been presented to pretty much everyone currently residing in Bath with any pretentions to gentility.

Unfortunately, her sister's dismissive remark about the calibre of the resident bachelors had been all too correct. Even Aunt Gussie had admitted herself rather disappointed at how thin on the ground eligible bachelors were, comparing the current landscape unfavourably with what the city had been like thirty years ago, when she'd been a single young miss.

'You could find almost as many eligible *partis* walking in the gardens here as you might find strolling in Hyde Park,' Aunt Gussie murmured, shaking her head as they passed yet another old gentleman being wheeled around in a chair. 'There were, to be sure, a contingent of the elderly and infirm come to drink the waters, but a large number of the Upper Ten Thousand also chose to spend the Season here! Well, we shall just have to do the best we can with what's available.'

'Speaking of which,' Pru replied, her voice lowered to a murmur, 'isn't that Lord Halden, walking with the older woman over there?'

'It is indeed!' Aunt Gussie said, her face brightening. 'That's his mother's cousin, Lady Isabelle Dudley. Keeps a house here as well as in London, generally residing at one or the other for most of the year. Apparently she doesn't much like the country, even though her husband's estate, Cliffacres, reputedly rivals Blenheim Palace. An earl's daughter who married a commoner, but one from an old and fabulously wealthy family, it's said she makes all her extended family dance to her tune.'

Pru's hopes in Lord Halden's direction took a plunge. Just what she needed—someone else who would probably dismiss her without a glance because of her mother. 'A high stickler?'

Aunt Gussie chuckled. 'No, just a tyrant. She caused her share of *on dits* in her day! A Beauty who had half the men of the *ton* dangling after her before she settled on Dudley.'

Prudence cut a covert glance towards the woman, noting the high cheekbones and tall, elegant figure that testified to how lovely Lady Isabelle must have been in her prime. She looked exactly as Aunt Gussie had described her: rich, handsome—and reigning regally over her family.

'Reformed sinners are usually more disapproving than most of those they consider to have fallen off the straight and narrow,' Pru observed.

'Perhaps. But it's also said her primary qualification when evaluating possible wives for "her boys" is fortune,' Aunt Gussie said. 'Shall we go greet them, my dear? If Lady Isabelle is determined to blight your chances with the most attractive marriage prospect currently in Bath, better to discover that early rather than late, so we may shift our focus elsewhere.'

The image of a certain tawny-haired lieutenant flashed into her head before she dismissed it. Even with Lord Halden eliminated from consideration, the globe-trekking Johnnie Trethwell wouldn't make her list of desirable prospects. Better to concentrate her efforts on the sort of respectable country gentlemen she sought.

'True enough.' Bracing herself for what might be a humiliating set-down, Pru laid her hand on her aunt's arm, summoned a smile, and prepared to brave the lion.

'Lady Isabelle, Lord Halden, good morning,' Aunt Gussie said as they caught up to the couple. After exchanging bows and curtsies, Aunt Gussie continued, 'Lady Isabelle, may I present to you my niece, Miss Prudence Lattimar?'

After her scanning her so thoroughly, Pru felt like a prize cow whose worth was being assessed by an auctioneer, the older woman gave her a nod. 'Miss Lattimar. My young cousin, Lord Halden, was just telling me how he'd met you in the Pump Room yesterday, and been charmed. Now I see why.'

Pru exhaled a shaky breath. Though Lady Isabelle most assuredly knew her history, evidently she'd passed muster anyway. Even better, Lord Halden's relation would have fully acquainted him with her circumstances. If he knew them, and still found her 'charming', the biggest obstacle to developing a relationship with him had just been hurdled.

For perhaps the first time in her life, she silently thanked her father for being such a careful curator of his vast wealth.

'You've just come from London, haven't you?' Lady Isabelle said. 'Walk with me, Lady Stoneway. You can acquaint me with all the latest happenings while these young people become better acquainted.'

That was so bald, Prudence had a hard time not blushing. The auctioneer, turning the prime merchandise over to the potential buyer. Dutifully taking the arm Lord Halden offered, she tried to settle her nerves.

Once they were a short distance down the pathway, she said, 'I hope you don't feel coerced into escorting me.'

The Duke's son laughed. 'My cousin isn't very subtle, is she? Completely accustomed to getting her own way, too, so there's little use trying to resist her. However, I don't need any coercion to walk with the most beautiful lady in Bath.'

Gratified, she smiled. 'You are very kind. I understand Lady Isabelle has a house here. Are you staying with her?'

'No. Not that she wouldn't have me,' he added. After that curious statement, he continued, 'It would be rather…restricting to live under the roof of someone bound to observe every detail of your comings and goings. A man needs a little freedom, after all.'

Prudence suppressed another pang of envy. If he considered living in his cousin's house chafing, he should try being an unmarried young woman of suspect character, whose every word and movement were scrutinised. Trying to summon up some sympathy, she said, 'Yes, a young man should be able to stay out late playing a hand of cards or finishing a fine ale, without having someone waiting on him, watching a clock.'

'Exactly!' he exclaimed, looking on her with approval. 'I'm so glad you're not one of those missish girls, who thinks I should stay at home with my cousin, holding her yarn while she knits, or something equally rubbishy.'

He stiffened when Pru, after trying to suppress a giggle, finally laughed. 'Sorry, I simply can't envision you dutifully hefting a skein of yarn! Does she knit?'

Relaxing, Lord Halden grinned. 'Heavens, I don't know. If she does, the stitches had better do what she tells them.'

Prudence shook her head. 'Alas, mine never do.'

'Not a needlewoman?'

A potential clergyman's wife would be expected to knit and sew for the unfortunate, she realised in a flash. 'I confess I'm not the most talented, but I am committed to doing better.' She bit her tongue to avoid adding, *Despite the fact that I detest needlework and would much prefer to be outside, riding or mucking about in the garden.*

'What amusements do you favour?' she asked instead, preferring to bring the focus back to him and avoid any potentially damaging questions about her other interests—or her *too* interesting, scandalous family.

'Besides drinking and cards?' he riposted, still smiling. 'I'm quite enthusiastic about horseflesh. There's nothing finer than a prime beast in full gallop, outstripping all the others on some track! Or on the hunting field. I generally spend the entire hunting season following one or another of the best hunts. Lady Isabelle rents a box at Melton Mowbray, and we get to the Belvoir as well.'

'You must be a capital rider, then.'

'Oh, yes. Sat my first pony when I was only three. Evaluate and purchase all my own mounts, too. Wouldn't leave so important a task to some groom!'

'Have you acquired any new horses lately?'

That simple question was enough to set him off on an enthusiastic recital of the merits and fine points of the perfectly matched pair of blacks he'd just purchased for his new high-perch phaeton, several hunters he was currently training for the upcoming season, and the flashy, high-stepping chestnut he kept for riding in Hyde Park.

Her contributions to the conversation limited to an occasional 'Oh, my!' or 'How excellent!' they'd made almost a complete circuit of the main pathway before he paused for breath.

'I dare say, it's capital to discover a young lady who appreciates horseflesh,' he said at last, giving her hand a hearty squeeze.

Before she could think of an appropriate response that wouldn't set him off again, the group of soldiers they'd seen in the Pump Room the day she met him rounded a corner.

'Lord Halden, well met!' Lieutenant Lord Chalmondy cried. 'And Miss Lattimar. How lovely you look.'

After giving Pru an inspection that lingered on her bosom so long she felt her face colouring, he murmured to his companions, 'What a hot little charmer she is, eh, boys?'

A flash of anger deepened the heat. Evidently Lord Chalmondy thought that, in the open air of the park, surrounded by his companions, he could get away with a crude remark he would never have chanced having overheard within the proper confines of the Pump Room.

Either not hearing or not realising how insulting the comment was, Lord Halden said, 'With this pack of half-wits about you, no wonder you were looking for some clever company.'

Lord Chalmondy laughed. 'There is that. But there's also some capital sport going on this afternoon.' He lowered his voice, although not so low that he wasn't perfectly aware she could still hear him. 'A cockfight down at the Mare's Tail and then a sparring match between the local champion and a man from Liverpool. Supposedly he used to work the looms in some factory. A regular bruiser! Should be a prime dust-up.'

'No gentleman with red blood still running in his veins would want to miss it,' Lieutenant Broadmere said.

'Sounds like just the thing for you soldiers to while away a dull afternoon,' Lord Halden said.

'Zounds, man, we're on our way now. Why not come with us?' Lord Chalmondy gave Pru another leering glance. 'You'll have all evening to charm the ladies. Or do you feel you may need a glass of Pump Room water to make it through the day?'

Lord Halden hesitated, obviously drawn by the prospect of sport—and unwilling to be thought less virile than his former university mates. 'Very well,' he conceded after a moment. 'Just let me escort this lady back to her aunt.'

There was a snigger and Pru was certain she heard one of them mutter 'lady?' in a contemptuous undertone.

Giving her another appraising glance that said exactly what he thought about her character, Lord Chalmondy said, 'Good heavens, it's mid-morning in a public park. I think Miss Lattimar is clever enough to find her way back without your help. Aren't you, Miss Lattimar?'

Resisting the strong urge to slap the mocking smile off his face, Pru hesitated. No gentleman, having received permission to take a young lady for a stroll, would go off to do something else until he'd returned her safely to her chaperon. Lord Chalmondy was making it quite clear that, though her fortune might have rendered her acceptable to Lord Halden's cousin, this duke's son did not consider her deserving of being treated as a gently born maiden should be.

He was obviously fully aware of her reputation, and would treat her—at least where there was no one from society to reprove him—as one of the Scandal Sisters.

Furious, but determined not to let it show, she said, 'Clever enough to need no further encouragement to quit the company of *gentlemen* such as yourself.'

'Excellent,' Lord Chalmondy replied, appearing not at all disturbed by her thinly veiled rebuke. 'You see, Lord Halden, the lady has released you.'

'You are sure you don't mind, Miss Lattimar? I'll see you somewhere later, then. You'll tender my farewells to your aunt and Lady Isabelle, yes?'

At her curt nod, he dropped her arm, left her there on the pathway and set off with the soldiers.

Fuming…and humiliated, for a few long minutes,

Prudence simply stood, watching them lope down the path and out of the park, their loud laughter and jesting trailing after them. Lord Halden never gave her a backward glance.

Still angry, worried her debut in Bath might turn out to be as disastrous as a foray in London would have proved, with dragging steps, Prudence turned around and set off to find her aunt.

Meanwhile, Johnnie Trethwell was limping through his second circuit of the paths at Sidney Gardens. He'd been happy to drop his aunt off to visit one of her cronies rather than have her accompany him, which allowed him to walk at a faster pace. Pushing himself and his knee to the limits of its endurance was the only way he was going to regain its full strength—no matter how much he was going to regret that determination come evening, when it would likely pain him in earnest.

He'd just turned the corner of the outer pathway when he spied Miss Lattimar, walking alone a dozen yards in front of him.

Johnnie halted, stifling his immediate impulse to go to her. He'd felt only too keenly the anxiety on her face in the Pump Room when Markingham had pulled him into the group of soldiers conversing with her and her evident escort, Lord Halden. Not that he'd been insulted by her obvious reluctance to have the Duke's son know they were acquainted. Though his attentions had been keenly sought the world over by bored matrons with more lust than morals—an arrangement that suited him perfectly well—he was only too aware that keeping company with a man of his reputation would do nothing to help her efforts to entice a proper suitor. Not burdened as she was with *her* questionable reputation.

He remembered the bleak resignation in her eyes when she stated she had no choice but to adhere to every rule of propriety. For a lady whose extraordinary beauty would normally have given her licence to be as capricious as she chose, that was the saddest comment yet.

He should remain silent and let her go her own way.

But the pathway ahead of her was deserted. There was no one about to see or disapprove. With that treacherous fact to encourage him, he couldn't quite defeat the desire to talk with her.

Still debating, he quickened his pace, closing the distance between them. Then, as he got nearer, he noticed how dawdling her steps were, how her head drooped and her arms trailed loosely at her sides, her reticule dangling by twisted cords, unnoticed. She looked the picture of—dejection?

Concerned in spite of himself, over his bad leg's protest, Johnnie pushed harder, until he was within hailing distance. 'Miss Lattimar!' he called. 'What's this, walking alone? Has a press gang rounded up every man in Bath, or have they all gone blind?'

Under his keenly observing eye, she first stiffened, then straightened, then slowly turned towards him. Hurt and mortification in her expression, she opened her lips to speak, must have thought better of it and forced a smile instead. 'It's such a lovely morning, I thought I'd have a stroll while Aunt Gussie rested on a bench.'

He was fairly certain, according to his vaguely remembered standards of conduct for single young females, that walking alone in a respectable garden in a genteel city like Bath with her chaperon nearby wouldn't be considered precisely *fast*. But he did clearly recall his more adventurous sister being roundly scolded for leaving her maid behind on such a foray, her governess emphasising that 'a well-bred young lady never walks *anywhere* unaccompanied. Never!'

Her troubled expression revealed the same distress he'd read on her face in the Pump Room. As he stood, watching her, something flashed between them, some wordless connection, spurring in him the urge to move closer. He had the absurd wish that he could take her in his arms and somehow ease her burden.

'Is something wrong? How can I help?'

Her eyes widened with alarm before, shaking her head, she said, 'How did you know I was upset? I've worked so hard on the ability to appear serene, regardless of the circumstances!'

That response was so unexpected—and delightful— he had to laugh. 'Well, I did come upon you from behind, when your guard was down.'

'Then you couldn't have seen my face.' Her exasperation deepened. 'Or did I give myself away when I greeted you? Please, let me know! In my circumstances, I *must* be able to control my demeanour, or the wolves truly will devour me alive.'

That truth was enough to extinguish his amusement. 'I suppose you're right. But don't worry too much. Most people see only what they expect to see. Half the time, they are too occupied with their own needs and desires to notice much of anything around them. If I'm a keener judge, it's because I've had to be. Travelling among various native groups in India, most of them hostile to one another and often to the English, one had to be a keen observer. Able to evaluate a man's stance and expression to fill in the many gaps in my comprehension of the local dialect, so I might accurately assess whether I was being invited to join a hunt—or was the object being hunted.'

As he'd hoped, that teased out a genuine smile—and he had to suck in a breath. The effect was like coming out of a dark cave into brilliant noon sunshine.

Basking in it, he said, 'May I escort you back to your aunt? Perhaps we can scandalise and confound a few disapproving matrons on the way?'

But she hadn't completely recovered, for his joking suggestion brought an immediate, alarmed widening of those enchanting blue eyes. Hastily he added, 'Excuse me, I was just funning. As you can see, the gardens are deserted. I should be able to return you safely to your aunt without endangering your reputation.'

She looked at him, the wry smile on her lovely lips making him wish she *were* as scandalous as society branded her, so he might kiss that luscious mouth, right here in the park.

While he beat back the desire, she said, 'You're right and I apologise. I've been suspicious of you at every turn, while *you've* done nothing but seek to protect me.' She sighed. 'If only my reputation were less...tarnished. I wish it were sterling enough to allow me to associate openly with the only man I've ever met, outside my own family, who hasn't judged— and dismissed—my character without meeting me or having me utter a word. How I wish we could be friends!'

Somewhat to his surprise, Johnnie had to acknowledge he shared that wish. Outside his own sisters, he had next to no experience of gently bred maidens, having left England right after university and having carefully avoided newcomers from the Fishing Fleet during his time in India.

Not that avoiding them required much effort. With the dearth of single English females in India, the ladies venturing out in search of husbands on the yearly voyages from England had no trouble finding partners. Even those with little beauty and few charms had numerous suitors, clearing the field for him to turn his attentions to the more dashing married matrons.

True, he found Prudence Lattimar's beauty arresting. He sensed a fire beneath her carefully controlled façade, no matter how stringently she was trying to mask it, that couldn't help but draw him like the proverbial moth to her flame. He had the tempting suspicion he might be just the man to coax that flame into a very satisfying conflagration.

More surprising, though, he was discovering himself equally captivated by Miss Lattimar's lack of artifice, her directness and honesty—traits he suspected were in short supply among females looking to attract a husband. Not just husband-hunters, he amended. He'd found those qualities lacking in virtually every female he'd ever known.

'I would enjoy your friendship,' he acknowledged—though what he'd do with the friendship of a woman he could neither bed nor wished to marry, he didn't know. Dismissing that qualm, he said, 'We must consider ways to make that happen. But not at this moment. Now, let us just enjoy as much conversation as we can squeeze in before I must surrender you to your aunt. So, how goes it with your Duke's son?'

She tilted her head at him. 'You truly want to know? I got the impression you didn't like him very much.'

'Just because he looked at me in my regimentals as though I were a slug that had just crawled on his shoe, before dismissing me as a nonentity? Excuse me, not just a nonentity, but scapegrace rakehell who shouldn't be allowed within speaking distance of his—or your—pristine person?'

While chuckling at his description, she shook her head. 'He did treat you badly, which was not at all well done of him.'

Johnnie shrugged. 'One can't expect wisdom or discernment from a university dandy—or a bunch of play soldiers who've never been within a musket-sound's distance of a real battle.'

'Unlike you, who are a real soldier?'

Grief and pain twisted in his gut. Fortunately, she could have no idea the cost of being a 'real' soldier, he thought before he shut down the memories and summoned a smile. 'Now you've caught me being as dismissive of them as they were of me! I admit, I have something of a distaste for Fitzroy-Price's ilk. I served under too many colonial officials whose chief qualification for the job was their papa's elevated title or connections. However, though I may have spent most of my adult life outside England, even I am not too dim to recognise that wedding the son of a duke must top even "wealthy", "young" and "charming" on every fond mama's list of the sort of husband she'd choose for her daughter.'

She nodded. 'He would be accounted a prime catch. Especially for someone like me.'

He frowned. 'Someone like you?'

'Yes. He's to receive a living from his uncle, Aunt Gussie tells me. How better to redeem my reputation, than to become the blameless wife of a clergyman?' Her enthusiasm faded a bit. 'Though I would hope he would learn not to be drawn in by rough companions and to treat all people with more respect. But he's young. His solemn role as a spiritual advisor will mature him and endow him with wisdom and compassion, I'm sure.'

With an effort, Johnnie restrained himself from rolling his eyes. In his experience, pampered, wealthy young men went on to become self-important, pompous older men, supremely confident in their superiority and disdainful of the rabble—which included most everyone else in society—beneath them.

But, as young and sheltered from the world as unmarried maidens were, Miss Lattimar had probably not yet learned that lesson. It wasn't really his place to teach her.

While he worked hard to keep from expressing his opinion, Miss Lattimar said, 'Enough of Lord Halden. Might I ask you a question?'

Primed now to expect almost anything, he immediately replied, 'Of course! Although if it deals with society, I can't promise to have the expertise to accurately answer it.'

'You absolutely have expertise about this society! I've never seen more of the world than our estate in Northumberland, the town house in London and the little I've experienced so far of Bath. I'm so envious of the travels and the adventures you've had! Please, can you tell me what it was like, living in India?'

'Tell you about India?' he echoed, surprised. 'Ladies usually beg to hear about storms at sea, or pirates. Generally, only men ask me about India.' *And then, mostly for tales about the women.*

'I'm sure you're a marvellous storyteller. And I truly would like to hear about your life there.'

'Very well, India. Let me see if I can pick out the bits best suited for a maiden of your tender years.'

She giggled. 'Oh, no! I want to hear all the spicy bits, too!'

Did she have any idea how irresistible she was? he thought, totally charmed. 'All right, then. Let me see if I can find bits spicy enough to titillate you without losing whatever credit I might have with your aunt for protecting you on your walk back.'

Quickly searching through memory to select a story that might entertain her without veering into the salacious, he launched into a description of the grand procession in the State of the Nawab of Surat in which troops from his regiment had participated. 'After the termination of the fast of Ramadan, one of the holiest events in the Muslim year, the Nawab ordered a grand parade from his durbar to the principal mosque. A select few of us British regulars marched after him, followed by elephants and camels carrying kettle-drummers and musicians, local men on horseback, their mounts as richly dressed as they were, and finally a state *palankeen* bearing representatives of the East India Company, members of the ruling British council, the Governor of the castle and the Admiral of the Mogul's fleet, all in dress uniform. Ah, the noise of the excited crowds calling and hooting, the women ululating, the tramp of boots, hooves and elephant feet! The sound of the drums and the strange melodies of the native lutes, the scent of marigolds, incense, perfume—and dung. And clouds of dust, enveloping us and coating our mouths and uniforms.'

She laughed, her eyes shining. 'You describe it so vividly I can almost hear it—and smell it! You *are* a marvellous storyteller! My twin sister, Temperance, who has a great desire to explore foreign places, has collected all the travel journals and memoirs she can find, but hearing such episodes described by someone who actually lived them is so much more fascinating than merely reading about them. Tell me more!'

So he did, secretly delighted when she begged him to continue his tales through one more circuit around the park before he returned her to her aunt.

When they finally turned down the pathway and saw Lady Stoneway and another matron sitting on a bench, her rapt expression faded. 'I hate it that it isn't wise for me to associate with you. It was so…energising to talk about something truly interesting, rather than having to confine my remarks to innocuous observations on the weather, or monosyllabic murmurs of appreciation for whatever a gentleman is prosing on about!'

'Good heavens! Is that what you have to do to look respectable?' When she nodded, he shook his head. 'How…stifling. And how much I admire you!'

She gave him a sharp look. 'It isn't polite to mock.'

'No, I'm entirely serious! It's fortunate I have no desire to mingle in polite society, for I probably wouldn't last half an hour before I got thrown out on my ear. I'm far too prone to ignore convention and say exactly what

I think, hang the consequences.' He chuckled. 'Which, probably, is why I was never a success at school and the Army in India looked askance on me. I ask too many questions and probe into too many areas they would prefer left unexplored.'

Miss Lattimar smiled—and she really was temptation incarnate when she smiled, he thought. A soldier ought to get a medal for bravery or restraint for resisting the completely understandable urge to kiss her senseless on the spot.

'My governess was for ever warning me and Temperance against doing that,' she was saying. 'Although Temper is so much braver and bolder than I am. She *does* tell people what she thinks. Defies them about casting us in the image of our mother, too, instead of trying to deflect them and please everyone, like I do.'

'It takes self-control and admirable discipline to limit what one says. Particularly when the comment one struggles to suppress is bang on the mark. I'd say that makes *you* the one who is strong and brave.'

She looked startled, as if she'd never thought that of herself. 'How kind of you to say so! I only wish I could believe it. Much as I try to be perfectly behaved, so that society will come to believe I am *not* my mother, I must confess, sometimes I feel like giving up the effort. Abandoning prudence and caution, raising my skirts and running through Sidney Gardens shrieking, just to see the look on some censorious matron's face. Or stripping off my stockings and wading in the fountain—like Temper and I used to wade in the river at home.'

'Probably best to suppress such impulses,' he said— even as it pained him to think she felt compelled to restrain that bright, exuberant spirit. 'I doubt they would be considered very suitable in a vicar's wife.'

He regretted the words immediately, for they extinguished the merriment on her face in an instant. 'I might be able to wade in a fountain, in the privacy of my own garden, with my children accompanying me,' she said after a moment.

'I hope you will.' Yet, he couldn't help a probably futile wish that somehow, she would avoid a fate that, to him, seemed destined to lock her for ever in a role where her natural charm and zest for life would be straitjacketed.

Just beyond speaking distance from her aunt, she stopped, as if she needed to armour herself to return to the world of rules and subterfuge. Lips parted, she gazed over at him, regret at having to part and longing on her face.

A wave of desire swept through him to carry her away from the propriety-bound world she was about to re-enter, off somewhere they could be alone. Where he might succumb to the urge to kiss her that had dogged him from the moment he saw her again.

From the widening of her eyes and the little intake of breath, he knew she felt that sensual pull as strongly as he did. And he was as helpless to resist it as a cobra hypnotised by a mongoose.

Giving him a tiny negative shake of her head, as if wordlessly acknowledging both the desire and the impossibility of indulging it, she said, 'I have to go back.'

'To the world of society and its rules.'

'Yes. But I can't tell you how much I enjoyed our walk. Maybe…maybe we *can* find a way to walk together again in future. I imagine my aunt will be fatigued and want to return home at once, so I'll say good day to you now, Lieutenant.'

He bowed. 'And to you, Miss Lattimar.'

They had nearly reached the bench on which both women sat before their approach was noticed. 'Prudence—and Lieutenant Trethwell?' Lady Stoneway said, looking both surprised and confused.

'Miss Lattimar!' the other woman exclaimed. 'Where is my cousin?'

'Lord Halden…encountered a group of friends, who pressed him to accompany him immediately on a…a mission of some importance.'

'But—he just *left* you, unaccompanied?' Lady Stoneway cried.

'Fortunately, Lieutenant Trethwell was at hand to make sure I returned safely,' Miss Lattimar said, giving him a quick, silent plea that he not contradict her slight alteration of events.

His lips tightening, he understood all too well. He'd already overheard some salacious remarks made about her by several of the soldiers joking with Fitzroy-Price that day in the Pump Room. Men who spoke of her like that would have no compulsion about insulting her by carrying off her escort and leaving her to fend for herself.

But it didn't say much for her escort that he'd agreed.

No wonder she'd been looking so dejected when he came upon her!

'Well, Lord Halden shouldn't have left me here, without proper escort back to my house!' the other matron said angrily. 'And so I shall tell him, when next I see him. Careless boy!'

Johnnie's cynicism deepened. He had no idea of

the identity of the overdressed, self-important woman with Miss Lattimar's aunt, but she conducted herself just like the wives of the high-ranking men he'd known in India. Concerned only with her own consequence and well-being, sparing not a thought for the beautiful young woman her cousin had left alone, vulnerable to attack by any ruffian who might have come upon her. No matter how unlikely it was that a ruffian would be roaming about Sidney Gardens on a sunny morning.

'Shall we all walk together to engage a sedan chair, Lady Isabelle?' Lady Stoneway suggested. 'I'm sure that's what Lord Halden expected we would do.'

The matron visibly brightened. 'You are right, Lady Stoneway. Of course that's what my cousin must have thought. No need of him to keep his friends waiting, when we might escort each other.'

'Before we go, Aunt Gussie, don't you want to thank Lieutenant Trethwell for making sure I came to no harm?' Miss Lattimar said, her voice calm, but something steely in her eyes. 'And present him to Lady Isabelle?'

Lady Stoneway looked uncertain for a moment before nodding assent. 'You are quite right, Prudence. I do thank you for safeguarding my niece, Lieutenant. Lady Isabelle, may I make you acquainted with Lieutenant Lord John Trethwell? His elder brother, as you may know, is now Marquess of Barkley.'

Lady Isabelle's cool expression indicated she knew exactly who he was and, for a moment, Johnnie wondered if she were debating whether or not to give him the cut direct. Which wouldn't bother him in the slightest, except for the embarrassment it would certainly cause Lady Stoneway and Miss Lattimar.

The latter, he noted with no little amusement, despite her self-professed craven submission to society and its dictates, was staring almost defiantly at Lady Isabelle, as if daring her to refuse the introduction.

Not at all to his surprise, the older woman capitulated—barely. 'Lieutenant,' she acknowledged with the slightest incline of her head.

'Lady Isabelle,' he replied, offering a bow considerably more polite than the one he'd given Lord Halden.

'Shall we be off?' Lady Stoneway said, obviously reluctant to press her luck any further with the matron. Her aunt's kindness—and concern for Miss Lattimar's status—were the only reasons Johnnie resisted the urge to further tweak Lady Isabelle by insisting he accompany them.

'I should be going myself,' he said, with an ironic quirk of his lip. 'Good day to you all. Miss Lattimar,' he added, unable to stop himself as they turned. 'Safeguarding you was a pleasure.'

Her eyes lit up and the smile she gave him was pure enchantment. 'I very much appreciated it,' she replied, before taking her aunt's arm and walking off, Lady Isabelle beside them.

Johnnie stood and watched them until her lovely figure disappeared from view.

Reviewing his impressions after their second meeting, Johnnie found Miss Lattimar's appeal had only increased. Along with the physical attraction he would expect her beauty to evoke in any red-blooded male, he'd felt an unexpected and disturbingly powerful connection on some deeper level. Having had a glimpse of the exuberant, uninhibited character she was trying to suppress—he chuckled, envisioning her, skirts held up, wading in the Sidney Garden fountain—he felt a strong urge to prompt her to be herself, without restraint. Even though the woman she became when she did so was not just more natural, she was even more devilishly attractive.

He sighed. He very much wished he could pursue her openly—in spite of the fact that he had never previously pursued, nor had any use for, a well-bred virgin. Following that trail led to marriage, something he had always avoided. Not just because he wasn't sure, with the vast floral garden of the feminine beauty and charm the world had to offer, he'd be able to limit himself for a lifetime to plucking just one bloom.

He also knew his wanderlust nature too well and the chances that he'd ever want to stay for long in one place were slim. A good English wife would probably prefer a settled countryside home with a husband in it to look after her and any children. To offer marriage without being able to pledge that wouldn't be fair to any lady, no matter how much she attracted him.

And when he travelled, he travelled alone. He'd witnessed first-hand the agony of someone who'd lost a beloved. He might sometimes be lonely enough to wish for a heart's companion, but loneliness was an old friend, something he'd grown accustomed to enduring. Better to suffer a quiet flame than to open oneself to an all-consuming conflagration.

How unfortunate the enchanting Miss Lattimar wasn't the worldly-wise *Mrs* Lattimar! Were she a dashing widow, he would have free rein to indulge in the delightful dance of desire. Sadly, seducing and then abandoning a well-born innocent was out of the question.

To experience the charm of Miss Lattimar's intriguing personality, he was pretty sure he could settle for *friendship*—novel as the notion was of being merely a friend to a desirable woman. But if he respected her desire to change society's perception of her from a scandalous young woman to a well-behaved, conventional Beauty, he couldn't lure her into solitary rendezvous. No matter how attractive the prospect of amusing her with further tales of his exploits or exchanging philosophical observations on the world.

For the first time, he regretted spending his adulthood roaming the world, collecting the stories and lovers that made him unsuitable company for a girl trying to redeem her reputation.

Never one to dismiss a desired goal as impossible, he put aside for the moment the problem of how to become her friend without compromising that quest and shifted his focus to the next issue.

What about Lord Halden Fitzroy-Price?

He'd heard that the Duke's son—handsome, well born, and behaving like he knew it—was languishing in Bath, supported by the beneficence of his rich cousin while he awaited a desirable sinecure as a cleric.

Johnnie might not be intimately acquainted with the inside of a church, but based on his few exchanges with the man, Lord Halden appeared to be less well suited than any individual he'd recently met to become a clergyman. Unless a parish wanted as pastor of their flock a self-important, arrogant man faintly contemptuous of those he believed were beneath him.

If that were truly his character, Johnnie wouldn't want to see a lady as lovely, charming, and innocent of the ways of vice as Miss Lattimar wasting herself on him.

He stopped short, surprised at the ferocity of that feeling. Why should he feel so protective of a girl he barely knew?

He might have only met her twice, but her unique personality intrigued him. He genuinely *liked* her. Almost immediately, there had sprung up a sort of... kinship between them.

Maybe he felt so strongly because he understood all too well what it was like to be a member of a disreputable family, to be accused of the same faults and vices by people who knew nothing about one but the family name—Lord Halden's dismissive remarks recurring to irritate him again.

He had no doubt whatsoever about *his* ability to best the Duke's son and any of his toy-soldier compatriots, but a gently born female like Miss Lattimar had few weapons with which to counter their malice. The warrior in him naturally felt compelled to defend someone smaller and weaker.

For all those reasons—admiration, desire, anger on her behalf about how she was treated—he felt linked to Miss Lattimar by the same sort of bonds a soldier develops for his fellows, a loyalty that propels him to watch out for and protect others in battle, even at the risk of his own life.

Dismissing the 'why', his officer's brain shifted to the 'how', mulling over the best strategy for his next move. He had to admit, having suffered slights and insults in the past from men of Fitzroy-Price's rank and birth, the man's position as a duke's son automatically prejudiced Johnnie against him. He really ought to reserve judgement until he had observed him long enough to make a dispassionate assessment of the man's character.

After a bit more reflection, he came up with a plan. It might, he thought with a grin, astonish his aunt, but it would also accomplish both the goal of keeping an eye on Fitzroy-Price and allowing Johnnie to satisfy his pressing desire to see more of the delectable Miss Lattimar, without risk to her reputation.

After all, even his aunt would have to admit that staying near enough to make sure Miss Lattimar came to no harm would be the noble act of a selfless friend.

Chapter Four

Returning to his aunt's town house in Queen Square, Johnnie tracked down Aunt Pen in her private salon, where she was dozing, some needlework abandoned in her lap.

He paused on the threshold, his fond glance tracing over a figure that radiated confidence and independence even in sleep. Penelope Woodlings wasn't just the most interesting of his relations, she was also the one who'd been least interested in society—and the sole encourager of an energetic young boy, youngest of a large brood and left to his own devices. The happiest memories of his childhood had been created while visiting her and her reclusive scholarly husband at their rambling country estate, joining her and her two sons in collecting rocks and bugs, chasing butterflies, climbing up trees after bird nests and crawling into dens to inspect the homes of badgers and foxes.

But it didn't end with the quest. In the evenings, she sent the boys into the library to discover more about the treasures they'd uncovered. Along with finding out facts about rocks, frogs and trees, he'd stumbled across volumes of memoirs and travel journals.

Those accounts had awakened a keen interest in the world around him and a burning desire to explore it, not just England, but beyond her shores.

It had been Lady Woodlings, not his impecunious and uninterested family, who funded his Oxford education, equipped him for the army and continued to write him letters of encouragement that followed him on his adventures to India.

A wave of affection and gratitude washed over him as he watched her dozing. 'Who will care for you, if I do not?' she'd gruffly replied when he'd thanked her for taking him in after he'd dragged his lame and still fever-ridden body back from the subcontinent. In all his turbulent existence, she'd been the one rock he could count on, no matter how stormy the waves and winds of his life became.

Though she'd never been much interested in society, marrying over her family's objections an unfashionable young scholar she'd pronounced the most intelligent of her suitors, she kept abreast of its news, as she followed all the developments in the world.

So of course, she'd known about Miss Lattimar's family background. Being normally the most reasonable and least judgemental of individuals, he knew it was her desire to protect him that made her urge him to court any wealthy lady but *that* one, whose purported propensity for infidelity might break his heart if he were unwise enough to fall in love with her.

But then, Aunt Pen had no idea of the true character of the lady. He would just have to see that she discovered it.

As he cleared his throat loudly, she startled, her eyes flying open.

'Johnnie, you're back. How was your walk? You didn't push that leg too hard, now, did you?'

Probably. 'I don't think so. Did you have a good visit with your friends?'

'Just a comfortable coze with some old acquaintances from my come-out days.' She shook her head, smiling. 'Still occupying their time with society events and gossip, and trying to lure me into doing the same.'

'Maybe you should attend more society events. The Subscription Balls, for example. Some concerts and plays.' He paused. 'I'd be happy to escort you.'

Any lingering drowsiness dissipated in an instant. 'You would be willing to *escort* me? Into society, where you might meet some *eligible* ladies?'

'I did some thinking during my long walk. Perhaps it's time I took more part in respectable society. After all, it's not fair to dismiss it as a boring waste of my time when I left England before I could ever truly become involved in it.' *Though I saw enough of its copy in India to know it doesn't interest me.*

'So you no longer fear that participating will make it look like you *wish* to find a wife? Excellent!' Aunt Pen exclaimed, jumping up to give him a hug. 'I would be happy to go about more! There are some events which aren't *too* dreadful. Balls—I've always enjoyed dancing. But do you think, with your—?'

'I can manage,' he cut her off.

'Balls, then, and supper events at which dancing will follow. Concerts, if the performer is proficient. I promise, no evenings listening to some young female with more elegance than musical talent! And theatre, if the play and the company are good. I wouldn't drag you to some dreary event I wouldn't enjoy myself.'

'Thank you. So...' he paused '...could you apply for Subscription tickets. Today, perhaps?'

'Today? Even better!' Looking delighted, she said, 'You know I hope you may meet some charming, rich young lady who will persuade you to remain in England, although of course you need not do so, unless...' Her enthusiastic speech trailing off, she tilted her head, inspecting him with suspicion. 'Why this sudden anxiety to get started?'

Before he could come up with an innocuous introduction of his intent—for she was sure to balk, if he began by admitting the only reason he was doing this was to be able to encounter Prudence Lattimar—she crossed her arms over her ample bosom and looked accusingly at him.

'This is about *her*, isn't it? That Lattimar chit!'

He might have known she would be downy enough to figure it out. 'Yes,' he confessed. 'I *was* about to explain, Aunt Pen. I know what it is to be condemned on the basis of your family's reputation, before you yourself have uttered a word. Miss Lattimar has scarcely been out in society yet and I've already heard... insulting remarks made about her by gentlemen who've not even met her. Which, I admit, rouses my fighting instincts.'

While she stood, arms crossed, looking dubious, he continued, 'Come now, be fair, Aunt Pen! Shouldn't she have a chance to prove her reputation one way or another, before those who would condemn her ruin her ability to form a connection based on her true character? I'd like to be around to keep the riffraff away and let her have that chance. Since the only way I could do that without making matters worse for her would be under the watchful eye of that censorious society, I'll have to endure it—put up with the silly, petty rules and the boredom.'

'She accomplished a great deal in one little walk around the Pump Room. Aroused your sympathy *and* enlisted your support!'

Not thinking it prudent to mention their recent stroll in Sidney Gardens, he replied, 'No, you're wrong. She made no attempt to recite some sad tale to arouse my sympathy—I simply observed how others treat her. Nor did she ever ask for my support. This campaign is my idea alone and she knows nothing about it. Yet, of course.' He laughed. 'She knows being seen with me anywhere else would serve to confirm, rather than refute, the reputation she is trying to overcome. Only with your approval, and in the full glare of society, would my attempts to help her not end up doing the opposite.'

'I don't care a fig about *her* reputation!' his aunt returned with some heat. 'It's *your* future that concerns me and I'd not favour you doing anything that might end up hurting you—like tying yourself to a known wanton. Any other lady of modest reputation would be fine.'

She fixed a concerned glance on him. 'You must have some source of income and the safest way I know to do that is for you to marry one. I know I'll only be able to coax you to stay with me until your leg has recovered and I really don't want to see you go back to adventuring all over the globe. Trading for treasure! That might take you into areas even more dangerous than the Army would.'

'I am not keen on pitching myself needlessly into

danger,' he admitted. 'But neither do I think I could stand to be leg-shackled to a country estate and a town house in London—however bewitching the owner.'

'Marriage doesn't necessarily mean you'd be tied down to England,' she argued. 'It's always possible you might find a girl who'd be willing to go adventuring *with* you. Adventuring which would be a great deal more comfortable if you had adequate funds to fuel the journey!'

'I hope to obtain those funds another way,' he countered. 'But finding a wife who'd go *with* me?' He shook his head dismissively—and then felt a rush of enthusiasm as the image of Miss Lattimar's beautiful face flashed into his head. Now *that* was a travelling companion who would truly excite him.

Too bad her dearest wish was to settle in some quiet English village, raising children and chickens while her husband wrote sermons.

Then again, much safer for her to remain in the peaceful English countryside, far from attack by dacoits and deadly diseases. Safer for him, not to risk finding a travelling partner who might truly capture his heart, promising desolation if he should somehow lose her.

Shaking off that disturbing thought, he said, 'You can't honestly think some sheltered *ton* miss who can hardly abide being stuck in the country, deprived of the shops and entertainments of London for several months a year, would be willing to go adventuring to some primitive hinterland?'

'Well, it's not *im*possible. I would happily have accompanied Everard on a journey to Greece and Egypt, if he'd had an urge to study the antiquities *in situ*.'

'Ah, but you are a most unusual female, Aunt Pen.'

Pinking at the compliment, she opened her lips to speak, then fell silent. His always-honest aunt couldn't refute the fact that she was probably the only female of her acquaintance who would be willing to undertake such a journey.

Before she could marshal her forces for a new attack, he said, 'Won't having me out and about at society events, keeping an eye out for Miss Lattimar, provide me a better chance of finding this rich but adventure-seeking paragon you talk about?'

'Considering you've hardly done more than accompany me to Sidney Gardens and occasionally to the Pump Room, I expect it would,' she allowed.

'Exactly. But I won't put myself to the pains of behaving through a long series of probably uninteresting events unless you will allow, if not support, my intention of talking and dancing with Miss Lattimar. It's all or nothing.'

His aunt sat for some minutes, frowning at him, her desire to bring eligible females to his attention obviously warring with her goal of preventing his further association with the dangerous Miss Lattimar.

As he'd expected, the inducement of having him meet someone more acceptable won out. 'Very well. You may present me to her and I will endeavour to be polite. However, if she displays the slightest sign that she might be embroiling you in a scandal, I'll carry you off to Woodhaven myself!'

Chuckling, he leaned over to kiss her forehead. 'We've a bargain, then?'

'We have. Off with you, now. I need to write notes to some friends who said they'll be holding entertainments, so they know to send us both an invitation.'

Johnnie groaned. 'Evenings of cards and conversation?'

'You'll have your lovely Miss Lattimar to console you,' his aunt said tartly.

'A consolation which I intend to fully *embrace*!' he said, laughing as he walked out at the reproving finger she shook at him.

Several days later, Prudence stood beside her aunt in the ballroom, having just been returned to her chaperon by the elderly gallant who had squired her through a country dance.

'One has to admire General Gaulford's vigour,' Lady Stoneway said.

'Yes, though I did worry he might have a seizure of the heart during some of the livelier movements.' Pru sighed. 'And he's becoming rather difficult to discourage.'

'Having a coterie of admirers about you isn't a bad thing. I just wish more of them were *younger* and eligible.'

Pru laughed. 'I can't make up my mind whether it would be preferable to marry a septuagenarian and spend my days caring for an invalid, or remain a spinster.'

'I hope it won't come to that, my dear,' Aunt Gussie replied. 'Although, sadly, the number of single gentlemen currently in Bath who are both "young" and "eligible" is disappointingly slim.'

Prudence's thoughts immediately flew to one who was young and *in*eligible…for her, at least. Oh, to be a rich widow, who might make a friend of whichever gentleman she chose! A friend, or *more*.

A wave of delicious sensation rippled through her at the thought of taking Johnnie Trethwell as her lover. Despite growing up in a household tinged with scandal, she had virtually no experience with passion. Mama might have been profligate in taking lovers, but her dalliances had always been discreet. Though they'd overheard stories and read about lovemaking—Papa's library contained a copy of Ovid they'd pored over, titillated—neither Pru nor Temper had ever witnessed so much as the exchange of a kiss.

Still, she knew instinctively that what she felt around Johnnie was sensual. That tingle of her nerves, the melting feeling in her belly and the heat and warmth below… It was probably well that she had to watch her behaviour so closely, for if she were able to do what she truly wished, she would be scheming ways to get him alone and have her first taste of kissing—in Johnnie Trethwell's arms.

'Now, there's a gentleman I hadn't expected to see!' Aunt Gussie exclaimed.

Jolted out of her naughty reflections, Pru found her attention immediately drawn to a tall, thin man wearing his scarlet regimentals with flair, several women gathered around him. A shock of recognition and pleasure zinged through her even before he turned, caught her watching him and gave her a little wink.

'Johnnie Trethwell,' Pru murmured. 'I wonder what he is doing here?'

'Lady Woodlings must have finally persuaded him to come out in society. Perhaps he *is* on the hunt for that rich widow. Or perhaps just staying in her good graces by accompanying her to the entertainments she enjoys.'

'He's not having any trouble finding feminine company,' Pru said, irked more than she would have liked by the evident admiration of the two ladies now conversing with him.

And looking thoroughly charmed.

Why shouldn't they be? She knew only too well how beguiling he was.

A little imp of envy came and sat on her shoulder. If Lieutenant Trethwell were going to appear at respectable gatherings, why hadn't he come over to beguile *her*?

'One would expect a rake to be irresistible,' Aunt Gussie observed. 'Though it is good strategy on Lady Woodlings's part to bring him here. If Trethwell can behave himself long enough to win the approval of the matrons who rule Bath society, he'll expand his opportunities to marry into the wealth he needs. Rather than just the willing widows he can encounter elsewhere, he'll be introduced to respectable maiden heiresses, too. I do wish him luck!'

Surprised, Pru looked over at his aunt. 'You do? I thought you warned me against him.'

'So I did, with good reason. While you try to overcome the rumours, it still wouldn't be wise for *you* to associate too much with him. But his kindness in keeping you company in Sidney Gardens the other day says a good deal about his character. He could easily have pressed his attentions on you, were he as profligate as he's been painted. Instead, he protected you—without any attempt to take advantage.'

'More's the pity,' Pru muttered.

'Prudence!' her aunt exclaimed—and then chuckled. 'He is devilishly attractive, isn't he? No wonder he has the ladies fluttering about him like bees around some exotic flower.'

'Bees around an exotic flower?' a low masculine voice repeated. 'That exotic flower would have to be you, Miss Lattimar. How beautiful you look this evening. And you, too, Lady Stoneway.'

Pulled from contemplating the tawny hair creeping over the collar of Johnnie Trethwell's regimentals—while imagining what it might feel like to be wrapped in his arms—Pru turned to see Lord Halden Fitzroy-Price bowing to her and Aunt Gussie.

Conscious of a little pang of…disappointment, she curtsied. 'Lord Halden. You are looking very fine yourself tonight.'

'Can I beg you ladies to accompany me to take some refreshment? That was quite a lively country dance, Miss Lattimar. I'm sure some punch would be welcome.'

'Very kind of you, sir,' Aunt Gussie said. 'I don't care for any myself, but please do escort my niece. I've just seen an old friend I'd like a word with.'

Lord Halden held out his arm. 'You'll do me the honour, Miss Lattimar?'

Surprisingly reluctant, Pru took his immaculate sleeve. Perhaps she was still angrier than she'd thought about his choosing his friends over her at Sidney Gardens.

'I am glad your aunt saw a friend, for I am mortified enough about my behaviour without having another witness to my chagrin,' Fitzroy-Price said as he walked her towards the refreshment room. 'I must apologise for leaving you stranded in Sidney Gardens after our walk the other day, Miss Lattimar. It was thoughtless and careless of me and I most sincerely beg your pardon. You may be sure my cousin roundly abused me for that inexcusable lapse in courtesy.'

His tone held just the right blend of penitence and boyish charm. Heartfelt—or practised? Pru wondered. And how much of that regret was due to the peal Lady Isabelle had evidently rung over him—not, Pru would wager, for abandoning *her*, but for leaving his cousin without a male escort?

'You hesitate so long, I fear you are not going to forgive me,' Lord Halden said.

Though she was finding it more difficult than she'd originally imagined to fit him into the mould of what she wanted in a husband, he was still her best prospect. He'd made a mistake and apologised for it. Wasn't that what she would want an honest man of character to do?

Summoning up a smile, she said, 'Of course I forgive you, Lord Halden. We all get carried away on occasion by the…exuberance of our acquaintances.'

'We do, don't we?' he replied, looking encouraged. 'How delightful to find you understanding, as well as beautiful.'

Ignoring the little voice that noted his acquaintances were insulting as well as exuberant, she pressed on. 'You must be looking forward with great anticipation to beginning a career as inspiring as the ministry. While you were preparing at Cambridge, which of your studies did you find most engaging? '

He gave her a self-deprecating smile. 'I'm afraid, as I already confessed, I wasn't much of a scholar.'

Hopefully he at least knows his Bible, Pru thought. 'The living is in the gift of the Earl of Riding, you said. Where is it located? Is the countryside suitable for hunting? I imagine you would very much like to continue one of your favourite pursuits.'

'It's in Hampshire. I haven't yet visited there, so I don't know much about the location. But your suggestion is an excellent one! I must discover the nearest hunt of repute. If it's not too distant, I might be able to stable horses there.'

At what expense? Pru wondered. *And how diligent would you be, leaving your parish for days at a time to gallop over the fields?*

'But so pretty a lady couldn't be concerned about the mundane details of a country living. Especially not while in a town as charming as Bath. Have you visited many of the sights yet? Surely you'll indulge in some shopping in Milsom Street. The shops are quite superior. After a stroll, one can take tea, or sample some of the famous Sally Lunn cakes at the bakery. You must let me escort you! Then, a drive along Lansdown Hill towards the racetrack is quite refreshing. If I may say so, my team is well matched and beautifully paced. Riding in a high-perch phaeton might appear a bit frightening at first to a lady, but I've such an experienced hand at the ribbons, you need not worry. You must promise to ride out with me, the next fine day we have.'

He certainly was trying hard to redeem himself— though whether from the charms of her person, or his cousin's exhortation that he should redouble his efforts to secure the largest dowry in Bath, she wasn't sure.

'Tea, Miss Lattimar?'

'Yes, thank you, Lord Halden.'

'Where would you prefer to be, then, if not in Bath?' she asked after taking a sip.

'Oh, in London, of course! One could never be bored there! So many sights to visit, the coffee houses and clubs, boxing and fencing and driving in the parks, and then the evenings! Balls, musicales, concerts, the opera, the theatre! Are you fond of the theatre, Miss Lattimar?'

'I confess I have not been much yet. My sister and I used to put on impromptu theatricals for our brothers, so I look forward to seeing more of it. Though I understand, many of those attending are more interested in visiting with friends and commenting on other attendees than watching the play.'

'Well, naturally,' he said, evidently finding ignoring the efforts of the actors on the stage perfectly understandable. 'Always fascinating to see who is attending and with whom. Never a dull moment in London! Nor any danger of being reduced to taking a solitary ramble along some country pathway in search of amusement. Always interesting company about, ready to accompany a man to some frolic or other.'

'Like a sparring match, a cockfight or some late-night cards at a gaming hell?'

Smiling, he shook a finger. 'No talk of that around a lady!'

You may not talk about it...you'll just go off and do it, she thought. His enthusiasm about the metropolis paradoxically dampening her spirits, she said, 'The lending libraries are excellent. Do you like Hatchard's?'

'I seem to recollect picking up a package for my sisters,' he said, shaking his head. 'Not bookish, myself, you'll remember.'

'So you told me.' Somewhat desperately trying another tack, she said, 'There's prime horseflesh to be found at Tattersall's, if my brothers can be believed. I'm very fond of horses myself. I'd love to view the offerings there.'

'Oh, no, that would not do at all, Miss Lattimar!' he said, looking appalled. 'You must know Tattersall's is a *man*'s domain, no ladies permitted.' He softened the stricture with a smile. 'Nor would a lady choose to be present. There are not just gentleman in attendance, but coachmen and grooms as well, with their vulgar talk and coarse ways. Not at all suitable for one of refined sensibilities. Ladies keep their own company during the day, with calls and visiting.'

And shredding reputations over their tea. How difficult it was going to be for someone like her, who would never fit the mould of a society lady, to survive a Season and accomplish her goal! 'No, we females must confine our excursions to shopping for gowns, bonnets, gloves and reticules,' she said with asperity.

'Such a wonderful variety to be found in London,' he agreed, oblivious to her ironic tone. 'Everything in the height of fashion, which one can't always guarantee about establishments outside the metropolis, even here in Bath. I quite enjoy escorting Lady Isabelle to her favourite shops. The haberdashers, bootmakers and tailors do exceptional work, too.'

'As evidenced by the elegance of your attire, Lord Halden.'

'One does one's possible,' he said modestly, flicking a speck of dust off his otherwise immaculate coat sleeve.

At least he wasn't a coxcomb, she thought. He took care with his appearance, but hadn't seized upon her opening to launch off into a monologue about sartorial splendour and how he achieved it—unlike one or two others among the few young men who'd squired her through dances at the last parties she'd attended.

'Perhaps we might ride together some time. I understand the area you mentioned, up Lansdown Hill, offers lovely vistas, while the open down land beyond allows for long, uninterrupted gallops, if one rides early enough.'

'I imagine you ride delightfully. But not early, surely! When one of the points of riding in a public place, rather than someone's private estate, must be to let others admire the handsomeness of your mount and the proficiency with which you control him.'

No, the point is to have a rousing gallop. Realising it was no more politic to express that view than it had been to admit a desire to visit Tattersall's, she stifled the remark.

By this time, they'd finished their tea. Talking of London all the way, Fitzroy-Price returned her to her aunt, Pru promising him a waltz later when Lady Isabelle arrived and bore him off.

To Lady Stoneway's enquiring glance, Prudence gave a sigh. 'I'm beginning to think General Gaulford might be a better option after all.'

'Truly?' Aunt Gussie said, immediately concerned. 'Surely he didn't say or do anything—'

'No, no, he was perfectly proper.' *And with his enthusiasm for London and society, perfectly—dull.* Pushing away that discouraging reflection, Pru said, 'It's just he seems…much more enthusiastic about living in London than in taking up the duties of a country cleric.'

'You mustn't fault him too much, my dear,' Aunt Gussie said. 'Most young gentlemen would prefer to be in town, where there are always friends to see and things to do. I'm sure he'll...settle into his responsibilities quite well. As one grows older, those shiny amusements lose their sparkle.'

That observation cheered her...a little. 'He is a capital horseman, so we can share that enthusiasm. Surely after he discovers the enjoyment offered by riding and driving through the exceptional vistas only the countryside can offer, he will become more enamoured of it.'

'I'm sure he shall. What could be more entertaining for a man than chasing *you* about some meadow on that great black beast you prefer?'

'I'd probably have to let him catch me, though.'

'Yes, you probably would,' Aunt Gussie allowed. 'Few gentleman can tolerate being bested by a lady.'

'At least I'll be in the country while I'm doing it,' she observed, trying to put the most encouraging shine on it.

Aunt Gussie patted her hand. 'You've always loved the countryside, haven't you, my dear? Even that vast stone pile in Northumberland that the rest of us find so dreary!'

'His living will be in Hampshire, he said. That's a lovely county, isn't it? Rolling hills and meadows, fine woods and quaint villages?'

'So the guidebooks say. I've never visited myself.'

Another of Pru's elderly courtiers arrived then to carry her off for the next quadrille, ending the conversation. As she went through the figures of the dance, Prudence tried to find some encouraging bits in Lord Halden's conversation.

Of course, he was young and would be enthusiastic about indulging in a young man's usual fascination with gambling, dicing, racing…and women? With the expectation that maturity and repetition would diminish the attraction of shallow pursuits, she thought she could tolerate the former.

She wasn't so sure about the latter.

Though aristocratic women since time immemorial had learned to look the other way about a husband's dalliances, with observation of her parents' arrangement to scar her, she didn't know how well she could tolerate having her spouse spending time with another woman. To say nothing of the fact that such behaviour would be highly inappropriate in a clergyman.

Not that she had any real hope of finding the absolute, all-consuming love her brother had discovered with his Ellie.

Christopher was a man. He could marry whomever he chose, even a former courtesan, and still be received by his family and friends, if not by larger society.

Though she wasn't prepared to accept just anyone who wooed her with an eye to her fat dowry, with her restricted prospects, she'd settle for mutual esteem with a kind man who had a settled occupation. Lord Halden's attentiveness to his aunt argued that he was kind—if occasionally thoughtless, she allowed, the incident at Sidney Gardens still grating. They did share a love of horses, surely an enjoyment they could pursue together. And a clergyman's wife took an active part in the business of the parish. Assisting her husband with his tasks and responsibilities would bring them closer.

The greatest point in his favour, though, was that of all the men who had thus far paid her particular notice, he was the only one whose future included an occupation more likely than any other to mould a man into a more perceptive and compassionate individual. And to allow his wife, in turn, to become known as a model of gentility, modesty and virtue.

Despite her misgivings, she wouldn't give up on Lord Halden—yet.

As the evening transpired, he squired her for the waltz she'd promised—and then another. The marked attention he showed her confirmed her impression that he'd decided to court her in earnest.

She ought to be thrilled.

Even if being with him had none of the ease and excitement she felt when walking with Johnnie Trethwell.

But then, how could it? With a rake who wasn't a serious marital prospect, she didn't have to watch everything she said and did, lest some inappropriate observation escape—like that bit about wanting to attend an auction at Tattersall's. And, as Aunt Gussie observed, one would expect a rake to be amusing and full of interesting banter—how else could he attract enough ladies to be considered a rake?

Lieutenant Trethwell certainly hadn't had any difficulty attracting ladies tonight. She couldn't help noticing as she changed partners and chatted with other gentlemen that he'd been surrounded the entire evening by a bevy of laughing, admiring females.

Not that she blamed them. He alone, among all the unattached younger gentlemen, possessed an air of being completely at ease in his own skin, radiating a calm self-confidence that said this man could handle whatever might happen with aplomb and, yes, a certain swagger. The dashing regimentals didn't hurt either.

He'd even managed to get that old dragon Lady Arbuthnot laughing.

She should be happy that his aunt's campaign—if such it was—to lure him into entering society was working. She tried not to feel bereft and envious that he'd made the rounds of so many other ladies but neglected to approach her.

He was keeping his distance to protect her. It was an act of kindness, she told herself. She should appreciate it.

Maybe, but she didn't have to like it.

So, later in the evening, when she walked back at the end of a dance on the arm of yet another retired gentleman to discover Johnnie Trethwell conversing with her aunt, her heart leapt.

The shiver along Pru's nerves increased and her stomach did a full swoop when he took her hand. 'Miss Lattimar, may I have this dance?'

'I—I'm afraid the next set has already formed,' she stuttered, unable to rip her gaze from that handsome face and those arresting hazel eyes.

'A pity. You'll walk with me, then? With Lady Stoneway's permission, of course.'

Scarcely waiting for her aunt's nod, he took her nerveless hand and bore her off.

Chapter Five

As Johnnie led her away, Prudence felt both fully energised and truly relaxed for the first time in that long evening. It was more than just being freed of the burden of keeping constant watch over her speech and behaviour—being with him seemed to heighten all her senses. The candlelight reflected more brightly off the mirrors, the chandeliers, the ladies' jewels. The music sounded more lively and tuneful, the room seemed warmer and more fragrant with the pleasantly mingled scents of wax, perfume and savouries from the tea room.

The compelling aura of confidence, the sheer *maleness* emanated by the man on whose arm she walked made her feel giddy.

For once, she'd not even try to suppress that alarming reaction. For the next few moments, she'd simply enjoy being with him.

'I must admit, I'm surprised to see you, Lieutenant Trethwell.'

'Surprised? How could you be? We traded glances hours ago, the moment I first entered the ballroom.'

'No, I meant surprised—' At the twinkle in his eyes, she broke off. 'You're teasing me,' she accused.

'Guilty,' he admitted. 'But that confused look is so delightful, Miss Lattimar. How can any man resist trying to provoke it?'

'Wretch,' she reproved, letting herself be charmed. 'As you know very well, I meant "surprised to see you at this gathering".'

He grimaced. 'Aunt Pen, trying to enlarge my acquaintance. She believes, if I only spend some time in it, I will discover that I actually enjoy participating in society.'

She couldn't help smiling. 'So…are you enjoying it?'

'Gad, no! The evening has seemed interminable, waiting and waiting until I could approach you.'

'Waiting? Why, waiting?' she asked. 'Or are you just trying to "confuse" me again?'

'Not this time. First, you see, I had to make the rounds of all the dragons. Ply them with just the right blend of flattery and respectful attention, so they might come to believe that the wild beast they've heard about can be tamed into a polite society lapdog.'

She laughed outright at the image. 'Sounds dreadful!'

'Not really, aside from the fact that it took too much time to visit them all. Making a lady feel attractive and appreciated, regardless of her age and degree of beauty, is a worthwhile endeavour, don't you think?'

You are a kind man, Johnnie Trethwell. 'I never thought of it that way, but I suppose you're right. Most men only flatter a woman when they want something.'

'Well, I'm not a complete altruist. I did need to

charm them into approving me before I dared approach you. You should commend me for endurance and patience, as well as caution, for beginning the process of gilding my reputation just so I might stroll with you without endangering yours.'

She was about to accuse him of teasing her again, until a swift procession of images made her stop. Recalling all the ladies—mostly older, married ones—with whom he'd danced or spoken, she realised he *had* approached every influential matron present at the ball tonight.

Surprise, delight—and gratitude—warmed her. 'You truly have been watching out for me.'

'Of course. After that…episode in Sidney Gardens, I wanted to make sure you get your chance.'

With other men…not with him. Banishing that poignant truth, she said, 'Then I must humbly thank you.'

'As you'll recall, we were both hoping to find a way to spend time together without inviting the censure of society. So, behold me, storming the barricades of the Subscription Room, battering down the walls of disapproval surrounding you so I may claim the prize of true friendship.'

Yes, friends. At least she could hold on to that. 'Like a true medieval knight.'

He chuckled. 'Or something. So, how are you finding your partners tonight?'

She shook her head ruefully. 'Mostly ancient.'

'True, though General Gaulford and Captain Mc-Query were very attentive, they were a bit…full in years. Mr Pleasance Wellington-Foxe, too, although I understand he's quite rich.'

'He would have to be, to support all those expensive sons. Most of whom are older than I am.'

'There does seem to be an unfortunate dearth of younger men.' He paused, then added casually, 'I haven't seen any other gentlemen in regimentals—Dawson, Broadmere, Truro or their group.'

'No,' she said shortly, having to quell a flare of anger as she recalled the sniggers, the insultingly disrespectful gazes they'd raked her with in Sidney Gardens. 'I imagine this entertainment is far too tame to tempt them.'

'Fitzroy-Price seemed to find it to his liking.'

She looked up and stared at him. 'You *have* been watching me all evening!'

He shrugged. 'Of course. I told you, being able to meet you was the only reason I came here. I admit, I'd much rather we meet in Sidney Gardens for a stroll, exchanging opinions and views on the world in quiet and privacy, but intimate walks alone would undo all the good work you're been doing, attempting to shore up your reputation. If that means accepting the chafing confines of a ballroom and having to spin a lot of moonshine to soften up a bunch of starched-up old dragons too full of their own power, I'm prepared to do it.'

His exceptional kindness—and his championship of her—brought a burn of tears to her eyes. 'I... I don't know what to say.'

For a moment, he simply gazed at her. She stared up, lost, the world narrowing to encompass only the warm sympathy in his grey-green eyes, the mesmerising spotlight of his close attention. Something tingled in the air, arcing between them, making her catch her

the strength emanating from that lean, whipcord body, she couldn't help wanting *more*.

The following afternoon, Prudence accompanied her aunt back to the Assembly Rooms, where Lady Stoneway had engaged to meet some old friends at the Card Room.

Which was, Prudence reflected, perhaps a better venue for speaking with eligible gentlemen than the Subscription Ball, since the lure of gambling during daytime hours enticed even the younger set to attend.

Spotting among the group the soldiers who'd insulted her at Sidney Gardens, she initially stiffened. But, under the close scrutiny of Lady Stoneway and two of her friends, Lieutenants Dawson, Broadmere and Truro offered her bows and perfectly respectable greetings.

Relaxing after having passed that hurdle, she was able to enjoy herself, cheerfully greeting the elderly gallants who came at once to pay their addresses and enjoying a light banter with two bachelors her aunt's friend presented to her, whom she'd not previously met.

The only thing to mar her enjoyment was the absence of Lieutenant Trethwell. But since her aunt had not announced her plans for today's meeting until they were on their way home from the ball, and thinking it imprudent to try to send him a note, she'd had no way of letting him know they would be here this afternoon.

As Pru was indifferent to both cards and gambling, before her aunt settled in with her friends for several hands of their favourite piquet, Lady Stoneway sent her off with one of the older gentlemen, advising her to take tea and chat with friends rather than bore herself to flinders playing badly a game she didn't enjoy.

She'd just walked back into the card room after sharing tea with the ever-gallant Sir Reginald, when, rising from one of the gaming tables at the far side of the room where the serious gamblers had gathered, she spotted Lord Halden.

Who, spying her in return, gave her a smile and immediately headed in her direction.

She told herself it was a happy chance that he'd decided to play cards today, affording her another opportunity to get to know the gentleman better and hopefully discover more interests they had in common.

'Miss Lattimar, Sir Reginald,' he cried as he reached her. Making his bow, he continued, 'I had thought to content myself only with winning a few guineas. What a delight to discover the company suddenly grown so much more charming!'

'It's good to see you, too, sir. And good to hear that your efforts were prospering.'

'Indeed. But I was in need of refreshment, which was why I had them deal me out of the next hand. Might I escort you for something?'

'Sir Reginald and I have only just returned from having tea.'

'Then you'll take a turn about the Octagon with me? Sir Reginald, having already claimed the lady for some minutes, it's only fair that you cede her now.'

Apparently realising the Duke's son was not to be denied, the older man bowed. 'Delightful to speak with you, Miss Lattimar. I shall look forward to having a dance at the ball Thursday night.'

As that gentleman walked away, Lord Halden

claimed her hand, patted it on to his arm and set off with her.

'Do you often play cards here during the day?' she asked—hoping through discreet enquiry to discover just how much a gamester he was.

'Yes. Lady Isabelle enjoys a round of whist and a chat with her friends. The play is rather tame, but one can usually win a few guineas, enough to make it interesting, before the more serious gaming in the evening. Do you play?'

'I'm afraid I've never been much interested in games of chance.'

'Not interested?' he exclaimed. 'However do you pass the long winter nights? One cannot count on having every evening an entertainment worth the trouble of braving the weather.'

It wouldn't be helpful to admit she preferred to spend such evenings reading—an activity in which she already knew he had little interest. Neither could she prevaricate by stating she occupied herself doing needlework, which she detested, no matter how suitable that pastime might be for a vicar's wife. Instead, she turned the question back to him. 'Do you have any particular favourites among games of chance?'

'Piquet and whist are the usual fall-back, since most older gentlemen can be induced to play when there is no livelier competition about. But I much prefer hazard and faro. Faster paced and usually the stakes run far higher.'

'And it's more exciting to play for high stakes?'

'Of course! Even my old great-aunt gambles for chicken stakes. But ah, there's nothing like testing your skill against other masters of the game when an amount of true substance is riding on the outcome!'

Not if it were going to be her dowry that funded the truly substantive amount, Pru thought, her unease growing.

'What's this, Fitzroy-Price, you've discovered a game where "amounts of true substance" are being wagered in the middle of the day? You must let us know where!'

They turned to see Lieutenants Dawson, Broadmere and Truro approaching.

'If there is such a game, I'm sure Miss Lattimar would excuse you—again,' Lieutenant Lord Chalmondy said.

'Or perhaps she could accompany us to the hell,' Lieutenant Broadmere said with a smirk. 'Joining other…ladies of her ilk. I understand her mother often does.'

Fury and chagrin held Pru speechless. No young lady of quality would dream of setting foot in a gaming hell, which was patronised only by men—and women of the demi-monde. As these Lieutenants knew quite well. To state that truth—or attempt to defend her mother—would probably only result in more snide comments.

She was debating whether she should deliver some blighting set-down—if she could think of one—and walk away when a tingling along the back of her neck and a sense of charged energy alerted her. She knew Johnnie Trethwell was approaching, even before she looked over her shoulder to see him drawing near.

'Why would you believe Miss Lattimar would even consider visiting a gaming hell, Broadmere?'

he asked in a pleasant tone at odds with the steely look in his eyes.

'Well, I...um...' the Lieutenant stuttered.

'If you know something detrimental about the young lady's character of which society should be aware, by all means, do reveal it.' Ignoring the look Pru sent him, begging him to desist, Trethwell continued, 'Do you have such information?'

Pinned like an insect to a display board by John-nie's implacable stare, Lieutenant Broadmere mum-bled, 'I have...it's nothing specific. Just...just an idle remark.'

'I would rather call it ungentlemanly, hurtful and censorious. Lady Vraux may have made a name for herself, but Miss Lattimar is not her mother, is she? In my observation, she has been everything that is gently bred and pretty behaved. She's here under the patron-age of Lady Stoneway, a matron of impeccable reputa-tion, and since her arrival has conducted herself with the utmost propriety. Has she not, Lieutenant?'

'I...suppose so.'

'Suppose—or know?' Johnnie persisted.

'I... I know that to be true,' the Lieutenant replied, by now red-faced and looking back at Johnnie with undisguised animosity.

Something about the intensity of the exchange must have telegraphed itself around the room, for the as-sorted groups who'd been conversing near them had at first fallen silent, then edged nearer to better over-hear the unfolding drama.

While Pru stood frozen, wishing a sudden earth-quake would create a convenient crevasse for her to disappear into, Johnnie said, 'Then I believe you owe the lady an apology—if you wish to continue calling yourself a gentleman.'

For a long silent moment, the two men stared at each other. Finally, Broadmere looked away. Clearing his throat, he said ungraciously, 'I beg your pardon, Miss Lattimar. My remark was…undeserved.'

Hoping her face wasn't as scarlet as the Lieutenant's, Pru gave him a tiny nod.

'We're finished here, don't you think, Broadmere?' Lieutenant Lord Chalmondy said. 'We'll look for you later, Lord Halden.' And with that, the three soldiers sauntered off.

'Nothing shows an individual to be more petty and mean-spirited than indulging in unfounded, malicious gossip,' Trethwell announced. Giving a significant look to the group who stood about gawking, he added, 'Do you not agree, good people?' in an ironic tone that, had she not been so mortified, Pru might have appreciated.

Trethwell waited until the group around them had dispersed before turning back to her. 'Miss Lattimar, will you accompany me for some tea?' he asked, holding out his arm. 'I'm feeling devilish thirsty.'

Head held high—she'd take him to task later for prolonging a humiliating interlude she'd have preferred to snip off in the bud—Prudence was about to refuse when Lord Halden, tightening his grip on her arm, said in an angry undertone, 'I imagine the last thing she wants is to take tea with *you*! Whatever possessed you to make such a scene? A woman of sensibility would just have ignored Broadmere. Now you've made the incident the talk of Bath!'

'If you understand that little about human nature,

Lord Halden, I wonder at your presuming to think you can guide a flock,' Johnnie replied. 'Surely you know Broadmere's nasty remark would be repeated and sniggered over regardless of how blamelessly Miss Lattimar reacted, reinforcing an image she has been at pains to dispel. Instead, society will now be tittering about how Broadmere was forced to admit his innuendo was false and agree she has conducted herself impeccably, then offer her a very public apology. However grudging.'

He was right, Prudence realised, impressed. Johnnie Trethwell was a keener student of human nature than she'd realised.

'Observers of the scene will also pass along their impressions of Miss Lattimar's response to the attack,' he was continuing. 'Not the defiant pique of an amoral Beauty who believes herself above the rules, but a true lady's distress and embarrassment. Making those who would condemn her on her mother's behalf reconsider their opinions. A far better outcome, I would argue, than having Broadmere's insulting innuendo circulate unrefuted.'

Turning to Pru, he continued, 'I'm sorry to have caused you additional distress, Miss Lattimar. But since that reprobate's remarks were already distressing you, I thought we might as well use them to best advantage. Now, Lord Halden, if you feel my behaviour had made Miss Lattimar too much an object of speculation to be seen with, I invite you to return to your card game.'

Lord Halden paused, irresolute, obviously enough of that opinion that Pru's humiliation deepened. 'N-no,' he said at last. 'Better that she go with me.'

'Since your consequence is enough to shield hers? But wasn't enough that you were willing to defend her to those louts? I think not. Miss Lattimar?'

Trethwell held out his arm to her again. This time, Prudence didn't hesitate to take it. 'I expect I shall see you later, Lord Halden,' she said coolly and walked off with Johnnie.

Chapter Six

But instead of guiding Prudence to the tea room, Johnnie led her into the mostly deserted ballroom. Angry as he was at Broadmere for his malicious attack, he knew the object of it might be almost as furious with him for dragging out the scene. 'Now you may blister my ears with that reproof for my presumption in intervening, without half of Bath society overhearing you,' he said as he escorted her to an unoccupied bench.

'It was presumptuous!' she replied—but with much less heat than he'd anticipated. 'Do…do you really think it was wiser to make a scene, rather than just let it go?'

'I know it's easier for a man than for a lady to insist on confrontation, but in my experience, it's always a mistake to let your enemies get their punches in unopposed. If the jackals learn that they can attack with impunity, the pack becomes even more vicious. Once word of Broadmere's rout makes the rounds of the gossips, others of his ilk will think twice about attempting to circulate unsubstantiated rumour. Attack is the best defence, I've always found.'

Pru sighed. 'Temper thinks so, too. I've always tried to…avoid and evade.'

'It *is* wiser to avoid a pitched battle—when you can. But when the time comes to make a stand, best to initiate the fight on your own terms, on your own ground.'

She gave him a little smile, still looking unsettled—as well she might. He felt another stirring of rage against the cur who'd casually smeared her name.

'It did feel…satisfying to watch him squirm. To have *his* conduct held up as reprehensible, rather than my own.'

'Attack being best defence,' he repeated, smiling. 'Which is why, after I return you to your aunt, I intend to make the rounds of all the important matrons, giving them the story first-hand, while apologising that a uniformed officer of his Majesty's service would treat a gently born maiden so poorly.'

'Many of the matrons probably believe what he said. They just don't have the temerity to say it to my face.'

'Oh, those are the ones I shall talk with first. Assuring them that I knew *they* would never judge hastily based only on rumour, when their own observations show the contrary to be true. I'll also appeal to them to show extra kindness when next they meet you, as an innocent maid could not help but be cast down by having to endure such an ugly episode.'

She raised her eyebrows. 'Don't empty the butter boat completely, or they will be sure to suspect something.'

He grinned. 'Suspect me? I'm finesse personified.'

In an instant, her reproving look faded. Tears sheening her lashes, she said softly, 'Thank you. For that swift and eloquent defence. For taking the time to explain it to me afterwards. You are a true friend, Johnnie Trethwell.'

His grin faded as he gazed into those big, cerulean-blue eyes, losing himself in their luminous beauty. As he watched her, gratitude sharpened into something else, something hot and needy that arced like a flame of pure energy from her to him, from him to her. Sucking in a breath, he felt compelled to draw closer.

'Oh, my dear, there you are!'

Lady Stoneway's voice dispelled the tension of the moment. Prudence stepped back, only then making him aware that she, too, had moved closer as she lifted her face to his.

'Yes, I'm here, Aunt Gussie,' she replied a little breathlessly. 'It was so…stifling in the Card Room, Lieutenant Trethwell escorted me here so I might have some…air.'

'After giving you a rousing defence, I hear! Whatever could that Lieutenant Broadmere have been thinking, to have tried to humiliate you so publicly? I have a mind to write to his commanding officer, asking if he's aware what sort of gentleman he's accepted into his company! Thank you, Lieutenant Trethwell, for defending my niece and sending that scapegrace off with his tail between his legs!'

Lady Stoneway halted, touched her hand to his sleeve. 'This is not the first time you've come to Prudence's rescue,' she said softly. 'We are both much in your debt.'

'Not at all, Lady Stoneway. No man with blood in his veins could stand by and let such slander be spread about a wholly blameless young lady. I only hope the story of Broadmere's comeuppance shields her from suffering such unwarranted abuse ever again.'

Lady Stoneway chuckled. 'Now that his ungentlemanly behaviour has been pointed out, the town's matrons will not be understanding. After all, if malicious gossip is going to be spread, *they* want to initiate it.' Looking at Miss Lattimar, she continued, 'I think you've had enough excitement for one afternoon, don't you, my dear? Let's engage a chair and go home.'

Turning back to Johnnie, she held out her hand. 'I'm under obligation to you, Lieutenant. If there is anything I can do to advance any cause of yours, you must be sure to call upon me. I imagine we shall see you at the ball later this week and I'll make sure Prudence saves you a dance or two. Now, come along, my dear.'

Prudence seized a moment to squeeze Johnnie's hand and murmur another 'thank you' while her aunt was making her curtsy.

'Lady Stoneway, Miss Lattimar,' Johnnie said, giving them a bow. 'I shall look forward to the ball on Thursday.'

As her aunt led her away, Prudence gave Johnnie a glance over her shoulder, full of gratitude, longing—and undisguised desire that sent a bolt of heat through him. And then she was gone, disappearing out the door of the ballroom.

His body humming in response, he had to blow out a shaky breath. Heaven forfend, she was both captivating—and provocative.

He'd just have to keep reminding himself that no matter how smoky her glances were, he absolutely could not seduce a virginal innocent.

No matter how much they might both want him to.

* * *

Late that evening, Johnnie sat at a table in the small, sparsely furnished rooms in Westgate Buildings occupied by his former army mate, Lieutenant James Markingham. Encountering the man in the Assembly Rooms after Miss Lattimar's departure, he'd been tendered an invitation to join the Lieutenant that evening for a convivial game of cards. Thinking it would be pleasant to revive a friendship that dated back to the first days of their joint service in India—and perhaps gather a bit more useful information—Johnnie had quickly accepted.

'How are you enjoying home leave?' Johnnie asked, throwing down the rest of his losing hand.

'I wish I could get as much time from the army as the Company gives its civil servants—three years, after ten years' service,' Markingham said.

'Perhaps, but you know how turbulent India is, always some nawab or prince scheming or revolting. Your regiment might get wiped out before you returned if you stayed away that long.'

'Or nearly,' Markingham agreed with a laugh. 'Needed time to recover from that fever I couldn't shake last summer, but I suppose it's best not to be gone too long.'

'You might miss out on chances for promotion, too,' Johnnie pointed out. 'As fast as India kills off officers, there are always vacancies—if you're present to claim one.'

'I just have to make sure it doesn't kill *me* off,' Markingham replied. 'Much as I was looking forward to getting away from the blasted heat, I have to admit, after years in India, last winter in Bath chilled me to the bone. But it's cheaper to put up here than in London, with almost as many entertainments available.'

'Seem to be plenty of officers about, with little to do.'

'Ah, yes, there's an encampment outside the city. Some sort of regimental exercise, supposedly, though they seem to be idle more often than they're exercising.' Markingham shrugged. 'Peacetime army in England—what do you expect? Mostly a bunch of quarrelsome younger sons sent by their families into the army to keep them from stirring up so much trouble at home.'

'Yes, you introduced me to some of them,' Johnnie said drily.

Engaged in dealing the next hand, Markingham halted. 'Tore quite a strip off one of them in the Assembly Rooms today, I heard. That's our Johnnie, always valiant in defence of a lady! But…surely you haven't an interest in *this* lady? Not at all your usual type. A noble virgin, isn't she? Whatever can you do with a female like that?'

'Nothing,' Johnnie admitted. 'And definitely not the type of feminine company I usually seek. She's refreshingly different, though, and being unfairly tainted by the reputation of her apparently infamous mother. You know me—can't stand bullies. In fact, satisfying as it was to rout Broadmere verbally, I'd really like to teach the rogue a lesson in a more tangible way. Is there a place hereabouts where the soldiers go to box? I'd love to go a round or two with him.'

'Wasn't brawling one of the reasons you didn't rise in the army as quickly as your merit should have dictated? Along with seducing too many bored officers' wives, of course.'

'If setting straight some ne'er-do-wells who tried to impose their dictatorial will on the weakest amongst us constitutes "brawling", then guilty as charged. As for the other,' he added with a grin, 'if the husbands took better care of their ladies, they would never stray.'

'Returning home at daybreak in a gin- or opium-induced haze isn't conducive to marital satisfaction,' Markingham agreed. 'Still, there was no one like you in all the regiment for gathering intelligence. Done up in your robes and turbans, with your gift for those impenetrable native tongues, you could get yourself in and out of places the rest of us wouldn't dream of trying to enter!'

Johnnie shrugged. 'One does one's possible.'

'Arguing philosophy with half-naked religious mystics in some village?' Markingham asked with a laugh.

'Those half-naked mystics—and the greybeards at the mosques—talk politics as well as philosophy, which was information the army dispatched me to gather.' *While despising me for having the skill required to gather it*, he thought.

'But then, transforming yourself into a travelling pedlar with trinkets to offer also gained you entrée where virtually no other man, Eastern or European, could have gone. I didn't envy you slogging about in your rags, but getting a close-up glimpse of beautiful dark-eyed maidens in the *zenana*? It would almost be worth going about in dust and turbans. The stories you could tell! You ought to publish your journals, like Skinner just did.'

'Not me!' Johnnie protested. 'I'm the soul of discretion.'

'More's the pity,' Markingham said. 'Say now, if

you're truly serious about having a mill with Broad-mere, you might try the Pheasant & Quail on the west edge of town, closest to the army encampment—the men sometimes get up impromptu matches in the yard behind the inn. Of course, just because you challenge him doesn't mean he'll accept.'

'Probably not. Men who go about insulting de-fenceless women are unlikely to accept a fair fight with a man who's up to their weight. More's the pity. Do you know anything more about that threesome—Broadmere, Dawson, Truro? Seemed to me too much like limping dandies to be cut out for the army.'

'It's home country service, though. Getting sent on exercises close to cities full of amusement, like Bath? Don't need to be very intrepid for duty like that.'

'Unlike us India boys, eh? Enduring heat, dust, dis-ease, isolation and attacks.'

'Punctuated by months of boredom that can be even more lethal,' Markingham agreed. 'Except for you, of course. Whenever *you* got bored, you just threw on your native duds and went exploring.'

'Surrounded by all that was exotic and unfamiliar, how could anyone with an iota of adventure in their heart not want to explore?' Johnnie said wryly, then held up a hand. 'I know, I know. I was the odd man out there. Most of our countrymen wanted to refash-ion wherever they were posted into as exact a replica of dear old England as they could manage.'

'The sane ones, anyway,' Markingham retorted. 'Just surviving the hostile climate, strange food and deadly snakes, animals and insects was enough ad-venture for most of us.'

'What of Fitzroy-Price, who seems to be an old university mate of the soldiers? He wasn't intrepid enough even for a home service army?'

Markingham straightened. 'Ah, now that one is an entirely different breed of animal. First of all, he's a duke's son, so of course his feet don't touch the dust of the ground like us commoners. What need has he of the army?'

'Younger sons require some occupation and he seems to me a poor candidate for the clergy.'

'True. There are already too many men of the cloth who are well connected but ill suited,' Markingham replied with a shake of his head. 'Hardly surprising, when livings are often in the gift of some high-born aristocrat, who can always be counted upon to have a son or nephew or cousin in need of an income. Which is the case with Lord Halden, though I've heard that he'll only take orders if he can't turn up some other alternative.'

'A blessing to whatever parish he ends up not serving,' Johnnie said acerbically. 'What is he hoping to do instead—marry someone with a fat dowry, like Miss Lattimar?'

'Apparently, he initially intended to try to coax his wealthy cousin, Lady Isabelle, into settling an income on him. But since that lady seems more interested in trying to marry him off so he can spend his wife's money instead, the odds currently favour him wedding Miss Lattimar.' Markingham gave a short laugh. 'After which happy event, he can chuck all this talk of becoming a clergyman, drop the chit off at the country estate she apparently longs for and return to London to live in the style—and dissipations—to which a duke's son is entitled.'

At least the man wouldn't inflict himself on some congregation, Johnnie thought. But that didn't help Miss Lattimar. 'Poor girl. She deserves better.'

Markingham shrugged. 'Better than marrying a duke's son? If you like her enough to defend her, I can see how you might wish for her to avoid that fate—at least, with Lord Halden. Most females would probably be thrilled to land a duke's son—no matter how deficient his character.'

Not this female, Johnnie thought. But how to rescue her from it? For if Lord Halden had set his mind on wooing her, and she believed him destined for the clergy...

'Are you going to play a card, or not?' Markingham's derisive tone interrupted his contemplation. 'It's not chess, you know. The next trick hardly requires that much cogitation.'

'Just strategising on how best to confound you,' Johnnie said, turning his mind back to the game.

But later, he intended to give much more careful consideration to the matter of preventing Prudence Lattimar from wedding a man he was now convinced would make her miserable.

And so, some hours and a tidy sum won later, Johnnie quietly exited from his friend's rooms and headed back to his aunt's establishment on Queen Square. While keeping a wary eye out—Westgate Buildings, located in the Lower Town, adjoined streets whose poverty, dens of vice and gaming hells meant a man needed to watch out for pickpockets and worse—he continued to mull over what was to be done about Lord Halden.

On the one hand, he despised tale-bearers. Though

he trusted Markingham to disclose only what he knew from his own exchanges with the officers who had first-hand knowledge of Fitzroy-Price and his army cronies, the account was second-hand, at best. He'd prefer to hear the man admit his true intentions with his own lips. But he also knew his acquaintance with the Duke's son was neither intimate nor friendly enough that he had much hope of inducing Fitzroy-Price to disclose anything to him.

Perhaps he should just continue to stand by and keep watch. He had been able to do Miss Lattimar a signal service in the Assembly Rooms today, an act which, he thought, smiling at the recollection, seemed to have won over even her suspicious aunt, Lady Stoneway. Though Miss Lattimar was apparently still trying to persuade herself that Lord Halden could turn into the kind of marriage partner she sought, from her tone and her troubled countenance, he could tell that the evidence from her own eyes and the man's own conversation was beginning to make her doubt that fond hope. Sooner or later, she would have to realise what Johnnie already believed: that this Duke's son would make a poor clergyman and an even worse husband.

Crashing sounds and raucous laughter coming from around the next corner pulled him from his reverie. With the expertise forged by years of creeping through dark alleys, he eased himself back into the shadows, becoming invisibly a part of the building behind him, and crept towards the hubbub.

Illumined by the lamps flanking the entry and in the hall beyond the open door, several rouged and painted bawds lounged, while the burly man who must be the bordello's bouncer was helping a dishevelled gentleman, surrounded by a bevy of guffawing, red-coated soldiers, struggle to his feet.

A gentleman he suddenly recognised as Lord Halden Fitzroy-Price.

'Knew Sadie worked you too hard for you to get another rise,' one of the soldiers called.

'Too weak from your exertions for some dicing at The Golden Fleece?' another asked.

Shaking his head—a motion that momentarily threatened to overcome his shaky balance—Fitzroy-Price said, 'Never. Mebbe have a go at th' bones 'n' come back 'n' visit you ladies ag'n?' Looking over at the laughing bawds, he gave them a salute that sent him lurching sideways.

The soldier Johnnie recognised as Dawson caught and righted him. 'Have to sober up first, or you'll not be able to perform again.'

'Nonsense. Always ready to perform,' the Duke's son said, giving his nether regions a salacious rub. 'Aren't I, ladies?'

'You're a right randy one,' replied the taller tart, her voluptuous bosom almost fully exposed by the extremely low-cut gown. 'Won't have no more time for us, though, once you marry that rich girl you was talking about.'

'Nay, he'll have more time then,' Dawson said with a laugh. 'Send the wife off into the country to breed and dally here—or in London.'

'With more money to spend,' another soldier added.

Fitzroy-Price bobbed his head in assent. 'Lots 'n' lots of money. Rich, beautiful 'n' eager to live in th' country. Best kind of wife.'

'Yes—absent,' Dawson said, to the laughter of all.

Johnnie remained silently in the shadows until the bawds withdrew into the house and the group walked off, Dawson bearing up the inebriated Fitzroy-Price. Thoughtful again, he resumed his stealthy trek to the fashionable side of town.

Well, he had his first-hand knowledge now. He hadn't thought his opinion of the Duke's son could sink much lower, but that episode showed him he'd been wrong.

The very idea of that self-important toad touching the pure loveliness that was Prudence Lattimar made him want to punch something—or someone. But he still didn't fancy turning tale-bearer, even of the damning evidence he'd just witnessed himself.

After a few more minutes of reflection, he decided to stick with his original intentions. He'd keep silent and continue to wait, in the confident expectation that Lord Halden's disreputable behaviour would eventually be brought before Miss Lattimar's eyes or into her hearing. At which time, she would finally allow the doubts she already harboured to convince her to abandon Fitzroy-Price as a lost cause—thereby ensuring she did not mire herself in a disaster of a marriage.

And meanwhile, he'd maintain an even closer watch, to make sure the Duke's son didn't manoeuvre her into an entanglement before she'd got a clear picture of his true character.

Fortunately, the arrogant ass was probably so confident that a young, handsome duke's son far outshone any other competing suitor, he probably wouldn't be in any great hurry to press Miss Lattimar into an engagement.

Chapter Seven

As the warm rays of the sun emerged out of a rosy coral dawn, Prudence reached the summit of Lansdown Hill. Pulling her hired mount to a halt, she paused to admire the magnificent vista down over the city, the pale stone buildings golden and shimmering in the mist rising from the river.

Even better, though, was the prospect offered by open downland that stretched away behind her, wide, flat trails occasionally bordered by small copses of trees that practically begged a horsewoman to indulge in a hard gallop.

Which was just what she needed, Pru thought, a surge of anticipation running through her. Maybe luxuriating in a long ride, a beloved pastime she'd had to forgo since leaving behind the carriage parks of London, would soothe the restlessness that had broken her sleep.

Convinced when she awoke again in pre-dawn blackness that recapturing sleep would prove impossible, she'd abandoned her bed, apologising first to the maid who stumbled in half-awake to help her dress and then to the kitchen staff who scrambled to assemble a meal after she arrived in the breakfast parlour hours before the family normally came down.

The tea, toast and cold ham they'd hastily made ready assuaged her hunger, but did nothing to dispel the ache of unease that sat like a rock in her chest. Knowing only one activity might help, while she finished her coffee, she dispatched a footman to the livery to engage a horse and groom for her.

Of course, no hired hack would be the equal of her fierce black gelding, Fury, she thought, giving the grey livery mare a gentle scratch behind her ears. But even if this little lady turned out to be unevenly paced, a gallop would help clear the cobwebs from her brain and brighten spirits that still hadn't recovered since the ugly incident at the Pump Room yesterday.

Much as she appreciated Johnnie's efforts on her behalf, the very fact that he'd had to make them—and planned to reinforce the gesture by circulating his version of the event to every important society matron in Bath—confirmed the worst fears she'd harboured before leaving London. Aunt Gussie's brave hope that bringing her to the smaller, less fashionable city so she might outdistance the rumours and innuendoes that would have flurried about her, had she attempted a come-out in the capital, had turned out to be futile.

The fact that her behaviour since arriving had been impeccable didn't seem to matter.

If society could only appreciate what an effort it required to always stifle her opinions and reactions, to wear a smile, appear serene and seemingly indifferent to slights! When, outrage suffusing her, she would have loved nothing better than to have slapped the smirk off Lieutenant Broadmere's face, right there in the Assembly Rooms. Repaid the soldiers for their insults during the walk in Sidney Gardens with some scathing replies about their own deficiencies of character. Or pointed out to the snide Lady Arbuthnot how unattractive she looked yesterday in that awful puce bonnet.

But no matter how prettily behaved she forced herself to be, to Bath society she was still just a Scandal Sister, an epithet they might never allow her to outlive.

Not that she intended to give up, she told herself, trying by force of will to raise her sagging spirits. She might be a 'Scandal Sister' to society here or in London, but if she could make a suitable marriage, she might still hope to escape carrying that label for the rest of her life.

She just needed that man of impeccable reputation to wed her and carry her off to some small village that cared little and knew less about London society. A kind, thoughtful man who could see and appreciate her for who she truly was and stand behind his loving, blameless wife in his community.

Wedding a clergyman still seemed the most promising way to accomplish that goal. But yesterday's incident had underlined her doubts that Lord Halden Fitzroy-Price was the right clergyman for the job.

Much as she tried to find common ground between them, aside from a love of horses, they didn't seem to share any interests.

And after yesterday, when he was clearly uneasy about remaining in her company after an incident that was sure to be the first topic of gossip in every drawing room in Bath, she wasn't sure he would continue to court her.

She was even less sure she wanted him to.

But what other prospects did she have? Several elderly retired military gentlemen, like General Gaulford and Colonel McQuery. Mr Wellington-Foxe, with his quiverful of expensive sons to support, or Sir Martin, a portly widower she'd just met who had a rambling household and several young children in need of managing.

And what *choice* did she have, but to marry? There was no other occupation available to a gently bred female. Better to settle for affection, children and a home of her own than to remain her whole life a dependent, living upon the goodwill of her father and, after his death, tolerated as a nursemaid or companion in some other relative's household.

Sadly, none of the eligible gentlemen in Bath appealed to her nearly as much as one handsome, fascinating—and for her, *ineligible*—gentleman. Not the settled, well-respected country gentleman or cleric she needed, but wandering adventurer Johnnie Trethwell.

A flash of fury and aggravation blasted through her, heating her face and making her clench her fists. Damn and blast, she was tired of the endless mental arguments! For the next hour, she'd forget them all and lose herself in the pleasure of the wind in her face and the sound of pounding hoofbeats.

Turning back to address the groom trailing her, she said, 'I'm going to put her through her paces.' Touching her heels to the mare's side, she signalled her forward.

Pushing her mount ever harder, Pru leaned low over the horse's head, urging her onwards with the silent pressure of knees and urgent hands on the reins. To her joy, the little mare responded with a burst of speed.

Wind threatened to pull Pru's hat from her head as the horse flew across the ground, seeming as thrilled as her rider to race to the limits of her endurance. The landscape passed in a blur of trees and shrubbery, her heart exulting with the joyful rhythm of the pounding hooves.

Ah, after the steep-streeted confines of Bath, the endless biting of her lip and stifling of her opinions, to finally be free!

Not until the mare was sweat-slicked and obviously tiring did Pru force herself to ease the horse back to a trot, then a walk, then signalled her to a halt. Laughing with exultation, she slipped down from the saddle, giving the horse another rub behind the ears before taking the bridle to lead the animal forward.

'Let's cool you down while we wait for the groom to catch up,' she said, rubbing the mare's velvet muzzle. 'I wish I'd thought to bring a treat for you, for what a trooper you are, my little grey miss! I ought to buy you from that livery. A girl with such a stout heart should only be ridden by someone who appreciates her.'

For the first time in a long time completely content, at the sound of approaching hooves, Pru smiled. Did she dare tease the groom about being left in the dust? But no, like most men, he'd not appreciate the suggestion that he'd been outridden by a girl.

There was only one man she knew who, she was almost certain, would have the confidence to be amused or appreciative, rather than feel challenged, by a female's abilities.

Dismissing with some difficulty the foolish longing for that unattainable gentleman, she prepared a more innocuous greeting. But as she turned to greet the horseman pulling up behind her, she discovered not the disapproving and probably irritated groom—but a merry-eyed Johnnie Trethwell.

'Bravo!' he exclaimed, giving her a salute. 'That was quite a gallop! Truly *ventre à terre*, just as I'd imagined you would ride!'

Conscious of a soaring delight she made no attempt to suppress, she said, 'As I already said, is there any other way? And oh, how glorious it was, to feel the wind in my face and the strength of a good mount beneath me and to finally *breathe* again! I must do this every day.'

'I don't wonder you felt…stifled. Have you recovered yet?' he asked, raking her face with a concerned look.

Thankful that, with Johnnie, she could for once speak frankly, she admitted, 'I would feel better if I'd been able to give Broadmere the roundhouse punch my brother taught me to deliver. One I *could* deliver, were I a *gentleman* whose reputation he was impugning! But since that is clearly out of the question, I'll have to do with a ride.'

She resisted the strong impulse to give him a full account of her worries. He had shown himself a true friend—hadn't he? But an adventurer who'd explored the bazaars—and if rumour held true, the harems—of the exotic east was unlikely to be very interested in the mundane struggles of an English maiden trying to find a conventional English husband.

'Maybe I can deliver it for you,' he said as she hesitated, debating. 'I have to admit, I'd obtain almost as much enjoyment from giving him a roundhouse punch as you would. A man who attacks a woman?' He shook his head in disgust. 'Beneath contempt. I'm surprised any man in his regiment tolerates him.'

'Probably because they are all of his ilk. If they were truly manly and adventurous, they would be off somewhere else, not wearing army regimentals in placid old England.'

He grinned. 'My thoughts exactly. Shall I escort you back to that lumbering groom I passed on my way?'

She shuddered. 'Oh, please, not yet! Tell me another story first. Perhaps about hunting tigers.'

'Very well, a story,' he agreed. After swinging down from the saddle, he gathered the reins loosely in one hand and fell in beside her, the two horses nuzzling each other as they trailed their riders.

Having Johnnie so near triggered a familiar, prickling sensory awareness all over her body. Ah, that she might nuzzle *him*, run her lips over his mouth, his chin…

A fiercer heat washed through her. Trying to rein in her thoughts before they galloped any further down that path, Pru forced herself to concentrate on his words.

'Although tigers abounded, tiger hunts were actually less frequent than you might imagine,' he was saying.

'Why—were the beasts too fierce for hunters to want to confront them?'

'Not exactly. It's just that the Hindus have an entirely different view of animals than the English. Believing that humans live through many stages, including in animal form, on the path to enlightenment and perfection, they have a reverence for and desire to protect all forms of life—something I found wholly admirable. In addition to the incredible beauty and diversity of the land! They only hunted when they saw it as absolutely necessary.'

'When did they find it necessary to hunt tigers?'

'Among the mountain tribes in particular, the natives believe a treaty exists between tigers and humans. They never go after one unless a tiger "breaks" the treaty by attacking or killing a villager. Then they send out a hunting party, and after bagging several to "teach the tigers a lesson", they believe the treaty goes back in force, each side ready to co-exist with the other again. They don't even hunt wolves, which are often a nuisance around camps.'

'Why—is there a treaty with them, too?' she asked, fascinated by this glimpse into a foreign land—and the love and enthusiasm for that land that illumined him as he described it.

'No. It's believed that if a hunter slays a wolf, from out of the land where its blood was spilled, several, even fiercer wolves will spring, intent on exacting revenge upon the hunter or his family. I've heard of women or children being carried off at night from within their own houses, with the villagers doing nothing. They're sure that some member of the victim's family must have at one time injured a wolf, who came to invoke a rightful revenge.'

Mesmerised, she shook her head. 'How vividly you make me see it—revenging wolves and treaty-making tigers! What a fascinating land!'

'An exotic and beautiful countryside, populated with an endlessly intriguing variety of cultures and clans. I found it mesmerising.' He shook his head wryly. 'Not, I'm afraid, a view that was much shared by my fellow soldiers. Many of them loathed the place. Though to be fair, the troops have no choice about where their regiments are posted. The East India Company officers were usually more appreciative, since they volunteered to serve there and, as financial and governing agents, had more contact with the population and got to know them better. Though even some of them thought of India service just as a way to make a fortune as quickly as possible so they might return and enjoy it back in England.'

'Were there any who made a fortune and chose to stay in India?'

'A few, and mostly from the early days.' He chuckled. 'I did have the privilege of visiting with Colonel Gardner, an old India hand who actually married into a Hindu family. His sons also married native women and his granddaughter married a Hindu prince. His family was intimate with a famous Marantha princess, Baiza Bai, who, unfortunately, I was *not* able to meet. What a fascinating woman! After her husband's death, she attempted to take over political power in the areas he had controlled. Alas, Indian law was no more supportive of a female's political ambitions than the English.'

'And here I thought all Indian women were cloistered in the *zenana*,' Pru said, impressed. 'How illuminating it would be to speak with such a woman! What stories *she* must have to tell!'

'I'm sure she would,' Johnnie agreed. 'But here comes your groom, looking properly disgruntled. You must charm him out of the mopes.'

'Yes, I must, for having rediscovered the joy of riding, I intend to do so often. Since I must suffer having a groom accompany me, I'd prefer it to be one I can outride!'

'Rascal,' he said, laughing. 'One you can outride, so you may escape scrutiny and go where you wish?'

'That too,' she allowed. 'But I would also just as soon

not have someone capable of racing on my flank, urging me to slow down to a more ladylike pace. I do have a care for my mount and would never ride one harder than it could bear. But this little lady seems to enjoy a good gallop as much as I do.'

'Instructive as it might be to watch you perform your magic, I must get back.' He halted, hesitating as the groom approached ever closer. 'Do you intend to ride every morning?'

Outdistancing her groom, so she might escape scrutiny and have a private word with this man who so enchanted her?

As she gazed up at him, the delicious sensual thrill she'd felt the whole time they'd walked together intensified the desire, always shimmering at the edges of consciousness, to be held in his arms, feel his lips on hers.

Meeting him—especially if she contrived to do so after outrunning her groom—was clearly dangerous. Yet, along with the physical temptation he represented, being with him brought her such…*ease* and comfort. Somehow she knew that, for the short time they were alone together, she could safely relax her guard and be herself. Voice her true thoughts, no matter how unexpected, unladylike, or unconventional. A freedom she didn't dare allow herself in any other company in Bath.

Reasoning that, as long as she remained on horseback, the physical distance imposed would keep in check her desire to taste his kisses, she simply couldn't deny herself the pleasure of meeting him again. 'Yes, I shall attempt to ride every morning I can.'

He nodded. 'Then perhaps I'll see you on the trail, as well as at social functions.'

She didn't want to let him go, knowing the next occasion she was sure to meet him wouldn't be until the Subscription Ball, two days hence. 'Would you be available to come to tea today? And Lady Woodlings, of course. Aunt Gussie and I will be at home.'

As he paused, reflecting, she felt a blush tinge her cheeks, that sudden invitation revealing all too clearly how much she wanted to see him. Would her boldness frighten him away?

'I'm not sure about my aunt, but I have no other engagements. Yes, I should be able to stop by.'

Breathing out a sigh of relief, Pru said, 'Very good. I'll look forward to seeing you, then.'

'As I will you. Well met, sir,' he said, turning to the groom who'd just brought his horse to a halt beside them. 'As you can see, the lady is safe and sound. I'll leave her to you, but do have a care. There's an army encampment not far to the west and Miss Lattimar is far too lovely to trot about in that vicinity without a protector. Miss Lattimar.' Giving her a short bow to her curtsy, he swung himself back in the saddle and, with a little wave, rode off.

Pru watched him go, knowing she shouldn't be nearly this excited at the prospect of seeing him again today. They would just be chatting over teacups under the eagle eye of their respective aunts.

But she *was* excited—and energised to start planning more such meetings. As she allowed the groom to give her a leg up back into the saddle, she was already scheming how to persuade this slow-riding chaperon to continue accompanying her on early morning excursions—beginning tomorrow.

Chapter Eight

After bathing, eating and dressing with care, that afternoon Johnnie limped up the stairs of Lady Stoneway's town house at the Circus—alone. He'd been not at all sorry a discreet enquiry revealed his aunt did in fact have a previous engagement, which saved him a possible lecture about the danger of seeking out *more* opportunities to be with Miss Lattimar and perhaps an outright refusal to accompany him. As he handed his hat and cane over to the butler, he had to admit to a feeling of anticipation at seeing the delightfully unconventional Miss Lattimar again.

Furies, but the woman could ride! Watching her gallop down that lane on Lansdown Hill yesterday was like listening to one of Daya's tales about the goddess Durga mounted on her tiger, weapons furled, racing off to defeat the forces of evil. Or to return to Western mythology, the virginal goddess Diana, were she to be mounted for the hunt. Trapped beneath the serene veneer she struggled to maintain was something wild and passionate and, curse him, he was increasingly tempted to try to release it.

The devil of it was, he was almost sure he could. Even as he knew he mustn't. It would be a betrayal of the friendship he'd pledged for him to liberate a wild unconventionality that, combined with the reputation she already carried, would doom for ever any chance she had of contracting the traditional marriage with the proper, upright member of society she claimed to want.

Even though he found it increasingly hard to believe such a future would really make her happy. A proper, upright husband and living a life of pious duty as a vicar's wife in a small village might, after years of sterling conduct, finally put to rest the unfair allegations that she was the moral, as well as physical, image of her profligate mother. But it would also trap her into playing a highly visible role where restrained behaviour and submissive deference would be expected in every aspect of her life. He wasn't so sure bare-footed spring-bathing with her own children would escape criticism from the more narrow-minded and censorious parishioners. Could she really be content, if she were forced to suppress that passionate nature for a lifetime?

As much as she was beginning to fascinate him, he was honest enough to admit he could offer her no better alternative. Even if he was warming to the idea of limiting himself to just one woman—to claim a woman like Prudence Lattimar, he might just be able to make that work—at the moment, he was the least likely man to give her what she wanted. Though he had prospects of obtaining on his own the financial backing he needed, he intended to use those funds to launch back out into the unknown—not retire to that estate in the placid English countryside she yearned for.

Such a bright, engaging spirit deserved to find the upright, settled husband she sought—one who not only shared her love of the countryside, but a man who would cherish her for the wonderful woman she truly was. One who appreciated the enchanting, unconventional loveliness of her as much as Johnnie did.

He had to admit, the image of her married to someone else somehow…grated. What delights might he experience, were *he* allowed to free that tempestuous spirit! Had he the least desire to mire himself for a lifetime in the back country of England, he might be tempted to try to win her heart.

Even as the thought formed, he knew it would be the act of a villain to try. Perhaps she could be charmed into quitting her beloved homeland, but for very good reasons, he had always adventured alone. Those reasons were still valid, no matter how intriguing the idea of showing perceptive, receptive Prudence Lattimar the glories and mysteries of the wider world outside England's shores.

Sadly, their planets would not align, he thought as the butler conveyed him to the drawing room. But he could still stand her friend and, within the strict confines of a drawing room, indulge himself in the refreshing novelty of her company, without putting either of them in danger.

Though he wasn't surprised to find other visitors present at Lady Stoneway's at-home, his euphoric mood slipped further when he noted the guest seated beside Miss Lattimar was Lord Halden Fitzroy-Price. Stopping short just inside the room, he hesitated, not sure he could manage to remain politely silent while a man whose true character he knew tried to bamboozle a lovely innocent. Confident in her aunt's ability to keep her safe inside her own drawing room, he'd half-turned to leave again when he caught an urgent look from Miss Lattimar.

Rescue me, it said.

How could any soldier fail to respond?

Telling himself he'd maintain a tight curb over his tongue—and keep his hands, already curled into fists with the desire to plant the scoundrel a facer, close to his sides—he gave her a tiny nod before walking over to greet his hostess, who was seated on the sofa adjoining hers with Mrs Marsden and two other ladies.

'Good afternoon, ladies,' he said, bowing as they nodded. 'Lady Stoneway, so kind of you to include me.'

'Lieutenant Trethwell, you're always welcome! Please, make yourself comfortable,' she said, gesturing to the chair beside the sofa where Prudence and Fitzroy-Price sat. 'Prudence, my dear, offer the Lieutenant some tea.'

'Yes, do join us,' she replied, smiling at him. Nodding a greeting to Lord Halden, who looked frankly surprised to see Johnnie so warmly welcomed into the bosom of the family, he had a hard time suppressing a smile as he took a seat.

Turning his thoughts to a more worthy subject, he paused to admire Miss Lattimar. How lovely she was in an afternoon gown of soft blue that made the gold of her hair sparkle! Yet the hue was only an inferior echo of the magnificent blue of her eyes. She truly was a work of art come to life—though the appeal of the vibrant spirit housed within the beautiful body excited his mind and passion as much as her appearance.

He looked up from appreciating her gracefulness

as she went through the ritual of pouring tea to see Fitzroy-Price staring at him.

Having dismissed him as beneath notice at the first, this cosy interlude must be giving the Duke's son pause. He was looking at Johnnie as if seeing him for the first time and being forced to evaluate whether this nonentity could actually be a threat to his ambitions of securing Miss Lattimar's hand—and dowry.

More of a threat than you imagine, Johnnie thought, meeting the man's eyes with a steely look that had induced many an opponent's face to colour as he turned away. For once, he was glad rumour branded him a charming fortune hunter. The Duke's son might discount his present occupation and prospects, but he would take seriously the unwelcome discovery that another man, apparently approved by her aunt, might be competing with him for the prize of Miss Lattimar's wealth.

Not that he had any designs on that—his wistful but destined-to-be-unfulfilled hopes centred more on capturing her body and spirit. But he was glad Fitzroy-Price now understood that he would not have the free hand to beguile the heiress, unchallenged.

To his credit, the Duke's son held Johnnie's gaze, their wordless confrontation not broken until Miss Lattimar recalled his attention by handing him his cup.

Not offering Johnnie even the courtesy of a greeting, Lord Halden addressed his full attention to Prudence. 'Shall we resume our conversation, Miss Lattimar? I was telling you about the new matched blacks I procured at such a good price from Atley. So many gambling losses, he's had to sell off his stable, poor man!'

Wonder how you'll pay yours when you fail to secure Miss Lattimar's dowry, Johnnie thought.

Still ignoring him—and not pausing long enough for Miss Lattimar to reply—Lord Halden continued, 'Indeed, the afternoon promises to be quite lovely. Won't you ride out in my curricle with me? With my hands on the ribbons, Lady Stoneway,' he added, breaking in on that lady's conversation to address her aunt, 'she will be entirely safe, I assure you.'

Without giving her aunt time to reply, Prudence said, 'Perhaps another time, Lord Halden. Lieutenant, would you relate to my aunt and her friends something more about the treatment of animals in India? As I told my aunt,' she explained to the group, 'I met Lieutenant Trethwell by chance while I was out riding this morning. He very kindly rode with me for a while and regaled me with the most fascinating stories about tigers and wolves!'

'It sounds quite—fierce!' Mrs Marsden said with a little shudder.

'Oh, no! It's just that the Hindus venerate all animals, in such unusual ways,' Miss Lattimar replied. 'Knowing how much you adore animals, especially your darling pug Hero, I thought you'd find it interesting.'

'Venerate? In what way? Please tell us more, Lieutenant,' Lady Stoneway said.

'If you insist,' Johnnie said, trying not to laugh out loud at the shock, succeeded by fury, on Lord Halden's face at having his offer brusquely rebuffed in favour of a story spun about *India*.

'It's true, the Hindus believe all living things possess a soul. For that reason, many of them eat no meat and they try to make sure animals are never harmed.

Wild peacocks, partridges and ducks wander through the villages with no more fear of the human inhabitants as if they were domesticated fowl. After harvest, when the corn is threshed by oxen for the villagers to share, peacocks peck at stray kernels, while squirrels dodge around the oxen's hooves to snag a little. Often, monkeys hang about in the trees all around, darting in to claim a considerable handful, without anyone attempting to molest them.'

'Even when they are stealing food the villagers planted, tended and harvested?' Lady Stoneway exclaimed.

'All living things carry within them a part of the divine, the Hindus believe, and as such have a right to sustenance, which should be freely offered. Indeed, travellers going past villages are often brought jugs of water and offerings of bread, grain and fruit. Some villages even maintain thatched huts near the village entrance where travellers may spend the night.'

'How very hospitable!' Mrs Marsden said.

Johnnie chuckled. 'Even when it may not be to their advantage. There were always a plague of stray dogs hanging about the villages, existing on scraps, and sometimes they become rabid. To protect public health, the Company decided to round up the strays. They posted notices that on a certain day, any dogs found wandering unattended would be seized and destroyed. Just before the allotted time, the villagers herded all the strays into their houses, so when the inspectors came by, there were none on the streets to be found.'

'How curious—and fascinating!' Aunt Gussie said. 'You must join us for dinner some evening! I should love to hear more about your travels and experiences. Oh, and we will send you a card, too, of course, Lord Halden.'

'So I might listen to another lecture from the well-travelled Lieutenant? I believe my schedule might be too full,' he said stiffly.

'Yes, I'm sure you are extremely busy,' Miss Lattimar flashed back, her serene face at odds with the slight edge in her tone. 'Today as well, I expect. We'll understand if you wish to take your leave now, won't we, Aunt?'

'I should be leaving, too,' Mrs Marsden said. 'I promised I'd call on Lady Belk this afternoon. She's not been well of late.'

The company rose. Realising he'd eked out as long a visit as custom permitted—and satisfied to have rattled Lord Halden's arrogant complacency in regard to his hold over Miss Lattimar—Johnnie turned to depart as well when Miss Lattimar caught his sleeve, shaking her head with a silent 'no'.

Halting, he remained beside her as her aunt ushered out the other guests.

'You may be losing your admirer,' he told her *sotto voce.*

'Maybe I should be glad to lose him,' she murmured back, the serenity of her face momentarily breached by a fleeting expression of doubt. 'He was unaccountably rude to you—again.'

'You got back at him, though, inviting me to tell a story about India. I almost felt sorry for him.'

She gave a tight smile. 'He never enjoys a conversation unless he's the centre of it. Oh, my—that sounds unkind! But unfortunately, my experience with him shows it to be true.'

Delighted at this further evidence that the Duke's son's grip on her hopes appeared to be loosening, Johnnie bit his tongue before asking whether this was the kind of man she wanted to spend the rest of her life with.

No need to press. Despite a very strong desire to see her future settled in the manner she hoped, she was gradually coming to see for herself that Lord Halden Fitzroy-Price was not the man to fulfil those dreams.

He wished he were. Shocked by that errant thought, he shut his ears to the whisper before it could utter anything else equally heretical.

'I can't let you linger, unfortunately,' she murmured, recalling him. 'But I wanted to keep you for a moment, to thank you for coming today and sharing another wonderful story. Which I would have asked for, even if I hadn't wanted to rebuke Lord Halden's discourtesy. Will…will you ride again tomorrow?'

'You succeeded in charming the hired groom out of his disgruntlement?'

'No charm required. The promise of a hefty increase in his fee, if he agreed to have the grey mare ready and to accompany me any time I wished to ride, was enough.' She chuckled. 'For the handsome sum I offered, I believe he will let me outride him as often as I like!'

'Perhaps we can test that notion tomorrow.'

'You'll be there, then? Just after the sun is up?'

The ardent appeal on her face lit a little glow in his heart that shouldn't be there. Ignoring the bugle call of warning that fact triggered in his brain, he said, 'I'll be there.'

* * *

As the sun warmed the roofs of the buildings in the city below, sending a steam of vapour to mist the morning sky, Johnnie guided his hack on to the trail leading from the heights of Lansdown Hill towards the racetrack. His experience with society ladies, most of whom attended social events until the wee hours and rose correspondingly late in the mornings, made him sceptical that Miss Lattimar would actually make a habit of riding out just past daybreak—a time when generally only tradesmen and servants were up and about. But sure enough, as he rounded the next bend, he spied her on the grey mare she'd ridden the day before, trailed by the stout groom on his bay gelding.

His spirits rose and his body tightened in anticipation. With just the two of them, far from the censorious ears of polite society, what outrageous remarks, what unexpected observations would she gift him with today?

The royal-blue riding habit that hugged her generous curves made him glad they were both mounted. With that brilliant smile she turned on him when she saw him approach drawing him like iron shavings to a magnet, without the impediment of horses between them, he didn't think he could have resisted the urge to kiss her.

'Bravo again, Miss Lattimar. I wasn't sure you would manage to propel yourself from your chamber so early two days in a row.'

'What, you take me for a slug-abed? I've always loved being up early, watching the night recede and the day ride in on its golden chariot. Or wrapped in its mantle of weeping rain clouds, more often.'

'What shall it be first, a walk or a gallop?'

'A gallop, of course! While the road is still deserted. And if your black can match my grey, he's well worth the hire!'

With that, she touched heels to the mare, who leapt forward immediately, displaying the same impressive acceleration he'd admired yesterday.

As it turned out, his black could not keep pace. Some moments later, when he urged his tiring mount past another stand of trees, he found her already pulled up and waiting, sitting easily in the saddle as she retied the strings of her bonnet under her chin.

'Not a slug,' she said with a wave of her hand to his horse, 'but not the equal of my little grey lady.'

'She is exceptional,' he agreed. *Almost as exceptional as her rider.*

'Not that I think your pride is hurt, but I'm sure you'd have made a better showing on a different mount.'

He grinned. 'I think my ego will withstand the blow. However, if I had Stalwart, the horse I rode in India, I believe I could have bested you.'

She pointed her riding crop at him in a challenging gesture. 'And if I had *my* mount of choice, Fury, I am sure you could not! Shall we walk them?'

'Yes, let's cool them down. It will take a while for your groom to catch up. That bay of his didn't seem to want to break a trot.'

'He told me that as long as I don't ride towards the west, in the direction of the soldiers' encampment, he felt confident I could gallop ahead and still be safe for the short time it would take him to reach me. Come, let's walk them while you tell me another story.'

Matching action to her words, she slipped gracefully out of the saddle and gathered her mare's reins in one hand. After giving his valiant black's neck a rub, he followed suit.

'Now,' she said as they strolled forward. 'Since no society matrons are present to disapprove my choice of topic, I want to ask about Indian ladies. Did you take a *maharani* as your mistress, Lieutenant Trethwell?'

Surprised anew, Johnnie threw back his head and laughed. What other English maiden would dare ask him such a question? Even Aunt Pen hadn't been that indiscreet. 'You really don't have any maidenly restraint.'

'Not a jot. I didn't think I needed any, not with you. Given my upbringing, you could hardly expect me to be missish. Temper and I became aware of the significance of Mama's gentlemen callers when we'd barely reached our teens.'

'If we're to chat about something that scandalously intimate, you'd best call me Johnnie.'

'Then you must call me Pru. When no one else is about, of course.'

'Of course.' *Uninhibited, yet still quaintly cautious. Could she be more enchanting?* he thought, entertained by her intriguing mix of innocence and worldliness.

'So, tell me about the ladies of the *zenana*. Is it true that they are always cloistered away from men and cannot go abroad without their faces covered?'

'Yes, most practise *purdah*, a separation from men. But the females of the Mahratta were excellent horsewomen and would ride out unveiled. Peasant women also went to the wells to gather water, which is where soldiers usually encountered them. High-born women were more strictly cloistered, spending their days among other women and their serving girls. Generally a laughing, indolent lot, always exquisitely groomed, eyes accented with kohl, dressed and bejewelled as richly as their circumstances permitted, even in the middle of the day within the walls of the *zenana*.'

She gave him a saucy smile. 'Just how do you know so much about what happens in the *zenana*, if you did not have a liaison with a *maharani*?'

He laughed, recalling it. 'In my information-gathering forays, I sometimes posed as a travelling merchant. Wandering about with a sack full of trinkets, one was nearly invisible in the crowded markets. Then one day, I found myself pulled along by a servant boy into a nearby house. Apparently the mistress had observed me selling my treasures through her shuttered windows and sent the boy to fetch me so she and her ladies could inspect my wares. I must admit, after that fascinating encounter, I sometimes took a break from my intelligence-gathering mission to refresh myself with a vision of feminine loveliness.'

'And the master of the household did not object to this intrusion?'

'Those dark-eyed beauties can have fierce tempers! Once, when one attempted to object, his lady subjected him to such a string of abuse, he gave in.'

'What a shocking rogue you were!' she said, laughing delightedly. 'So, no *maharani*. What of the other native girls? I understand nearly all the British soldiers serving in India took native mistresses.'

Surprised again, he gave her a sharp look. 'What makes you think that?'

'Temper and I read Captain Mundy and Captain Skinner's journals of their sojourns in India.'

'Good heavens!' he exclaimed. 'Your reading material has been as unrestricted as your upbringing!'

'We've always had full access to Papa's library—some of the Greek and Roman translations are quite... sensual. Then, Temper has been obsessed for years by the desire to explore abroad and combs the bookshops for volumes about travel. Naturally, when she saw memoirs about a land as exotic as India, she snapped them up. So, did most soldiers take native mistresses? Did you? I'm sorry, you're not...offended by the question?'

As the bittersweet memories welled up, he shook his head. Having encouraged her to ask outrageous questions, it was hardly fair to object when she did—no matter how painful the nerve they struck. Nor, given her openness, did he feel it right to turn suddenly prim and refuse to answer.

'I'm not...offended, precisely. Many soldiers did take native wives. To some extent, the liaisons can be helpful—mostly for the soldier. He becomes acquainted with the manners and customs of the local people and is able to learn their language. He gains some vestige of a home life, with a kind partner to keep house, cook and tend him when he falls ill.'

'Was that how you learned the language and customs so well, you could pass as a travelling salesman?'

'If that's an indirect way of asking if *I* kept a native mistress, the answer is no. But you're correct, I did learn about language and culture from one such lady. Daya, the consort of my best friend, Tom Alcorn.'

She studied his face. 'It did not end well, this union?'

He'd never repeated the story to any English female—not even Aunt Pen. His regret, anger and grief over Daya's death, his guilty sense of responsibility for Alcorn's, were sores that had never healed. To those who asked about his days in India, he'd always confined himself to relating amusing stories. Why abandon that prudent restraint now?

He looked up to find her compassionate gaze on his face. 'You needn't answer me, if you don't wish to. I have no right to pry into the intimate details of your life.'

Could divulging the tale to this female, whose unusual upbringing had made her more interested in and less judgemental of others than any other English person he'd ever met, help relieve some of that lingering anguish?

Maybe it was having spoken so freely of intimate matters he'd seldom discussed even with the closest friends, but suddenly he felt moved to tell her the whole.

'Daya was a girl from one of the villages near our encampment. "Mercy", her name means, and she certainly exhibited that quality! As I think I told you, usually villagers are very hospitable, bringing water, dates, food, even garlands of flowers to greet visitors. But the towns near the cantonments had become rather wary of soldiers. When we approached the wells, the girls drawing water would usually scatter. Most did, the day Alcorn and I rode up to her village, dusty and thirsty. But not Daya. She walked right up to us, smiling, and offered us the water jug she'd just filled.

'She had a lovely smile and shining dark eyes,' he continued, gazing into the distance as the scene came back to him in all its vivid colour. 'The picture of grace and loveliness in her bejewelled sari. I was struck by her, but Alcorn was completely dazzled. He returned several times to the well, and the last time, he brought her back to camp with him. She was such a shining spirit, so bright, eager to learn English, eager as well to teach us her language and her ways. Her tales about the gods and goddesses, temples, debating scholars and holy beggars, inspired me to begin roaming about on my own.' He laughed. 'She was the one who advised me to dye my exposed skin with betel juice and brought me the native dress that would allow me to stroll about, unnoticed.'

'You were fond of her.'

He tilted his head, assessing. 'Yes, I was. But Alcorn loved her, which thrust him into a dilemma. He couldn't marry her and take her back to England. He knew any children born of their union were destined to be outcasts in both cultures. But he couldn't imagine life without her, either. If things hadn't transpired as they did, I think he would have married her quietly and remained in India, perhaps taking a position with one of the Company's military forces.'

'What did happen?' she asked softly.

'One of the conditions many men made for taking mistresses is that they would not produce children.'

She raised her eyebrows. 'That's not so easy to guarantee.'

'No,' he said shortly. 'Despite the native women's claims of knowing foolproof remedies to prevent conception, they didn't. Daya must have fallen pregnant, but though she had to know Tom would never have abandoned her, she didn't tell Alcorn. Apparently, after the potions failed to work, she went to a woman in the village who promised to take care of it. She bled to death.'

'How awful!' she gasped, reaching out to touch his sleeve. 'I'm so very sorry.'

Finding the gesture strangely comforting, he said, 'Alcorn was never the same after that. I guess we both went a little crazy, he drowning himself in drink, me frequently going off alone to explore. Trying to outrun my fury at inhabiting a world where both societies would allow something like this to happen, I suppose. After being several times reprimanded for it, some higher-up decided if I was going to roam about anyway, I might as well collect useful information while I was at it.'

'They must have found that *wonderfully* useful.'

He grimaced. 'Perhaps. But if I'd been something of a loner already, my expeditions sealed that fate. Although when the British first arrived, outnumbered on tiny outposts, contact between and cordial terms with the local people was tolerated, if not encouraged, but as the Company tightened its grip over the country, there were fewer and fewer exchanges. The English came to see their role as guiding a benighted backward people towards the light, religiously and culturally. All things Indian were disdained and any Englishman who admired their culture or wished to mingle with them was looked upon as peculiar and "un-British".'

She nodded. 'Yes, in our literary explorations of the wider world, Temper and I read Mills's book. He was quite dismissive of the native peoples and their heritage.'

She'd surprised him yet again. 'You've read Mills's *History of British India*? You are an unusual woman!'

'Whether I want to be or not,' she said drily. 'What happened to Alcorn? Did he stay in India after all, or resign and go home?'

Johnnie felt the knife of grief twist again in his chest. 'There were dacoits—outlaws—operating in the area, attacking traders. The army sent us out to investigate. Some of the renegades' scouts must have alerted them, because they had an ambush ready for us. Rather than fall back with us so we could regroup, Alcorn raised his sword and rode straight at them.' He took a shuddering breath. 'When I realised what he was doing, I rode after him...but I was too late. He was slashed to pieces.'

Tears in her eyes, she shook her head. 'Another terrible death.'

'Perhaps. But I think Alcorn wanted to die. Maybe he hoped, in some afterlife between the reincarnation of the Hindus and the heaven of the Christians, he and Daya might be united in death as they could not be in life.'

'You were wounded while going after him.'

He nodded. It haunted him still...realising, to his disbelief, that instead of riding back beside him as he'd expected, Alcorn had wheeled his mount and galloped off alone. He'd turned in the saddle, urging his mount forward again, shouting at his friend to retreat. Watched helplessly as Tom rode into that certain death of slashing sabres, then battled alone for his own life.

'Finally realising what was happening, the rest of the company rode into action behind me. They kept me from suffering the same fate Tom had.'

Their rescue couldn't assuage the terrible guilt he felt over not anticipating Tom's suicidal charge, the agonising doubt over whether there might have been any way he could have saved the closest friend he'd ever had. Nor could any relief over surviving himself mitigate the stark, soul-penetrating grief that came from knowing Tom and Daya had been taken, leaving him once again, as he had been for almost all his life, completely alone.

A devastation he never wished to experience again.

'There wasn't anything you could have done,' she said softly. 'I hope they did find peace together.'

It was only then, as he struggled to pull himself from the past, that he realised she'd somehow known what he'd been thinking—the guilt, if not the devastation. Feeling both warmed by her understanding and dangerously exposed, he pushed the thought away.

'Enough stories from me. What about your past? Your mother and how you deal with her? She must be an incredible beauty, if you are said to be her image.'

'Beautiful, yes. Also witty, well informed and alluring. Men fall for her in droves, even now. To be fair, she no longer looks to attract new lovers. Although her uninterest only seems to spur men on.'

'The lure of the unattainable. Do you admire her?'

She sighed. 'Admire. Resent. I even hated her for a while, when I grew old enough to envision a come-out and realised society would hold her sins against me. Temper was angry with her, too, until she turned sixteen. Then she suddenly decided she would never wed and would attack those who maligned Mama.' Prudence smiled. 'She's going to try to get our father to release her dowry, so she may travel the world, like Lady Hester Stanhope. Though I can't blame her for disdaining marriage. Our parents' union was hardly an advertisement for the estate.'

'My parents', either,' he agreed. 'If he is so indifferent to her activities, why did your father marry your mother?'

'Since his youth, he has collected beautiful things. The only explanation we've been able to come up with is that, having seen her, the most beautiful girl of her debut Season, he simply had to add her to his collection. He was wealthy, and her dowry was small, so her family pushed her into the union. It was only later, after he virtually ignored her, that she began to take lovers. Temper thinks she turned to other men to try to spark Vraux into some reaction. She never got one and, by the time she'd dallied with one or two, she'd acquired that notorious reputation. Defiant as my sister, she embraced it.'

Johnnie could hardly believe a man could possess a wife as beautiful as Prudence Lattimar and be indifferent to having other men seduce her. Were Pru his, he'd gut anyone who tried to touch her.

'Your father was never angry, or jealous?'

She shook her head. 'I've never been able to figure Father out. He seems to have this…horror of touching. When I was a child and tried to embrace him, he would push me away. Gently, but with such a look of…distaste in his eyes, I soon stopped trying. Once Mama produced an heir, he seemed content to let her go her own way. I'm not supposed to know, but I overheard Aunt Gussie telling my brother Gregory that when Mama was *enceinte* with Christopher, her unmarried lover tried to persuade Father to divorce her, so they might wed and he could claim the child as his own. Father refused. Christopher has…an accommodation with his natural father, who recognises him, and even supported him for his Parliamentary seat.'

'And what of your natural father? Do you have any contact with him?'

'None. Aunt Gussie told Gregory that Christopher's father was the love of Mama's life and, after she lost him, she buried her grief in a string of lovers, one of whom fathered us. But unlike Christopher's father, who only married when he could not have Mama, this gentleman had no wish to acknowledge us.'

As lonely and unappreciated as he'd felt in childhood, how much worse had it been for her? Abandoned by her natural father, pushed away by her legal one.

No wonder she yearned for a man to love and care for her. Compassion welling up, wishing he could do something to ease the pain he read in her tear-bejewelled eyes, he grasped her chin. 'Mine had no time for me, either,' he told her as he lifted her face towards his. 'Too bad you weren't born a man! You could have consigned them all to perdition, as I did, and gone adventuring.'

Gazing into her eyes, he was overcome by the awe and wonder her beauty always evoked in him. But her loveliness was as sensual as it was pure.

The softness of her face burned into his fingers, firing again the passion that always smouldered beneath the surface, stealing his breath, holding him so spellbound he could scarcely move. 'Right now, I am very thankful you're a woman,' he whispered.

The silence of the copse of trees sheltering them hummed with the force of attraction between them. Finally giving in to it, as her eyes fluttered closed and she raised her face, Johnnie bent to kiss her...

And heard the clip-clop of approaching hoofbeats. Heart racing, he released her chin and stepped away. An instant later, the groom came trotting past the greenery, spotted them and redirected his mount.

Fisting hands that still trembled, half-furious, half-relieved at the interruption, he laughed.

Her eyes startled, her face went pale, then coloured with a blush. 'What?' she demanded, her tone gruff.

Was she as disappointed as he was to have been cheated of that embrace?

'A fortuitous, if infuriating, interruption.'

Apparently, she only then noticed the approaching groom. Jerking her gaze away from Johnnie, she gave a gasp. 'Oh! Stebbins. You're…here.'

'Yes, miss. Sorry it took so long.'

'Just as well,' Johnnie said. 'We've had time to walk the horses and cool them down.'

'Shall I give you a leg up, miss?' the groom asked.

Giving Johnnie a regretful look, Pru said, 'Yes, please. I suppose it's time we were heading back to the city.'

Once remounted, they signalled the horses to a trot side by side, the groom trailing behind.

Knowing the moment for scandalous exchanges was at an end, Johnnie said, 'What would you do, if you could not marry a vicar?'

She sighed. 'Retreat to Entremer, I suppose. Work with the horses. Among other things he collected, Papa acquired some magnificent Arabians and some prime Irish hunters. I'd love to try breeding his prizes.' She laughed ruefully. 'I do love the country. I'm the only one in the family who doesn't see living in Northumberland as punishment and exile.'

'Surely you could go to London next year and have your Season then.'

'What, as long in the tooth as I'll be? I'd be considered past my last prayers by then! Besides, how could I expect to be received more favourably by society there than I have been here? London is even more critical and censorious than Bath.'

'Perhaps. But you can't consider Bath a reasonable test. There are hardly enough eligible young gentlemen to qualify it as a proper Marriage Mart. And while you'd not wish to marry a man who was interested only in your dowry, surely among the many who gather in London, there'll be several wise enough to see the gold of your worth through the dross of gossip surrounding you. Maybe even a clergyman.'

Her eyes had dimmed, but at that, they relit. 'You truly think so?'

In trying to lift spirits that an imminent return to the city had obviously sent tumbling, was he giving her false hope? 'Surely not all young gentleman are as block-headed as the handful you've met here in Bath.'

'Many of them seem to be.' At her suddenly acerbic tone, he turned towards the direction in which she was looking—and spied her three tormentors, Dawson, Broadmere and Truro, riding up Lansdown Hill. Their path back to the city, and the soldiers' towards the encampment, were about to converge and there was no way to avoid them.

Pru stiffened, her expression going blank. Johnnie could almost see the mantle of serene, eminently respectable young lady fall back over her. Raising her chin as they approached, she greeted the soldiers politely.

Perhaps Broadmere had been sufficiently chastened, or perhaps it was Johnnie's glowering presence beside her, but the trio replied with unexceptional greetings of their own. With neither party slowing their pace to allow for conversation, they were soon past them and descending into the city.

Once they were out of sight, Prudence blew out a breath. 'You can rest easy. I resisted the urge to jump out of the saddle, run over and punch Broadmere.'

Surprised again, but delighted by her fierceness, Johnnie laughed. 'A fortunate thing. Once you began pummelling, I'm not sure I could have pulled you off him.'

'They seemed rather subdued. They must have been up early for them to be already returning from making their purchases in town.'

'My poor innocent! They're probably just now returning from their night's revels.'

Obviously embarrassed by her naivety, her cheeks pinked. 'Yes, you're undoubtedly correct.'

There it was again, that flash of innocence in the midst of her worldliness. He felt like gathering her up and running off with her, so she might be his alone.

This will never do, he told himself, trying to cram the potent mix of desire and affection back into whatever crevice of his soul from which it had escaped. Distracted by that struggle, he found himself saying, 'Will I see you again later today?'

'Probably not, unfortunately. I'm accompanying Aunt Gussie to visit a friend who's been ill, after which we'll dine *en famille* with Mrs Marsden.'

'You'll ride tomorrow?'

'In the morning, if the weather holds fair.'

He scanned the sky, frowning. 'With the way the clouds are scudding in, we should look for rain.'

'If it's too wet in the morning, I'll try for the afternoon. We have no other engagements and, having resumed the pleasure of a daily ride, I would hate to miss it.'

By now, they had reached the city, where a bustling transit of pedlars, workmen, maids and footmen running errands, and sedan chairs carrying residents for their morning ablutions at the baths, made conversation more difficult.

Bringing her horse to a halt, Prudence raised her voice. 'I'll head off for the Circus now. Thank you for your company, Lieutenant Trethwell.'

Conscious of a curious little sinking feeling in his chest at the prospect of leaving her, he bowed. 'The pleasure was mine, Miss Lattimar.'

Holding his mount steady, he watched her ride off, trying to resist the ridiculous notion that happiness rode with her.

Turning his mount towards Queen Square, he ignored the urge to ride after Prudence and find some excuse to prolong their encounter. He had no business seeking out additional opportunities to be with her—almost daring himself to fall deeper under her spell. Once his leg had adequately healed, he intended to go to London and approach the men who had indicated interest in sponsoring his work.

While Prudence would doubtless make an observant, curious companion on his travels, as Tom and Daya's deaths had taught him, he'd be wise to stick to his resolve to always travel alone. Leave Bath, before she could engage his emotions any further. Safer for *her* to remain in her beloved England, where, never having truly possessed her, he wouldn't have to worry about how catastrophic it might be to lose her.

And then he had to laugh. Why was he expending all this needless angst? He just needed to remind himself that while he burned to travel the globe, all Prudence yearned for was to settle quietly in the English countryside.

Chapter Nine

Rain coming on as Johnnie had predicted, it wasn't until the afternoon of the following day that the showers eased and Prudence was able to ride up Lansdown Road on to the heights about the city.

Resisting the urge to gallop immediately, she trotted the mare for a time, hoping to hear behind her the welcome approach of Johnnie on his black. But after nearly an hour of proceeding at a sedate pace, restless, she reluctantly concluded that he'd not been able to get away and put spurs to her mare.

Pushing away the questions and worries circling in her head, Pru lost herself in the sound of thundering hoofs, the rush of the wind whipping at her face. Racing around a sharper curve, she had to suddenly veer on to the verge to avoid running down a group of soldiers riding at an easy pace in the direction of the racetrack.

Dawson, Broadmere and Truro among them.

Damnation, did those fellows never go off on military exercises? she wondered as she guided the mare around that obstacle and back on to the trail. As eager to put them behind her as she was to outrace her dilemma, she urged the mare ever faster. So fast, a sudden gust of strong wind ripped the bonnet from her head.

Unwilling to pull up and retrieve it, she drove the horse onwards until the mare's slowing pace and sweating neck indicated her mount had reached the limits of her endurance. Pulling the grey to a halt, she patted the horse's slick side.

'Sorry to push you so hard, my beauty, but what a game speedster you are!' she murmured. 'This time, I thought to bring you a treat by way of apology. Then we'll fetch my hat.'

Slipping from the saddle, she offered a bit of apple, then gathered up the reins and turned her tired mount back towards the city. After a time, she came upon the small grouping of trees and shrubs where she thought the bonnet had gone flying.

Nothing clung to the branches nearest the road, but there was a gap in the trees leading into a wooded copse beyond. Walking the mare into it, she spied the errant bonnet caught in a tangle of hawthorns on the leeward side of the enclosure. Looping the mare's reins around the closest bush, she set off to retrieve it.

Returning with it to where she'd tethered the mare, she shook off the dust, pulled off the leaves caught in the feather trimming and was retying it on her head when she heard the clop of hoofbeats and a murmur of approaching voices. Realising the riders must be the soldiers she'd bypassed earlier and not wishing to encounter them while alone and unprotected by even the groom, she quickly led her horse deeper into the shrubbery.

True to the adage that one never hears any good when eavesdropping, as the voices grew close enough to be distinguishable, she realised, to her chagrin, that they were discussing *her*.

'Galloping like a circus performer at Astley's, not even a groom in sight!' one voice said derisively.

'Maybe heading to an assignation?' another suggested. 'I wouldn't mind an afternoon interlude at some shepherd's cottage with that little beauty.'

As the voices grew louder, one she recognised as Lord Chalmondy Dawson's remarked, 'An assignation, without doubt. Fast as she was riding, I'll bet she's as hot for it as you would be.'

The voices were now passing the entrance to her hiding place. Incredulous and outraged that they would discuss her so contemptuously, she was torn between running out to confront them—and the wiser course of ensuring she was not discovered. Conflicted, Prudence forced herself to remain immobile, barely breathing. If only there were a way to stop her ears from hearing their degrading remarks!

'Can't you just see it?' Dawson said in mocking tones. 'Our good friend Lord Halden arriving home from his parish church, his virtuous little wife greeting him on the doorstep with open arms extended—to unbutton his trouser flap. Then falling on her knees to pleasure him while he offers a welcome home prayer!'

'Can you imagine anything more ridiculous than that wanton creature thinking to play a vicar's wife?' Truro said scornfully.

'But as he's several times said, once Fitzroy-Price has her money, he won't need a parish,' Dawson reminded. 'He can tether her in the countryside and sample her delights whenever the mood strikes, then leave her there and repair to London.'

'With blunt enough to sample as many other delights as he chooses,' Broadmere said.

Their outburst of raucous laughter gradually faded as the hoofbeats retreated into the distance, their voices reduced to an unintelligible murmur.

Too shocked and horrified to move, Prudence's hands shook as she gripped the reins. Her chest ached with the effort of suppressing the outrage, fury and mortification triggered by the soldiers' crude, humiliating remarks.

She knew that among the privacy of their friends, men probably discussed women in the most base and graphic of terms. But this was *her* they were describing so degradingly. The raging part of her wanted to run after them and abuse them as roundly as they'd just abused her.

But with her face framed by the strands of hair blown out of her coiffure after she'd lost her hat, her bonnet dusty and its once jaunty feather drooping, storming out to confront them would probably only reinforce their view of her as an ill-behaved wanton.

Looping the reins over a bush again, she used her fingertips to comb back under her hat as many errant wisps as she could locate without a looking glass to assist her. She'd remain here another few minutes to make sure the soldiers were too far away to spot her when she emerged. And to master completely the useless rage, burning humiliation and a foolish, juvenile *hurt* she should be far too cynical to feel.

Minutes crawled by while she stood there, taking deep breaths to stave off the stupid urge to weep. As intolerable as it had been to overhear herself discussed in such a disrespectful manner, even more shocking was the casual assertion she'd heard—offered by Lord Chalmondy Dawson, the man who supposedly had known him since childhood—that Lord Halden had no real vocation for the ministry and, if he could gain another source of income, would not take holy orders.

So much for her optimistic hopes that maturity and immersion in the solemn duties and responsibilities of the priesthood would correct the deficiencies of character that had troubled her, turning him into the kind of man she could admire and support.

Instead, he was, in essence, just another fortune hunter, however highly born. Marrying him would gain her, not a respected place in the community as a vicar's wife, but solitary exile in the country—the only safe place to immure a wife with a wanton reputation.

Feeling too heartsick and weary to maintain the cool, calm façade she must present to the world, once she could safely emerge from her hiding place, she would ride back to the sanctuary of her bedchamber as quickly as her mount could carry her. Where, hidden even from Aunt Gussie, she could allow herself to mourn the two bitter truths she could no longer deny. The duplicity of Lord Halden Fitzroy-Price and the death of her dream of attaining respectability by marrying a respectable man.

So upset was she, it wasn't until she led her horse out of the copse a few moments later that she realised the obvious fact that her homeward journey would not be swift. Without a companion and with no convenient log or fence nearby to assist her, she'd be unable to clamber back into the saddle. Until she reached the clearing where the groom should be waiting for her, she could proceed no faster than a walk.

Somehow, that additional delay, a minor irritation she would normally have shrugged off, seemed the last straw. Though she was able to hold back sobs, she couldn't halt the tears that began sliding down her cheeks, blinding her as she trudged back in the direction of Bath.

Too numb and miserable to even care how she looked, when a horseman approached at a canter, she merely swiped the tears from her face with her sleeve and looked to the side, pretending an absorbing interest in the distant vista of trees and fields.

Until a familiar voice shocked her back to the present.

'Prudence!' Johnnie cried. 'What happened? Did you take a fall? Are you all right?'

To her dismay, the concern in his tone, so at odds with the callous disregard of the soldiers, seemed to make the tears flow faster. Shaking her head in the negative, she tried without success to manufacture a smile while she steadied her voice enough to speak. 'N-no, I... N-nothing happened.'

'Don't be ridiculous! Something happened,' he snapped as he jumped down from the saddle. 'Come, let's get you tidied up.' Snagging her horse's reins with one hand and adding them to his own, he took her elbow, guiding her off the road and behind the partial shelter of a broad oak. 'Your hair's coming down and your bonnet's a disaster. You're sure you didn't fall?'

Looking up at him defiantly, her chin still trembling, she said, 'I never fall. I... I lost my hat while galloping and had to dismount to retrieve it.'

'Oh, truly?' he asked sceptically. 'The disarray of her coiffure and the destruction of her hat was all it took to move the intrepid Miss Lattimar to tears?'

Damn him, that reminder of the cause of her distress increased the flow of tears she was trying so hard to stem. 'Is...is it truly so impossible for me to ever be thought respectable?' she whispered, tears once again blurring her vision.

She heard what sounded like a strangled curse. Then he pulled her directly behind the broad tree trunk and took her in his arms. Where, to her added mortification, she could no longer restrain the sobs.

Feeling again like the lost little girl crying after a fall who'd been passed by, unnoticed, by a mother on the arm of her latest lover, she lay her head on Johnnie's chest and wept out her grief, chagrin and searing disappointment.

The flood finally slowed to trickle, then stopped. She pushed against him and immediately he let her go. Ignoring the sense of being bereft that swept over her once she lost the comfort of his protective arms, she muttered, 'Sorry. I'm not usually prone to waterworks. It's your fault, for being so sympathetic.'

That evoked the wisp of a smile. 'So, seeing you in tears, I should have pulled you up short and slapped some sense into you?'

'It's what my brother Gregory would have done. Or Temper. She says tears are a waste of emotion.' In truth, she felt no better for allowing herself the deluge. 'She's probably right,' she added with a sigh.

'Whatever brought them about had nothing to do with the destruction of your headgear. What did happen? Did you encounter some soldiers? I heard in town there was to be a race this afternoon.' His eyes widening, he grabbed her shoulders. 'You weren't *assaulted*,

were you?' he asked roughly. 'You're not protecting...
someone, are you?'

'No, you mustn't think that! I didn't precisely *encounter* soldiers. If I appear in disarray, it's because I
galloped past a group of them and lost my hat. I thought
it might have blown into a little woodland glade just
off the road, so I walked my mount back to look for it.
I was retrieving it when I heard the soldiers passing by.
And I didn't confront them—I remained hidden, like
a coward. Even after I discovered they were discussing me...in all the low, degrading ways you would expect soldiers to talk about a *doxy*,' she ended bitterly.

Johnnie sighed. 'You want them punished?' he asked
after a moment. 'I can probably find a reason to challenge them—especially Broadmere. I assume he was
among the group?'

'What, you're going to fight them all?' she asked.
Despite her scornful reply, the wave of gratitude and
warmth at his understanding almost brought on another
round of tears. Suppressing it, she continued, 'There are
too many of them and boxing their ears wouldn't change
their opinion of me. If they figured out the reason for
the challenge—and after your previous exchange with
Broadmere, they very well might—it would only reinforce their view of me. They would simply believe *you*
were the man that they assumed I was galloping to meet
at some clandestine rendezvous and be certain you are
already enjoying my salacious charms.'

'Ah, would that it were true,' he said with an elaborate sigh as he tapped her nose with a finger, obviously trying to cheer her. '*Chahna*, you mustn't upset
yourself over what that worthless bunch of malinger-
ers think. They've most likely shredded the reputations

and mentally disrobed every female in Bath handsome enough to catch their eye.'

'I wouldn't concern myself—if their views weren't probably also shared by much of Bath. And if I hadn't learned something else...so very distressing.'

Suddenly alert, his amused smile vanished. 'About Lord Halden?'

Her initial surprise at the accuracy of his guess deepened into dismay as she realised its implications. 'You know about him, too? Am I the only one in Bath who didn't?'

'About his hopes of marrying money, so he need not take orders? Or his women and his gaming?'

'His desire to marry me and conveniently deposit me somewhere in the country so he could go to London and use my money to disport himself?' she asked, hoping to have him confirm or deny that awful conclusion by appearing to be already aware of it. Johnnie might not tell her something he thought would distress her—but she knew he wouldn't lie to her.

Struck anew when he merely shrugged, she made herself press harder. 'Do you know for a fact that he gambles extensively and frequents...houses of ill repute, or is that just rumour?'

'You truly wish to know?'

'Heavens, Johnnie, I've been considering *marrying* the man! Don't you think I need to know the truth about him?'

'Most women wouldn't need—or want—to know more than the fact that they'd be marrying a duke's son.'

'But I'm not "most women", am I?' she tossed back bitterly. And then was totally stopped in her tracks by the penetrating gaze, full of wonder, admiration…and *tenderness* he fixed on her.

'No. You are extraordinary,' he said softly.

Before she had a chance to consider the implications of that look and tone, he continued brusquely, 'I'm not privy to Lord Halden's intentions concerning you, though I've heard his…acquaintances declare that is his plan. I have observed his gambling and…sporting proclivities first-hand, however.' He shook his head. 'In any event, he hasn't given much indication he possesses the character one would hope to find in a man about to take holy orders.'

'Spoken as one who shares his proclivities?' she said sharply, then felt ashamed. 'Excuse me, that was unfair. As an unattached gentleman who has made neither overtures nor promises to any lady, you may enjoy whatever pleasures you wish without censure.'

'I'm not all that much a rogue!' he protested with a laugh. 'I'll admit to enjoying a little gaming among friends, but I've never thought it amusing to play Johnnie Raw to the sharps at the hells and my liaisons have been…discreet. I do see others about, though, when I'm walking out late.'

At her eyebrows raised in enquiry, he made an impatient gesture towards his leg. 'Sometimes, when it won't let me sleep, I try to ease it by walking. Not wishing to wake Aunt Pen and have her fuss over me, I leave the house.'

The reminder of his injured leg made her feel even worse for snapping at him. 'I'm sorry again. It's not my place to criticise your activities, of whatever sort.' She took a deep breath. 'I'm calm now. If you'll give me a leg up, we can ride back.'

Instead of moving to let her walk away, he tipped her chin up, so she had to look directly into his eyes. 'You lose nothing by giving up on Lord Halden. The man's not worthy of you. Switch your efforts to enticing someone who is.'

'And who might that be?' she asked wryly. 'As you've already noted, Bath isn't exactly thick on the ground with likely prospects. Besides, if you knew of Lord Halden's true intentions, every man in Bath, if not ladies, know it too. After being so closely associated with him, it's difficult to think about turning my attention in some other direction, knowing th-that—' the very thought of it brought the anguish back, making her voice hitch '—that everyone in Bath is laughing at me for thinking I might retrieve my reputation by marrying a respectable man, and then fixing my efforts on...on a fortune hunter like Lord Halden.'

He shook his head. 'I doubt the rest of society thinks anything more than that you were trying to entice a duke's son—and isn't that what every society mama trains her daughter to attempt?'

That truth cheered her—at little. 'I hope you're right. That's far more flattering than thinking of myself as a...a laughing stock,' she said, once again choking back tears of anger and humiliation.

'Nonsense!' he said bracingly. 'If you are disdained at all, it's only because the other ladies are jealous of your beauty and wit.'

She sighed, not quite believing him, but grateful for his efforts to bolster her spirits. 'Regardless of what others think, it's humiliating to realise how long I persisted in encouraging Lord Halden, in spite of the doubts about his character that have troubled me almost from beginning. Well, enough! I shall encourage him no more. In truth, I wish I could cut him—or treat him with disdain for deceiving me about his true intentions. But alas, I suppose I shall have to at least be polite.'

'If you don't plan to look for other suitors in Bath, what will you do?'

'I'm not sure yet.' What *would* she do, now that her whole purpose for coming to Bath had been exposed as a ridiculous dream of a foolish, naïve girl? That stark realisation lanced through her again, reviving her anguish so that she could no longer hold back the question that had been hovering on her tongue. 'Is it truly so ridiculous to imagine me as a vicar's wife?'

His expression softening, he gently brushed away the tears from the corners of her eyes. 'Not for someone who truly knows you. You're worthy of a man who answers to the highest calling…and ought to be rewarded by finding exactly the sort of gentleman you seek.'

Then, the concern in his eyes changed to another sort of warmth and his fingers on her chin tightened. Muttering something that sounded like 'damn and blast,' as if he couldn't help himself, he bent down—and kissed her.

Surprise shot through her, but she didn't feel the least urge to pull away. Instead, she marvelled at the never-before-experienced sensation of a man's lips on hers, gentle, soft and comforting. Yet at the same time, the sensual charge always in the air between her and *this* man, momentarily suppressed by her emotional turmoil, surged back to life, overwhelming her with an intense awareness of his heat and closeness.

With a murmur, she leaned into him, instinctively seeking the feel of his body against hers. Sparks seemed to ignite wherever her torso touched his, burning along the length of her, urging her closer still. Awkward, but driven, she reached up to clasp his neck.

Suddenly his arms encircled her again, in possession rather than comfort. Ah, what a glimpse of Heaven, that delicate, wet touch of his tongue, tracing her lips! A wash of heat engulfed her entire body, until she felt like she was melting from inside out. Had he not been holding her so tightly, she might have collapsed, her knees buckling under her. When his tongue probed at her lips, begging entry, she opened to him, allowing him to slip into her mouth and explore its moist softness—until his tongue found hers.

Sensation exploded, rippling out in waves from her mouth all over her body. She felt compelled to match him as he led her in a rapier's dance of tongue on tongue, following as he thrust and parried. Her body overheating, she wanted to rip open the thick confines of her wool jacket, unbutton his tunic coat and yank loose vest and shirt. Slip her hands underneath to touch bare skin…

She was fumbling at his buttons to do just that when he suddenly pulled away, setting her roughly at arm's length. His breathing erratic, he gasped, 'It's my turn… to apologise.'

Bereft, protesting, befuddled, she stared at him. 'Why?'

He gave a strangled laugh. 'For almost leading you down the path to become what the soldiers accused you of being. It was wrong of me, so wrong! You deserve, not rough wooing under an oak tree, but a warm chamber, a soft bed—and most of all, your wedding lines.'

As the heat of passion faded and cold reason elbowed

its way back into her consciousness, her instinctive dismay over his sudden retreat faded. He was right— were they discovered, she would be irretrievably ruined. Though it was her supposed wanton character that would be affirmed, he, too, would be censured for dallying with an unmarried maiden of good birth.

While she struggled to recover her disordered senses, he tucked wisps of hair back under her hat, straightened her pelisse and attempted to right the drooping feather on her bonnet. She would have been furious at how calm he appeared while she was still reeling…had not his fingers continued to tremble.

'The feather is beyond hope, but I think the rest of you will do,' he said, his voice almost returned to normal range. 'Let's get you back to the city. Wherever is your groom, by the way? He must be riding the slowest piebald hack in equine history.'

'He's not riding after me, he's waiting for me,' she replied, thankful to find she sounded almost recovered as well. 'There's a stand of trees just at the top of Lansdown Hill—not far away from the Feather & Arrow on the Bath Road. I told him he might nip down there and have himself an ale and I would meet him back at the grove after my gallop.'

'He's as useless as a slug for protection, if he's let this much time elapse before coming to look for you. What if you *had* taken a tumble? I know, I know…' He held up a hand to forestall her reply. 'You never fall. I suppose you assured him of that, too. I think your horse is sufficiently rested. Shall I give you a leg up? I'll escort you back to the grove, so he can get you home.'

Home. Where was her home to be now? Would she ever find one?

Though he'd managed for a moment to lighten her mood, in the cold aftermath of frustrated passion, the disappointment and doubts about her future overtook her once again.

'Yes, I should get back,' she said, her voice as listless as her spirits. 'Aunt Gussie will be wondering what happened to me.'

Seeming to sense she had no more taste for discussion, he rode beside her in silence to where the road began its descent back to Bath. There they found the groom, who was dozing on his placid mount.

'Thank you for your escort, Lieutenant,' she said, nodding to Johnnie.

'Shall I see you at the Subscription Ball tonight?'

'I believe Aunt Gussie plans on attending. Though I'm not sure what good it will do.'

His sympathetic gaze raked her face. 'Never give up, Miss Lattimar. When one advance is blocked, shift your attack in another direction. Often, it proves to be a superior one.'

Numbly she nodded. 'I hope so. Shall we go, Stebbins? Until later, Lieutenant.'

Having restored Prudence to the nominal protection of her groom, Johnnie gave her a wave and watched her ride away…his smile fading the moment she disappeared from view. Frowning, he set his own mount back on the road towards the racetrack.

He hated to see her upset, but he wasn't about to lie to cover for Lord Halden, even to spare her further distress. In fact, aside from his fury at discovering how deeply whatever vulgar comments she'd overheard had hurt her, he couldn't help being relieved she had finally discovered Fitzroy-Price's true character for herself, sparing him the unpleasant task of revealing it to her. Which, revolted by the idea of the lovely Prudence throwing herself away on someone so undeserving of her, he would otherwise have felt compelled to do.

The very idea of that womanising gambler forcing his hands on her—his first suspicion when he'd found her alone and in disarray—made him want to skewer the man on his sabre.

Especially given how much he wanted her himself.

Blowing out a frustrated breath, he urged his mount to a trot. When he'd first come upon her, her golden hair coming down, her bonnet dusty and rumpled, her skirts muddy and her glorious blue eyes swimming in tears, he'd been reminded of the barn kitten he'd once rescued as a boy from the dogs tormenting it—a soft, delicate creature attacked by uncaring beasts much bigger and stronger. He'd taken her in his arms, intending only to protect and comfort.

But Prudence Lattimar was not a helpless kitten. Virtually the moment his arms closed around her, his blood surged and his member, always half-aroused around her, hardened.

He thought he'd managed to control himself rather well—until she looked at him with those tear-rimmed eyes, asking if anyone could believe in her, and he'd just *had* to kiss her. And as he should have known the moment he touched her, one soft brush of her lips was not enough.

Not when she turned to fire beneath his fingers. Her initial awkwardness might have been eloquent of her innocence, but she learned quickly, her instinctive response to his caresses containing all the knowledge of every Eve since the dawn of time. With her tongue seeking his and her lush body pressing against him, when her fingers started scratching at buttons he would have been happy to tear loose, he knew with blinding certainty that if he didn't stop that moment, he would no longer be able to resist taking her where those sultry eyes begged him to go.

Fortunately, he'd been sensible enough to stop…this time. But he must take better care not to risk getting himself into such a position again.

Or so he instructed himself, as the little voice in his head argued that's exactly where he wanted to be—and go further.

Irritated with himself, he blew out a breath. Perhaps he ought to put an end even to circumspect rides and see her only in company. But how was he to determine what her plans were, if they could not talk freely? And how could he protect her, now that her hopes of Lord Halden had been dashed, if he did not know what she intended to do next?

He'd not worry about that now, he concluded, turning his horse back towards Bath. He'd see her at the ball this evening and try to ascertain how it went with her after she'd had time to recover from the distress of the ride.

And look forward to the glory of touching her hand and guiding her through the movements of a dance, protected by the public forum and the crush of spectators from the fierce desire to kiss her again—and claim her for himself.

Chapter Ten

Still too deeply distressed to want to discuss the appalling truths she'd discovered on her ride, Prudence decided it would be easier to face all of Bath at the Subscription Ball than to field the questions Aunt Gussie would surely pose if she tried to cry off from the engagement. And so she found herself later that evening entering the Assembly Rooms beside her chaperon, determinedly pasting her usual serene expression on her face.

A serenity that nearly faltered when, almost immediately after their entry, a smiling Lord Halden Fitzroy-Price walked across the floor to greet her.

Prudence forced herself to smile politely. But she couldn't keep the edge from her voice as, replying to his greeting with its obligatory compliments on her beauty, she said, 'I'm surprised to see you tonight, Lord Halden. From what some of your military friends said when I passed them on the road while I was riding this afternoon, I expected you would be at the track.'

'Ah, yes. But the races were all over by mid-afternoon.'

'And there were no card games to be had tonight?'

'There are always card games. But none that matched the allure of dancing with the most beautiful girl in Bath.'

Biting down the retort that the richest girl must of course be the most beautiful, at her aunt's nod of permission, she allowed Lord Halden to lead her on to the floor, where the next set was forming. Fortunately for her efforts to remain at least nominally polite, the dance was a pattern piece that afforded them little opportunity for private conversation.

She didn't think she could have endured a waltz in his arms.

Hardly had the music ended when she turned from him to walk off the floor, forcing him to trot after her. 'You left the dance so swiftly, you must be in need of refreshment,' he said, snagging her elbow. 'Allow me to escort you to the tea room. I can describe to you some of the excellent animals I saw at the race today.'

Before he could add anything else—and she lost control of her temper and informed him *she* was no longer horseflesh available for his exalted title's purchase—she made him a short curtsy. 'I don't believe I wish to hear about your horses again tonight. I must return to my aunt. Good evening, Lord Halden.'

With that, she left him standing alone at the edge of the dance floor. Fighting down the swell of emotion that continued to hold her on a knife's edge between tears and an explosion of rage, she had nearly reached Aunt Gussie—who was staring at her in puzzled surprise after her abrupt abandonment of Lord Halden— when a familiar uniformed figure caught her eye.

Johnnie came across the floor towards her, his rangy stride calm and masterful and his smile both intimate and welcoming. Her volatile emotions veering from rage to delight, Pru had to stifle the urge to run into his arms.

'Lieutenant Trethwell, a pleasure!' she said, holding out her hand to him. 'Did you enjoy the rest of your ride…after you rescued me?' she added *sotto voce* as he tucked her hand on his arm.

'A lonely ride it was, to be sure. And are you… recovered from your wild gallop?'

'And my unstable emotions?' she murmured. 'Thank you again for your…sympathy. You helped me more than you could ever know.'

To her surprise, he sighed, a rueful expression on his face. 'Would that I *could* help you in your quest. But at least, in the nick of time, I avoided doing you harm. You are impossibly tempting, you know.'

The unabashed hunger in his eyes seemed to steady her further. She recognised as clearly as he did the danger in the attraction between them. But it was an *honest* attraction, freely admitted. There were no subterfuges between them, no dissembling about wanting one thing while actually pursuing something quite different. She realised she valued more than ever before the frankness and openness she shared with him and perhaps no one else but her sister.

'You are impossibly tempting, too,' she replied—even as, relaxing in his company, she felt some of the weight of her uncertain future lift from her. Was that what it meant to find a true friend one could count upon? 'And since we do tempt each other so much, perhaps we should retire to the refreshment room and feast upon cakes and tea, an indulgence much less dangerous for us both.'

He laughed and she felt her spirits lift even further. *Ah, Johnnie*, she thought with an inward sigh. *If I believed there were any chance you might be content to remain in England, spending your life as a simple country gentleman, I might dare tempt you further...*

Alas, everything she knew of him told her that he would not be happy living the quiet, settled existence she longed for. Wanting to retrieve what was left of what had been a day of dismal revelations, she vowed to dismiss any further contemplation of her gloomy future and simply enjoy the delight of his company now, while she still had it.

Who knew where she—or he—would end up next and how soon they might have to part?

While they drank tea and nibbled on cakes, she encouraged him to tell her more stories about India. He soon had her laughing with his tales of snake charmers and *shakirs*, and elephant drivers leaning over the backs of *howdahs* to beat away pursuing tigers.

A touch to her arm made her jerk her gaze around—to discover Lord Halden, standing beside them. How long had he been there, listening, before he'd felt compelled to interrupt them?

'Ah, Miss Lattimar, here you are,' he said, according Johnnie a small, unfriendly nod. 'Your aunt told me you'd gone to have tea. I believe a waltz is forming. Will you do me the honour? No other lady here dances so gracefully.'

Prudence feared she might spit in his eye if he tried to hold her as closely as a waltz required. 'Very kind of you to say so, Lord Halden, but I do not feel inclined to waltz. Lieutenant, if you would return me to my aunt? I dare say she is wondering at my long absence.'

'Of course, Miss Lattimar,' Johnnie said. The gaze he fixed on Lord Halden, as if daring him to interfere, was even less cordial than the one the Duke's son had given him. 'It would be my pleasure.'

To Lord Halden's obvious *dis*pleasure, he led her off. Prudence could practically feel his anger and affront at her second snub in the gaze that followed them as Johnnie led her from the room.

'He should have no doubt now that you don't wish him to pay his addresses to you,' the Lieutenant remarked as he led her towards her aunt. That lady, seeing her still on Johnnie's arm rather than accompanying the Duke's son sent in search of her—the man one would have expected her niece to prefer—was once again staring at her, eyebrows lifted in surprise.

'I would be happy to know Lord Halden has taken that point,' she said, looking back to Johnnie, 'but I don't yet feel up to discussing it with my aunt. Could we…take a few turns about the room?'

'You know I can deny you nothing,' he said with a provocative smile.

'You truly can't?' she flashed back. 'Ah, then what might I dare ask for?'

His hand on her arm tightened, then relaxed. 'Best ask carefully, lest we both get burned.'

Oh, that I might dare let you, Prudence thought as he led her away from her puzzled aunt.

They'd made almost one full circuit of the dance floor before the waltz ended. As the last notes faded, Lord Halden emerged from the tea room with a group of friends. But to her exasperation, as the musicians began to strike up the next dance, Fitzroy-Price set his face determinedly and headed in her direction.

'Heavens, he's slow to take a hint,' she muttered. 'Lead me into this set, won't you?'

'Of course,' Johnnie replied promptly. As they took their places, Lord Halden continuing to glower at them, he said, 'This is almost as satisfying as pummelling him in the ring.'

'Much more civilised,' she said, chuckling.

'Probably. I'd still *prefer* to pummel him, but since that opportunity is unlikely to present itself, this will have to suffice.'

'He looks like a spoiled child denied the treat he was expecting,' Pru observed. 'Why did I not fully comprehend sooner how preoccupied he is with his own desires? As if he believed a woman should be grateful a man of his birth and breeding deigned to court her and not expect more than his escort. Especially one of my reputation,' she added with a sigh.

'Well, you need suffer him no more,' Johnnie said bracingly. 'Even an individual as self-absorbed as Fitzroy-Price will have to recognise the meaning of your continued refusal of his overtures.'

'I certainly hope so! I only hope his anger—for I cannot believe he has invested anything more than self-interest in pursuing me—doesn't get directed at you.'

Johnnie's lip curled in disdain. 'You need have no worries on that score. He may be a duke's son, but he's no match for me in a fair fight and he knows it.' Grinning, he added, 'He's even less a match for me in an unfair one.'

'Know some dirty fighting tricks, do you?' Pru asked. 'Would that you were my brother! I could get you to teach them to me.'

Johnnie uttered a strangled groan. 'I can't decide which would be worse. Becoming your brother and giving up the delicious contemplation of having you as a woman, or remaining simply a normal man, who burns to possess you.'

The sudden heat in his gaze brought back all the memories of their afternoon interlude and the wave of pleasurable sensations that had swamped her as he kissed her...as she kissed him back. 'You are not the only one who burns,' she admitted. 'Perhaps you should return me to Aunt Gussie. I think I've had enough of discouraging Lord Halden for one evening.'

'Perhaps it's best to let the lesson sink in, without the distasteful prospect of having to confront him again,' Johnnie agreed, offering his arm. 'To your aunt, then. Will you ride tomorrow?'

She made a grimace of irritation, unhappy both at having to miss a treasured activity—and the opportunity to spend private time in his company. 'I'm afraid not. You remember my aunt's dear friend, Mrs Marsden? After having rented a property in Bath for many years, she's decided to settle here permanently, and recently bought a town house. She's moving in soon and has asked if Aunt Gussie and I would accompany her tomorrow to a warehouse to look at furnishings.' Acting upon sudden inspiration and wistful hope, she said, 'You wouldn't be interested in coming along, would you? To give a masculine opinion?'

Lowering her voice, she added, 'We couldn't converse as freely as we do while riding, but it would be better than at these evening entertainments, where we are always surrounded by a crowd of onlookers.'

He hesitated and she assumed he was hunting for

polite words to refuse. 'Are you sure your aunt would approve of adding me to the company?' he said instead.

'She would appreciate having a gentleman's point of view,' Pru replied, delighted he hadn't turned her down and sure she could persuade her aunt to agree.

'Very well, then. I'm afraid my expertise at furnishing a lodging extends only to tents, but it might be interesting.' Giving her a teasing smile, he lowered his voice to murmur. 'Perhaps we'll discover some naughty pictures to furnish Mrs Marsden's private salon. Or some nude sculptures?'

'Wretch!' she scolded, feeling her face heat. 'If we should discover anything of the sort, you will *not* point them out to Mrs Marsden!'

'The best classical Greek and Roman sculptures are nudes,' he observed, grinning at her.

'I shall keep that in mind, should I have a need to redecorate my own rooms,' she shot back.

She might have known she couldn't shock him, for he merely laughed. 'I wager you would.'

Enjoying their sparring, she was about to embellish upon her reply when she spied Lord Halden at the other side of the room. Though she avoided meeting his eyes, a sideways glance showed he was crossing the floor towards her.

'Drat and blast, Lord Halden is coming this way again,' Prudence murmured. 'We had better find Aunt Gussie quickly.'

'At your service, ma'am. Shall we try the tea room?'

Walking across to that chamber, they discovered her aunt chatting with a friend. Just before they reached the lady's side, Johnnie said, 'You need only confide to her what you learned today about Fitzroy-Price's true intentions. That will be more than sufficient to explain your sudden lack of interest in him. No reason to mention…anything else you heard.'

He was right, she realised. Immensely relieved that she would not have to repeat the other, far more distressing words that had been spoken about her, she said, 'Good advice. Thank you. For once again coming to my rescue. Will you call for us at nine tomorrow?'

'It will be a pleasure. Lady Stoneway, may I return your niece to you? She was just mentioning how fatigued she is, so I'll bid you both good evening. Shall I summon chairs for you, ma'am?'

'Well—yes, I suppose so. If you truly wish to leave, Prudence?'

'I do, Aunt Gussie. And, no, I don't feel ill, so you mustn't worry. I'll explain later.'

'Then, yes, Lieutenant, I would be obliged if you would arrange chairs for us. Come then, Prudence, let us fetch our wraps.'

'Thank you, Johnnie Trethwell,' she mouthed as he bowed over her aunt's hand. Giving her a little wink, he walked off to do her aunt's bidding.

Chapter Eleven

Fortunately, the bustle required for her aunt to rise and ready herself to leave the house much earlier than usual kept that lady so occupied, she neither remembered to question Pru about her cool treatment of Lord Halden at the Assembly, nor added more than an absent, 'yes, that would be nice', to her niece's blithe assertion that she'd invited Lieutenant Trethwell to accompany them to the shops to secure a masculine opinion. 'After all,' Pru improvised, 'Mrs Marsden often has her sons to stay with her and she wouldn't want them to feel uneasy, having to tiptoe around furnishings that appeared too fragile or feminine.'

Johnnie appeared promptly at nine, chairs were engaged and soon they were disembarking at the warehouse in the lower part of town near the river where they were to meet Mrs Marsden.

'Gracious!' Lady Stoneway said, putting a handkerchief to her nose after she'd alighted from the chair. 'How…insalubrious it is!'

'Not a place for ladies to linger,' Johnnie agreed. 'Shall we ring the bell? I'm sure your friend awaits you within.'

A clerk soon appeared to usher them inside, where to Lady Stoneway's relief, no hint of the miasma from the river penetrated. They followed the clerk upstairs to a long, open room, lit by large windows at either end of the building, its floor space almost completely taken up by various objects of furniture, many of them under holland covers.

Mrs Marsden, attended by an older gentleman who soon identified himself as the establishment's owner, exchanged hugs with Lady Stoneway. 'Thank you so much for coming to assist me! I've never before made such a costly and important purchase, and I am grateful to have your advice.'

'My niece thought, to ensure that Randall and Thomas feel comfortable in their rooms when they visit, you would find a masculine point of view helpful—didn't you, my dear?' She gave Pru a speaking look, which told her though she might have been distracted earlier when her niece casually mentioned inviting the Lieutenant, Lady Stoneway suspected his presence was intended more to gratify Pru than to assist her dear friend.

Before Pru could reply, Mrs Marsden said, 'What an excellent idea, Miss Lattimar! I hadn't previously considered it, but having a gentleman's opinion truly would be helpful. Thank you, Lieutenant, for agreeing to assist.'

'I shall try to be as useful as I can.'

'If you will follow me, ladies and gentleman, I will show the section that contains the collection I described to you, Mrs Marsden. All the pieces were bought or commissioned by the late Colonel Charles McGreavy. The works are of fine quality and blend harmoniously together. Although some are quite rare and costly, rather than sell the pieces one by one, the colonel's heirs were hopeful a purchaser could be found to take most or all the pieces, so their father's collection might be kept together. Shall we have a look?'

Somewhat to Pru's surprise, Johnnie *was* useful. As they removed holland covers from various pieces, it was soon evident that Mrs Marsden was struck more by each item's ornamentation and style than its practicality.

'That gate-leg table does have fine inlay on the feet,' Johnnie said, rolling his eyes at Pru over the crocodile-like decoration. 'Do you intend it for a piece to decorate your reception room, or as a table for dining? If the latter, I fear the damage your sons' booted feet might do to such delicate carving.'

'I suppose you are right, Lieutenant,' Mrs Marsden said. 'Though it is so very handsome!'

'This other dining table is larger and would do better for company dinners,' Johnnie continued. 'It may be plainer, but it is matched by a fine sideboard. Only think how well it would display your china and crystal!'

In a similar manner, he advised her against a gaming table with legs in the Egyptian style, chairs with overlarge ball-and-claw feet just made for tripping over and side tables with startling stripes of zebrawood, recommending instead a number of elegant but sturdy mahogany pieces with a subtle rosewood inlay.

Following his advice, Mrs Marsden ended up selecting all but the most outlandishly decorated pieces in the colonel's lot. While Lady Stoneway and her friend circled the pieces again, refining the final selection,

Pru was at last able to have some private words with Johnnie.

'You must have had quite elaborate furnishing in your tents,' she observed with amusement.

'Actually, the Colonel's accommodation was rather splendid,' Johnnie replied. 'I never developed a taste for those animal-headed or footed furniture items that have become so popular, though.'

'The ones with Egyptian motifs?' Pru asked.

'Yes. Perhaps it comes from having forded rivers inhabited by crocodiles. I never wished to invite them into the house.'

As Pru chuckled, Johnnie stopped short. 'The late Colonel must have been an India-serving officer. The pieces under this cloth appear to be Hindu temple carvings.'

Pulling the cloth aside to reveal several stone figures, he pointed at a four-armed one. 'From the iconography of its decoration, I'd say that is a Vishnu and this one a Shiva. The colonel must have been an *early* India hand. It's no longer fashionable to admire native Hindu art or express any sympathy for the religion.'

'Is it so barbaric?'

'I didn't find it so. The idea of the oneness of creation and the respect for all living things I found admirable. I think barbarism depends more on the character of the individual than the religion.'

After rooting further under the cloth covering, he halted, chuckling. 'Then again, the good colonel might just have had a taste for the prurient. There are some statuettes of goddesses back here and, like the classics of Rome and Greece, they are nude. But their activities would certainly shock Mrs Marsden.'

'Let me see,' Prudence said, not sure whether he was being serious or teasing her.

'Better not,' he advised. 'This bas-relief is likely to surprise even a worldly-wise reader of Ovid.'

'Nonsense,' she said, pulling his hand aside—only to drop the cloth back over it a moment later, so truly shocked she felt momentarily light-headed. Knowing her face must be flushed bright red, she stammered, 'M-my goodness! That is...detailed.'

Looking contrite, Johnnie tucked the cloth securely back in place. 'I shouldn't have let you see it,' he apologised, his own face reddening. 'Though its true purpose isn't to...inflame the desires. The Hindus believed that pleasure between man and woman was a delightful part of normal life. There are Sanskrit texts, parts of which are devoted to advice about perfecting the pursuit of pleasure.'

'Texts you have studied?' she asked tartly, trying to recover her composure.

He laughed. 'Alas, my Sanskrit wasn't good enough. Although one can find carvings like this on the walls of many temples.'

'We shall definitely not point that out to Mrs Marsden,' Pru said, her cheeks still hot. She knew she'd not soon forget the expression of bliss on the face of the figure of the reclining woman, the nipples of her full breasts hard and peaked as a man buried his face between her legs.

'An old India hand indeed!' Johnnie said, his voice distracting her from the heated recollection. Reaching under the cloth on an adjoining table, he pulled out a long, carved sword. 'It's a *talwar*—an Indian cavalry sword.' After giving it a quick inspection, he replaced it on the table. 'There are several other good blades in there.'

'Perhaps the colonel was a collector.'

'Apparently there are quite a few collectors in England, not all of them old India hands. Or so the friend for whom I obtained a similar weapon told me. Now that my leg is mostly healed—or as healed as it's going to get—I've been preparing for what I mean to do next.'

'Not a return to the army, surely.'

'No, I've had my fill of that. But a letter I received this morning from my brother James reinforced my intentions to pursue a different possibility. Not that he suggested it directly—indeed, my entire family will probably have palpitations if I succeed at this venture.'

'What, cause your family further distress? Surely you wouldn't think of it!'

He smiled at her teasing. 'Even a family known for its reprobates will baulk at this. James mentioned a friend of *his* had recently bought some swords, scimitars and *talwars* from a dealer, at a price that made me whistle! I've recently discovered there are a growing number of wealthy men who collect weapons and, with Britain's expanding presence in India, an increasing demand for weapons from that region.'

'I'm not surprised,' Pru said. 'My own father has collected weapons for years.'

He nodded. 'I will soon be meeting with several wealthy men, including the one for whom I brought back the *talwar*, who have expressed interest in advancing me the funds to set up a business acquiring similar articles. Given my familiarity with the area and my contacts in the bazaars—where, I assure you, there are weapons to be had for a fraction of what James reported his friend paid for his—I'm sure I could sell the items back in England at a profit.'

'I imagine you could. And not just weapons. Men with time and money to spare collect all sorts of things. When you meet with your initial investors, you should ask them what other items their fellow collectors are looking for—artwork, gemstones, artefacts.'

'I hadn't thought of that—but you're right!' His face lighting with enthusiasm, Johnnie said, 'I've always wanted to penetrate further into the subcontinent than I was permitted to wander from the cantonment where I was posted. Who knows what other treasures lurk, waiting to be discovered?'

'And how many merchants, *shakirs* and *maharanis* there are to meet, entertain and bewitch?' she added, a pang of sadness going through her that she was not a foreign treasure he was eager to acquire, or a distant land he was drawn to explore.

No, she was only a straightforward, ordinary English Beauty who would never hold the attention of a man fascinated by the exotic.

Pushing away that depressing thought, she said, 'I think Mrs Marsden and my aunt have finished making their selections. Shall we rejoin them—before you give in to the temptation to shock her with those carvings?'

He offered his arm and she took it. 'I never shock ladies,' he said primly. 'Unless they want me to.'

She was saved from replying to that by Mrs Marsden coming over to pat her hand. 'Thank you so much for your help. Both of you! I feel much more confident now about how well the house will turn out. And I'm sure my sons will thank you, Lieutenant, for making sure they will feel comfortable around all the furnishings!'

'It was my pleasure, Mrs Marsden. I'm glad we were able to discover so many…evocative pieces.'

Pru felt her face heat again, certain he was referencing the one work they could not let Mrs Marsden discover.

'I'm not much acquainted with the lower part of Bath, but I believe we are not far from Sally Lunn's teahouse,' Mrs Marsden said. 'Let me invite all of you there for some refreshment.'

The party accepting her invitation, chairs were procured for the short transit—Prudence, briefly alone in hers, trying to keep her mind from dwelling on the erotic carving she'd witnessed. Just what was that man doing between the woman's thighs?

Whatever it was, the lady appeared to very much enjoy it.

Which she didn't doubt. Her whole body tingled with anticipation at the idea of Johnnie Trethwell touching her anywhere, much less in so…intimate a place.

They soon disembarked at the bakery and, after some of the famous cakes and some tea, the party decided to stroll up Milsom Street, Mrs Marsden being eager to acquire some linens and glassware to complement her furniture purchases.

They had turned the corner from Burton Street into Milsom when Pru spotted Lady Isabelle gazing at the window of a bonnet shop, Lord Halden looking bored as he stood beside her.

Before she could turn away, *he* saw *her* and, after a word to Lady Isabelle, headed in her direction. Johnnie must have seen him, too, for he tightened his grip on her arm and muttered a curse that echoed her own feelings.

'Don't worry. I won't let him annoy you,' he murmured.

The next moment, Lord Halden reached them. 'Lady Stoneway, Mrs Marsden and Miss Lattimar,' he said, bowing to the ladies. 'Trethwell,' he added frostily.

'Lord Halden!' Mrs Marsden said, beaming, obviously still believing that the Duke's son was a prime matrimonial prize whose escort Pru would certainly prefer to that of a lowly lieutenant. 'How good to see you! We're about to walk up Milsom Street. Would you like to join us?'

'Mrs Marsden, you must see that Lord Halden is presently occupied by his cousin Lady Isabelle—she's over there, at the milliner's,' Pru broke in before the Duke's son could answer. 'It would be most inconsiderate to rob her of her escort and I'm sure she is much too busy for a dawdling walk up Milsom Street. Another time, perhaps? Good day, Lord Halden.'

Inclining her head, she urged Johnnie to walk her past him. 'Now, Mrs Marsden, which shop was it that carries the linens you wished to see?'

Though Pru didn't look back, she could feel Lord Halden's fulminating gaze on her as they left him behind. But either he was too polite to charge after them and abandon his aunt—or more likely, too arrogant to consider running after any female, for fortunately, he made no attempt to follow.

Her snub of the Duke's son apparently recalled to Lady Stoneway Pru's similarly cold behaviour to him at the Assembly the previous evening, for she gave Pru a searching glance. However, thankfully deciding she would not quiz her niece about her puzzling behaviour on a public street, she bent her efforts instead on distracting Mrs Marsden from her shocked reaction to the cut by posing a series of questions about the colour and finish of the linens she sought.

'Perhaps now he will finally take the hint,' Pru murmured to Johnnie.

'Let us hope so,' he replied. 'A man of his birth and self-importance seldom expends much effort on a female who's made it clear she doesn't desire his attention.'

'Not when there will always be so many others who do. Sadly few in Bath, though, who possess so handsome a dowry.'

'Might be good for his character to be denied now and then,' Johnnie observed. 'I'm afraid I too must abandon you, though. I'm accompanying Aunt Pen to a concert this afternoon. Will I see you at the Harrison musicale tonight?'

'I'm afraid not. The removers come tomorrow and we promised to help Mrs Marsden choose which of her belongings she wanted to keep after considering the other furnishings she bought today.' Pru laughed ruefully. 'Which may serve to delay Aunt Gussie a bit longer from demanding why I'm suddenly snubbing Lord Halden.'

'Just tell her the truth. I'm sure she'll support your decision.'

Pru sighed. 'I hope so.'

'I'm afraid it must be goodbye, then, after I take my leave of your aunt and Mrs Marsden. Will you ride tomorrow morning?'

'I certainly hope so.'

'Then I'll hope to see you.'

He squeezed her hand, leaving her bereft when he pulled away and turned to bid goodbye to the other ladies. After more profuse thanks from Mrs Marsden, he gave them all a bow and walked off.

His limp *was* less pronounced than it had been, Pru noted as she watched him.

Which meant he would soon be recovered enough to leave Bath and go about setting up his trading company. It was just as well, she supposed, her spirits sagging. Now that she'd dismissed Lord Halden from contention, with few other suitable matrimonial prospects in the city, she wasn't sure it was worth remaining here for the rest of the Season herself.

Chapter Twelve

After a mostly sleepless night during which Prudence found herself repeatedly awakening from a fitful slumber to memories of her humiliating interlude hiding in the shrubbery, she rose early. Knowing only a hard ride would drive away the demons and restore to her enough serenity to finally have that talk with Aunt Gussie—she'd put off revealing her discovery of Lord Halden's true intentions towards her again last night, pleading an all-too-real headache—she resolved not to wait until later in the morning, when she might hope to encounter Johnnie.

He'd rescued her on several occasions now, she thought wistfully as her sleepy maid helped her into her habit. But much as she appreciated his protecting and encouraging her—and as keenly as she longed to be back in his arms—indulging in solitary interludes with him might tempt her to actions that truly would ruin her, should anyone discover them.

A wave of heat rippled through her, and once again, she had to banish thoughts of the well-pleasured lady in the temple relief. Though she was beginning to doubt she would ever find a suitable partner for a compatible marriage, she didn't want to make herself into such an outcast that marriage to a respectable gentleman at some time in the future would be impossible.

And Johnnie Trethwell, dear as he'd become to her, couldn't be part of that future. The best she could hope was that they might remain friends. Maybe when he went adventuring again, they might exchange letters, his relating more amusing, fascinating and exciting tales like those he'd already shared with her about the India he loved, the foreign lands so inextricably part of the man he'd become.

Surprising the livery groom, who had apparently only just arrived at the stable, she sent him off to saddle her grey mare with more than his normal fee to sweeten his reluctance to leave his steaming cup of coffee. And so, as dawn lightened the low-hanging clouds to the east, she was once again riding through the heavy, swirling mist up the road to the heights of Lansdown Hill.

For once, not even the prospect of a gallop cheered her. Which was just as well, for even when she reached the summit, a thick fog still blanketed the ground. Though her fresh mare strained at the bit, obviously eager for a run, Prudence held her to a trot, her mind going round and round as she tried to determine her best path for the future.

With Lord Halden's duplicity revealed, was there any reason for her to remain in Bath? Even if the Duke's son had deceived the matrons of Bath as effectively about his intentions as he had her, eliminating the added humiliation of being laughed at for encouraging him, it required only a quick run-through of her other would-be suitors to conclude that she felt nothing for any of them stronger than a mild appreciation. None had inspired in her a sense of connection or stirring of affection that hinted it might deepen into the love and admiration she needed to pledge herself to someone for a lifetime.

There was only one man who'd elicited a strong response from her—and Johnnie had no interest in marrying and settling down. Though she felt immensely drawn to him and freely admitted she yearned for his touch, she'd been too scarred by growing up with a scandalous mother to ever be comfortable living as his mistress, *carte blanche* being the only offer he was likely to make her. Worse than earning for herself the notoriety she'd tried all her life to escape would be knowing that, sooner or later, he'd grow bored with her or England or both and move on.

How odd that they'd made such an immediate connection, she thought with a wistful sigh. She, a girl who'd seldom been far from home and he, a man who'd travelled half a world away. But despite the vast differences in their experiences, she couldn't help but contrast the free and easy exchange of ideas they shared, the sense of being accepted and valued for herself Johnnie gave her, with the stiffness and disconnection she felt around every other gentleman.

If she were brutally honest, she was more than a little afraid she'd stupidly fallen in love with Johnnie Trethwell. There was a chance he might reciprocate her affections, though she was not at all sure he felt for her more than an indulgent fondness for a sheltered ingénue.

Perhaps, like Temperance, she was destined to remain a spinster.

And if that were the case, as often as her thoughts seemed to go back to that temple carving, perhaps she should remove herself from Bath before her senses outwitted her wit and the potent temptation Johnnie posed lured her into doing something that would disgrace her for the rest of her life.

The sound of hoofbeats approaching through the fog behind her pulled her from her reverie. But the anticipation that leapt in her chest died immediately as the rider emerging from the mist turned out to be not Lieutenant Trethwell—but Lord Halden Fitzroy-Price.

Though he was, as always, impeccably turned out in his dark riding dress and boots polished to a high shine, as he came close, she noticed his eyes looked red-rimmed and weary, and the curve of lips he accorded her when he realised she'd seen him seemed more grimace than smile.

Distaste and resentment bubbled up. Could she not even be allowed the solace of a solitary morning ride? It seemed ironic that, after several weeks of making every attempt to appear where she might encounter him, only now did he seem suddenly bent on making a concerted effort to seek *her* out—despite her pointed discouragement.

He must need her money very badly.

How lovely that she must no longer maintain quite so careful a control over her tongue.

'Lord Halden,' she said, giving him a slight nod, but neither pulling up nor slowing her mare's pace to accommodate his arrival.

'Miss Lattimar. Damn and blast—how can you enjoy riding at such an ungodly hour of the morning?'

'Perhaps because I've not spent my night submerged in brandy and revelry? If you're just returning from those, you're riding in the opposite direction from town, you know.'

'Of course I know!' he spat back, his tone aggrieved. 'As you must realise, I rode out precisely to encounter you.'

'I cannot imagine why. Or how you even knew I was riding, admittedly somewhat earlier than usual. Unless...surely you haven't paid someone to spy on me?' she cried, incredulous, but unable to imagine how else the Duke's son would have known she'd left her aunt's town house.

'I needed to keep track of you and a pretty penny it's costing me,' he replied. 'But since you've suddenly became so persistent about discouraging my escort, I needed to contrive some way to speak with you alone.'

She gave him a sharp glance. 'If you noticed my attempts to discourage you, you must realise there is nothing you need to speak about to me alone.'

'How can you say that, after the very great *encouragement* you've given me these past weeks?'

He had her there, she acknowledged, chagrin heating her face. 'That may be true. But a lady retains the privilege of changing her mind...especially when she discovers compelling reasons to do so,' she added, her tone turning acid. Hoping he wouldn't be arrogant or foolish enough to protest he had no idea what she meant, she kicked her horse into a canter. 'Good day, Lord Halden.'

'Not so fast!' he snarled at her. To her surprise, he

rode over and seized the mare's bridle, forcing the horse to a halt. 'How dare you presume to pass judgement on *my* desire to marry wealth? You, daughter of a whore who's shown herself as profligate as her mother, throwing yourself at that shabby-dressed half-pay cripple!'

'Who is ten times the man you'll ever be, despite his limp!' she shot back angrily. 'Release my reins, sir.'

Instead, in one swift movement, he sprang down from his horse, grabbing her hand and jerking her off her side-saddle as he did so. Flailing to try to prevent herself from falling, she found herself captured in his arms before her feet could touch the ground.

Truly furious now, she struggled to free herself. 'Let me go this instant!' she cried, turning her head away from the brandy fumes that emanated from his person.

'I shall not let you go,' he retorted, allowing her to step away, but tightening his grip on her arm. 'You think I intend to let a dowry as handsome as yours slip through my fingers?'

'When you are probably in debt to every tradesman and brothel in Bath, and have such *fond* plans of spending my blunt in future?'

He uttered a rough laugh. 'Precisely. So you found out about my little…excursions, did you? Your whey-faced soldier carrying tales?'

'I'd like to see you dare call him that to his face. But then, you'd risk getting your arrogant nose broken and your pompous behind tossed in the dirt.'

Apparently not quite self-deluded enough to deny that truth, he ignored it. 'Whatever your suddenly developed distaste for my company, we *will* wed,' he continued, seeming supremely self-confident. 'You've been far too encouraging of my suit for society to consider you anything but a tease and jilt if you don't. Even your papa's guineas wouldn't be enough to buy you a husband then.'

'Better to remain a spinster than marry a man like you.'

'Oh, come now,' he said, his tone turning more beguiling. 'You needn't get your nose in a snit. I've more than enough stamina to keep you satisfied, whatever my other…pursuits. Only remember, you'll spend most of your time running a grand household worthy of a duke's son and maintaining a position in society more elevated than you could otherwise ever hope to attain. And once I've got some brats on you, I won't be too particular about the company you keep.' He laughed. 'You could even entertain your cripple.'

She tugged her hand, trying to break his grip. 'This conversation is over.'

His good humour faded, his face hardening and his eyes turning cold. 'If you're going to be intransigent, we'll resort to persuasion of a different sort.'

With surprising strength, he yanked her towards him and wrapped his arms around her shoulders. Lowering his head, he attempted to kiss her.

Pru ducked away and pushed at him. 'If you don't let me go *this instant*,' she hissed, 'I can't be held responsible for my response.'

'Couldn't help yourself responding, could you, my hot little piece?' Loosening his grip long enough to pluck off her hat, he tore the veil as he tossed it away. In another swift motion, he pulled a handful of pins from her hair, sending a heavy cascade of tresses down her back as he forced her close again. Holding her in an implacable grip, he bent to kiss the bared skin of her neck, sucking hard on the sensitive skin.

Shuddering against the touch of his mouth, she finally understood his intention. 'You—you intend to compromise me!'

'Of course, my sweet,' he murmured against her neck. 'When you return to Bath looking dishevelled, people will be too delighted to confirm what they've always suspected about your wanton nature to refrain from gossiping. And if no one happens to observe you, I shall just drop a little hint about our *excursion* myself. You *will* wed me, or be irretrievably ruined. So why not relax and enjoy what we both know you want?'

'Let me go, you villain!' she cried. Wrestling to try to win enough space to free herself, she managed to elbow him in the side. Grunting, he tightened his hold, his fingernails biting into her arms through the wool of her habit.

'Witch!' he growled. 'Want it rough, do you? Despite your sweet-as-treacle ways, we both know under that bodice is the luscious bosom of a wench who's just as hot for it as her mother. Maybe I won't take you here…but I will have a taste.'

He was too strong for her, she realised. Thinking furiously of some other way to throw him off, she let herself soften a bit, so he was able to force her chin up and kiss her. His insistent tongue probed at her closed lips until, nearly gagging, she let him gain entry into her mouth. As he moaned, his tongue thrusting at hers, she bit down hard.

He cried out and jerked his head away, one hand going to his mouth. Bound to him now only by the one arm, she pulled back as far as she could and used the extra distance to slam her knee up into his tented trouser front, while using her free hand to rake her fingernails across his face.

Howling, he released her, both hands going to cradle his battered anatomy. Hoping she could somehow manage to remount her horse before he recovered enough to come after her—for she had no doubt now that, should he catch her, he'd be furious enough to violate her completely—Pru raced to where the horses had wandered, grazing on the verge.

Her heartbeat pounding in her ears, she grabbed the mare's reins, scrabbling with her other hand to get enough purchase on the horn of the side-saddle that she might be able to get a foot in the stirrup and swing herself up. Struggling with that near-impossible task, she kept a sidelong glance on Fitzroy-Price, still bent over and groaning half-a-dozen paces away.

Oh, how she wished she were free of these clinging, trailing skirts! Back in the meadows at Entremer in a pair of her brother's cast-off breeches, able to grab a horse by the mane and swing herself on to its broad, bare back unaided.

She got her foot up—*almost* into the stirrup before it slipped away. The mare danced nervously at this unusual mounting technique—no doubt further unsettled by the groans coming from the man a few paces away. Panting, Pru crooned to her, trying to soothe the little horse so she could make another attempt.

But, frightened, the mare jerked free, backing away from her. Just as Fitzroy-Price, finally straightening to his full height, headed towards her, murder in his eyes.

Chapter Thirteen

Pru was frantically looking about for a fallen branch, a rock, anything she might fashion into a weapon, when from out of the mist, a rider emerged at a gallop.

So consumed with the urgency of making an escape she'd not even heard its approach, she almost wept with relief when she saw that the man vaulting from the saddle was Johnnie Trethwell.

Before she could utter a word, he'd assessed the situation. Advancing on Lord Halden, he dealt him a tremendous blow to the jaw that sent the Duke's son reeling into the dirt. Following him down, he leaned over to grab Fitzroy-Price by the cravat and lift him up to deliver another blow to his chin. He was raising the booted foot of his good leg, obviously intending to deliver a kick, when Pru ran over to catch his sleeve.

'Enough, Johnnie!' she cried, pulling on him. 'That's enough. Let him go.'

He fixed his gaze on her, his grey-green eyes blazing such fury she took an involuntary step backwards. And then she realised how she must look to him—her hat gone, her hair half-down, her mouth reddened from the harsh pressure of Lord Halden's kisses, the mark of his mouth on her neck. 'I'm all right,' she said urgently. 'He didn't hurt me. Not really. Let him go. Please.'

She could feel the coiled strength of him radiating to her fingertips as he stared fiercely at her, anger humming through his body. At last, some of the tension eased. 'Very well. For you, I won't kick the life out of him like the cur deserves.'

Pulling from her grasp, he went over to Lord Halden, grabbed the man's hand and dragged him to his feet. 'Not a word, or I'll disregard Miss Lattimar's plea that I stop,' he warned as he pushed the man towards his horse.

After shoving him none too gently into the saddle, Johnnie said, 'Tell your friends you were bested in a friendly boxing match that got out of hand—though I'm not sure how you'll explain those scratches. If you breathe a syllable of what really happened, I'll come after you and there will be no Miss Lattimar to beg for mercy. Now, get out of my sight before I change my mind and finish you here and now.'

Slapping the horse on the rump, Johnnie watched as it leapt forward. A moment later, horse and rider had disappeared into the cloaking mist.

Limping back over, he placed one hand on Pru's shoulder and used the other to raise her face, closely inspecting it. Determined not to give way to tears, she managed a smile. 'As you see, I'm f-fine.'

She almost lost that battle when, with the gentlest whisper of a touch, he ran his thumb over her swollen lips, then traced the livid red mark she knew must stand out sharply against the pale skin beneath her ear. 'Damnation! I should have kicked the hell out of him. Sorry—but other than this, which is more than enough justification for a beating, he didn't…hurt you, did he?'

She shook her head rapidly to displace the few tears that had gathered, despite her best intentions. 'No. Thankfully, you arrived before he could. I… I don't think I could have managed to remount before he caught me.'

He shook his head. 'You can't imagine what went through my head when I heard you crying out, somewhere ahead of me in the mist. You're lucky I didn't kill him where he stood.'

Suddenly struck by an awful thought, her eyes widened. 'You—you can't think that I *asked* him to ride with me! Even to make him understand he must cease his courtship of me, I wouldn't have been so foolish as—'

'No, no, I don't think that. You rode out earlier than usual this morning. Did he meet you by chance on his way back from a night of gaming at the soldiers' camp?'

'It's worse than that,' she said bitterly. 'He paid to have someone watch Aunt Gussie's house and then followed me here. To press his suit. He said since I'd encouraged him so publicly for weeks, if I now refused to marry him, I'd be labelled a flirt and a jilt, and no other respectable man would have me. When I told him I'd rather live out my life as a spinster than marry him, he tried to…force his attentions on me, so that once he revealed what happened here, I would be so thoroughly ruined that no other man but him would wed me. He's certain to spread the word about the incident if I continue to refuse him, "regretfully" admitting he'd been swept away by my charms when I lured him into riding with me this morning, proving me a wanton no sane man would dare to marry. Either way, I end up ruined.'

'You think, with the way his face will look by the time he gets back to town, anyone will believe you submitted to him willingly?'

She shrugged. 'He's a duke's son. Whatever he says will be believed. He might even throw in a faradiddle about nobly sustaining those blows while rescuing me from *you*, after which, overcome by gratitude, I offered him my person.'

'That won't explain away the marks left by your fingernails! Besides, you think he will take my threat so lightly?' Johnnie said hotly.

'Oh, I believe he acknowledges the seriousness of it. But I also think he's arrogant enough to believe, when it comes down to it, I would choose miserable marriage to him over disgrace and spinsterhood. I expect most women would. But I will not.'

'Then if he dares repeat his falsehoods, he will get what he deserves.'

Pru shook her head, a dull resignation seeping through her. 'He'll probably send a note to Aunt Gussie's later, asking one final time if I will accept him—I doubt he'd dare present himself in person. If I persist in refusing him, he's too vain to tolerate such an insult without exacting retribution for having me thwart the easy path to the wealth he feels he deserves. And he's cunning enough to devise a way to ruin me while protecting himself against you. He need only do his damage and disappear into the home of one of his cronies for a while.'

She sighed. 'Johnnie, you of all people know what men of that ilk are like! He will rework this whole scene in his head until he's convinced himself that I am the villainess, he the upright gentleman who offered respectable marriage to a female who didn't deserve it. With his pride and vanity offended, he'll have no compunction about seeing me thoroughly ruined.'

He stood silently beside her, obviously considering her words. 'Damn it!' he burst out a moment later. 'Sorry again, but you're right. A man like that will take self-righteous pleasure in seeing you ruined. And short of tracking him down at his cousin's and putting a ball through him, I don't see how I can prevent it.'

Scorched bare by the emotional firestorm of the last half-hour, shock followed by fury, fear and a near despair, his concern touched her on the raw. 'Dear Johnnie,' she said softly, tracing his face with one finger. 'You've been such a champion for me! At least you know that, whatever Fitzroy-Price says, you got here in time to prevent him from truly ruining me.'

'His gain. If he'd managed that, he'd be a dead man, no matter where he hid and for however long.'

'Well, fortunately you won't have to delay your future plans to stalk him.'

He released her and walked over to pick up her discarded hat, frowning as he fingered the torn veil. 'Once again, you've managed to destroy your headgear. But if you'll accompany me behind another conveniently broad oak—not that, in this fog, anyone riding in this direction could see ten feet off the road anyway—I'll do my clumsy best to repair your coiffure.'

'Perhaps Temper was right all along,' Pru said as she followed him to the oak. 'Perhaps it's useless to try to play by the rules, when those rules have already condemned me, no matter what I do. A condemnation that will be unanimous and permanent, after Fitzroy-Price does his damage.'

'You…wouldn't consider marrying him?'

She gave him a withering glance. 'Would you consider wedding Lady Arbuthnot to have her additional wealth to fund your venture?'

'Point taken.' Chuckling, he gathered up some of her fallen tresses and attempted to wrap them back around her coiffure. 'Maybe if I coil it tightly, it will stay under your hat.'

'Yes, try that. If you're careful, you can slip out a few of the pins from the front to help secure the back.'

'Keep still while I attempt it.'

As she held herself immobile while Johnnie worked, something from deep within bubbled up, the lethargy of despair and hopelessness slowly overshadowed by a sense almost of…relief. As if a page had been turned, closing off the past and presenting her with a new future, uncharted but clear. A future that offered a freedom she'd never before allowed herself.

'Perhaps being ruined won't be so bad after all.'

He paused to look down at her quizzically. 'What, you're going to take on the whole world?'

'Isn't that what I *have* been doing? Now there's no need any longer. No more pasting an impassive façade on my face, considering every remark before I utter it, every action before I take it. All to meet a censorious society's expectations of how a virtuous young maiden should conduct herself—even as society inspected me like a specimen under glass for every tiny infraction, eager to justify its preconceived opinion that I was *not* a virtuous young maiden. Doesn't being ruined finally set me free to say what I want? *Do* what I want, without a care for what anyone else thinks?'

Giving her an indulgent smile, he carefully settled her riding hat back over the makeshift coiffure. 'And what do you want, *chahna*?'

With a joyous sense of release, she allowed all the pent-up passion for him she'd been restraining since the moment they met to flood out. 'This,' she whispered.

Reaching up to clasp his neck, she pulled his face down and kissed him.

Like many a soldier, Johnnie knew that being in the grip of some strong emotion—rage, fear, the driving imperative to protect one's men—loosened one's hold over all the rest. Like lust. And after rescuing her from being mauled by Fitzroy-Price, his anger was still white-hot.

So the moment Pru's mouth touched his, a little clumsily, the lack of finesse betraying her inexperience, he went from simmering desire to raging passion in an instant. His craving for her, muted but never subdued, overwhelmed him like that attack of dacoits riding at full cry, snuffing out before it could fully form any thought that this might not be wise, shutting down everything but the compelling need to possess her.

No gentle brush of her lips this time. Wrapping his arms around her and binding her against him, he possessed and ravished them, demanding entry, scouring her tongue with his as he licked and probed, nipped and suckled. Consumed by the fire in his blood, he slid his hands down her back, kneading, caressing, until he could cup her bottom and pull her against an erection so hard it was nearly pain.

She gave him every encouragement to continue, meeting the thrusts of his tongue with bold strokes of her own, her hands clawing at the knot of his cravat, the buttons on his waistcoat.

She broke the kiss, gasping, rubbing her face against his. 'I want you, Johnnie. I understand now why my mother, denied this by Papa, reached out for it with other men. But I don't want anyone else. Only you. Take me. Love me. Show me everything you make me yearn for.'

Her long speech gave sanity time to break through the haze of madness that had possessed him. It would be an unforgivable violation of their friendship for him to take her. But he could kiss and caress her for a while longer before the honourable part of him wrestled free of the grip lust had over him, and forced him to let her go completely.

'Touch me,' she urged. 'I want to feel your hands on me.'

Taking her mouth again, he unbuttoned the jacket of her habit and her blouse to run his hands over breasts so full, so voluptuous, his mouth watered to taste them and suckle the pebbled texture of her nipples. The impenetrable layers of shift and corset making that impossible, he gave her long, drugging kisses, licking her lips in rhythm to the stroke of his fingers over her breasts.

'Too…many garments,' she gasped between kisses.

She worked her fingers under his cravat, prying open his shirt front, sliding her hands down to rub her fingers over his chest. While he shuddered, breaking the kiss, jolted by the fire of her touch, she murmured, 'I want to feel your hands, your mouth, on *my* bare skin.'

Eager to comply, he kissed the tender area under

her chin, the velvet expanse of the neck she arched for him. He continued down her throat, his tongue seeking her collarbone, teasing below the edge of her chemise and corset to lave the full rounded tops of her breasts.

Until she shocked him again, leaving him paralysed by sensation as she fumbled open the straining buttons of his trouser flap and touched his rigid member. As he hissed between his teeth, her fingers on him stilled. 'Does that…not please you?' she whispered.

'It's…intoxicating,' he replied, then caught her hand before she could run her fingers down his length. 'But you mustn't.'

'I can't get out of this habit. But here,' she said, drawing up her skirt with one hand, 'I'm bare beneath. And I can bare…this.'

Slowly, tentatively, she stroked down his shaft. Obviously emboldened when, helpless to control his reaction, it leapt under her caressing fingers, she stroked him again.

'I'm not exactly sure how this is contrived between a man and a woman,' she said, nearly driving him to the brink as her even, measured strokes extended further and further, almost reaching the aching tip. 'But you can touch me with this, can't you? And that will bring us both ultimate pleasure?'

He could let her bare him, lay her on his coat, kiss his way up her sweet legs and inner thighs until he reached the throbbing centre of her. Plumb her depths with tongue and fingers until she reached a climax so powerful that, humming with satisfaction, she would probably not feel any pain when he pierced her maidenhood. Having breached that, he could still, letting her adjust to his invasion, kissing her lips, her neck until her body began to respond of its own volition, her hips rocking to invite him deeper. Then he could bury himself in her sweet centre...

And spill his seed, imperilling her with the burden of an illicit child that would complete the ruin of her future.

Sweat dripping from his forehead, he pushed away her exploring fingers and tugged down her skirts. 'A pleasure I have no doubt would be unparalleled. But, *chahna*, the risk is far too great. We have no means of preventing conception. It's madness to count on being lucky enough to avoid that.'

Not trusting himself to touch her, he stepped away, his body still on fire, his arms and hands trembling. 'It's not that I don't want you. I've dreamed of possessing you, almost from the moment I first saw you in Sidney Gardens. But you offered, and I accepted, *friendship*. It would be the act of a villain, not a friend, to steal your innocence and take you so irresponsibly.'

Absently she rubbed at the loose buttons of her jacket. 'Then...you will offer me—nothing?'

From some unfathomable recess of his brain, he heard himself saying, 'Well, I... I suppose you could marry *me*.'

She gasped, her eyes flaring wide...and then slapped him across the face with all her strength.

Reeling a little on his bad leg, he held up both hands. 'I didn't mean to insult you!'

'Bad enough that Lord Halden wanted to marry me for my money!' she raged. 'I'll not have you offer for me out of, of...*pity*! I'll have you know I won't settle for less than loyalty, devotion and *love* from a husband. You can't offer that...can you?'

Could he love her? Did he love her? Before he could put his rattled thoughts in sufficient order to even consider her question, she snapped, 'I thought not. Much as I desire you, I'll not live with you as your mistress.'

Stung, he retorted, 'I would never do you the insult of offering *carte blanche*!'

'Then you would leave me with *nothing* before we part? No taste of passion to warm the rest of my lonely life? Surely there is *some* way to pleasure that doesn't risk conceiving a child.'

Good sense insisted that he deny it and get her back to town. But an insidious little voice was whispering in his ear that he could give her—give them both— that pleasure. There were many paths to a fulfilment he just *knew* would be spectacular, without the threat of her bearing a bastard.

The randy, desperate, foolish part of him urged him to agree, to begin scheming immediately to discover a time and place to make such an assignation happen. The honourable part of him fought back, insisting that taking her innocence without being willing to pledge any commitment to her would be as infamous as making her his mistress.

Fighting that internal battle, he stood silent—until he looked up to see her smiling. 'So there is a way,' she murmured. 'Something sweet and pure and joyous, that will for ever remind me of you.'

Damnation, why couldn't he just lie to her?

Somehow, he couldn't. Clamping his lips shut, he reached over and brusquely began refastening the buttons of her garments. 'Time to make you presentable and get you back to Bath.'

'You said you could deny me nothing. Before you

hurry me back to Bath—and the imminent destruction of my reputation at the hands of Lord Halden—I insist on one more kiss.'

When he leaned over to give her a chaste peck on the forehead, she merely laughed. In her dancing eyes, he saw dawning the dangerous realisation of the sensual power she held over him.

Did she have any idea how close she was to breaking him, to cindering all his good intentions in an inferno of passion?

More shaken and unsure of himself than he'd been while facing down charging outlaws bent on his destruction, he finished her last buttons, righted his own dishevelled cravat as best he could with trembling hands and motioned her towards her grazing mount.

As he gave her a leg up into the saddle, she leaned down to touch his sleeve. 'Thank you,' she said softly.

'For what?'

'For not saying "no" to my request.'

Heaven help him, how *was* he going to deny her?

Trying to unstick a mind which seemed to have frozen on an image of pleasuring her, he threw himself back into his own saddle and nodded at her to follow as he led her back to the road and on towards the clearing where the useless groom waited. He shouldn't even consider fulfilling her request—which would be difficult enough to arrange, even if he were convinced it would be wise.

He'd been pursued by bored matrons before, but their invitations to seduction had always been subtle, delivered by passionate glances or in conversations full of innuendo and double entendre. And in the end, he'd been the one who controlled the situation and made the first move.

Then came unique and unparalleled Prudence Lattimar. Who stated her desire plainly and without subterfuge—as she spoke of everything else. Surely, once she regained her equilibrium after the emotional upheaval of nearly being violated by a man she'd trusted, her good sense would tell her such an interlude was impossible.

Saving him from playing the unprecedented role of the seducer trying to avoid seduction.

Chapter Fourteen

Thankful that Aunt Gussie wasn't an early riser, Prudence was able to slip up to her chamber for a quiet interlude after a protective Johnnie insisted on seeing her safely returned to the town house. Using some rice powder to conceal as best she could the mark Lord Halden had left on her neck—and thankful for the discretion of her maid, who asked no questions as she helped her change from her riding habit into a morning gown, then silently offered her a fichu to wrap about her throat—she was able to sit by her window and contemplate what she must do for the immediate future. And decide how to break the news to her long-suffering aunt that the goal that had brought them to Bath would be unattainable.

Despite the traumatic beginning of her day, by the time she walked down to the breakfast room at mid-morning to greet her aunt, she'd regained most of her usual composure. After joining Aunt Gussie for a cup of coffee, she invited that lady to take a turn around the Circus's elegant circle with her after her aunt finished her breakfast.

Though she'd thought her expression serene and her voice normal, upon hearing that request, Aunt Gussie set down her coffee cup, her eyes widening in alarm. 'Something drastic must have happened—I knew I felt something was amiss! And...' she lowered her voice to a murmur '...if you feel it necessary that we stroll in the Circus to tell me about it, it must be drastic indeed!'

There was no point pretending it wasn't. With a sigh, she nodded. 'I don't know how you knew, but it is rather drastic.'

'Fortunately, I've never needed to resort to smelling salts, so I shan't faint dead away on the flagstones,' Lady Stoneway said in a humorous tone, obviously trying to cheer her. Her expression going from amused to concerned, she reached over to squeeze Pru's hand. 'Whatever it is, my dear, we will weather it together.'

Pru swallowed the lump that had risen in her throat. Aunt Gussie had done so much for her, she hated to repay that kind lady with humiliation and scandal, even though it wasn't her fault. Though the unfolding of the upcoming disaster was out of her control, at least she could warn her aunt of the storm about to break over their heads.

'Thank you, and let me say in advance that I'm sorry.'

'No need for apologies. Well, I think I just lost my appetite.' Pushing back her half-empty cup, Lady Stoneway rose. 'It won't take me long to get into my pelisse, bonnet and gloves. I'll meet you downstairs in the drawing room in a trice.'

Pru nodded, then followed her aunt from the room and up the stairs to claim her own outerwear. Walking past the wardrobe where the rest of her clothing was folded, she wondered how soon they would be packing it all up and leaving…for where? Back to London? Or to Entremer?

Once the scandal broke in full force, there wouldn't be much point in remaining in Bath—subjecting her poor aunt to the prospect of being cut by almost everyone in society save her closest friends. At best, Pru might have a few days to settle some scores before most doors in society were closed to her and she shook the dust of Bath from her feet to go into permanent social exile.

A few minutes later, after accepting their cloaks from the butler, Prudence and her aunt exited the town house and began a slow circuit of the Circus's central garden. 'So, my dear, what is this news so alarming that you didn't wish to divulge it within hearing distance of the servants?'

'When you hear it, you may wish you had brought that vinaigrette. I'm afraid it's nothing less than my ruin.'

Omitting the calumnies she'd overheard from the soldiers the previous day, still too painful to repeat, Prudence briefly recounted what she'd learned about Lord Halden Fitzroy-Price's true intentions regarding her and the taking of holy orders.

'So that was why you were so cool to him at the Subscription Ball last night!' Lady Stoneway exclaimed. 'What a wicked man, to lead you on so duplicitously, knowing all along he had no real calling! But I don't see how his subterfuge means your ruination.'

'There's more, and it gets worse,' Pru said grimly, proceeding to give her aunt a carefully edited account of her encounter with the Duke's son during her ride earlier that day. Omitting mention of his threat to ravish her, she described his fury at her categorical refusal to marry him, his tearing of her veil and forcing a kiss on her so that he would be able to claim she'd been compromised—and would therefore be ruined if they didn't wed.

Though Lady Stoneway snorted with indignation when Pru revealed how Lord Halden had tracked her down on her ride, she remained otherwise silent until Pru finished her account. Then, halting, she took her niece's arm and looked at her searchingly. 'You are sure he didn't harm you?'

'No, Aunt, other than a punishing kiss, it was just threats.'

'You'll need to tie that fichu higher then, my dear.'

Her hand flying automatically to her neck, Pru flushed. 'I… I expect you are correct.'

'That…that blackguard!' her aunt exploded. 'One has a mind to call the constable and have him taken up for assault! How dare he try to ruin *your* reputation, when he has just shown his own character so lacking?'

'You can hardly expect him to admit that. He's probably been granted his every whim since childhood, so how dare I stand in the way of what he wants? There's more yet—I'm afraid. Lieutenant Trethwell heard the altercation and came riding up to rescue me. He… he dealt Lord Halden some serious blows to the face, which I suspect are going to leave him looking battered for some time.'

'Heavens! Was Lieutenant Trethwell injured as well?'

Pru laughed drily. 'I think you can guess the answer to that. Trethwell advised Lord Halden to claim he'd got the bruises in a boxing match with friends, else he would return to punish him again. Attacking the son of a peer was a dangerous move, but since I was the only witness—and he can hardly hope to induce *me* to testify on his behalf—he's unlikely to take legal action. I can only hope Lord Halden will take the Lieutenant's threat seriously and not claim he received the blows from the Lieutenant while trying to prevent *him* from pressing his attentions on me, thereby trying to besmirch the Lieutenant's reputation as well as mine.'

'He'd do better to claim a boxing match gone wrong—else it will be quite obvious, when the curious observe that Lieutenant Trethwell is entirely unmarked, that Lord Halden was thoroughly bested.'

'I hadn't thought of that!' Pru said, feeling better. 'Perhaps you're right. He wouldn't want to bring attention to the fact that he isn't up to Trethwell's weight—a man he sneeringly refers to as a "half-pay cripple".'

'I'm beginning to wish you *had* given Lord Halden the cut direct last night!' Aunt Gussie exclaimed. 'What a thoroughly vile remark! Bravo to Lieutenant Trethwell for once again proving himself your protector. But...' she pinned Pru with her penetrating gaze '...he felt it necessary to mill down Lord Halden merely because the man *kissed* you?'

Prudence felt her blush deepen. 'Lord Halden...might have threatened more,' she admitted in a small voice.

To her shock, her aunt spat out an expletive Pru would never have dreamed might emit from her ladylike lips. 'Then I can only thank Heaven that Lieutenant Trethwell happened along! I suppose it's useless for me to observe that if you hadn't out-galloped the protection of your groom, the encounter might have been avoided.'

Pru shrugged. 'Perhaps, but I doubt it. Lord Halden had only to give the man a charming smile, flip him a coin and suggest he take himself off for some ale at the nearest public house. Stebbins isn't one of our own servants, a long-time retainer who would feel responsible for my protection. He's employed by the livery and would surely think it ill advised to refuse the directions of a duke's son.'

'I don't suppose you could talk Lord Halden out of spreading the story.'

'What, appeal to his honour as a gentleman?' Pru said scornfully. 'Had he any honour, he'd have accepted my refusal with good grace and left me untouched. Besides, he as much as admitted he's deeply in debt. I suspect his family pawned him off on Lady Isabelle to keep him from running up any more bills in London, with the instruction that she find him a rich bride as soon as possible. Hence her willingness to accept even one of the Scandal Sisters.'

'You wouldn't consider giving in and marrying him.'

'Absolutely not! Surely ruin is preferable to the misery of being at the mercy of such a man for a lifetime!'

Lady Stoneway sighed. 'I agree, but it is a brave choice, my dear. No matter that it's the man to blame, the woman is always the one who suffers. With marriages often arranged for the mutual benefit of money and consequence, many would take the easier path. Compared with the prospect of becoming an outcast condemned to remaining single, they would console themselves in the knowledge that, by marrying the villain, they would gain a life of ease and a high position in society.'

'Advantages he himself pointed out, while he was still trying to cajole my acceptance. But I am not such a woman and, thank the Lord, I don't have to be. I'm fortunate that Papa's wealth protects me from having to earn my bread for the rest of my life as an unwanted poor relation—or something worse.'

After that remark, for a long time the two walked in silence. Finally, Lady Stoneway, linking her arm with Pru's, said with a sigh, 'I've racked my brain, but I'm forced to agree that if Lord Halden persists in this scheme to ruin you—and unless you hide yourself away until that mark fades, his accusations will have physical proof—I can't see any way to wiggle out of this. And to think I engineered your introduction to him and encouraged his suit! I am so sorry, my dear!'

'You needn't be, Aunt Gussie. You've done everything you could to try to get me accepted and settled. I admit, I'd begun to have doubts about Lord Halden's suitability before this incident, but even I didn't think him capable of…this.' She touched a finger to her neck.

'I could talk with my friends. Give them a true account of what actually happened.'

'You could try, but it's not likely society would accept my version of events over his. If some *have* heard whispers about his being in debt and amusing himself with ladies of the demi-monde, those are common enough faults many women would be willing to overlook to land a husband of such an elevated degree. Besides, even if some believe my account, they would hesitate to accuse a duke's son of lying and risk offending his powerful family and friends.' She gave a mirthless laugh. 'Especially when his version of events fits so neatly into what society wants to believe about me anyway!'

'Then what shall we do for you, my dear? Retire to London and wait for next year?'

'I don't see any purpose in that. If rumours about my likeness to Mama followed me here, my actual ruination in Bath is sure to become common knowledge in London society, probably before we could pack up and get ourselves back to town. I would spare us both the humiliation of being ignored—or cut—next Season. I think you should bid your friends here goodbye, have your maid pack your things immediately and return to London or Chemberton as soon as possible. I shall remain another few days before I leave for Entremer.'

Lady Stoneway gave her a sharp look. 'You can't think so poorly of me as to believe I would abandon you here alone, without any escort!'

Pru's face hardened. 'Before every door in society closes to me, I intend to set the record straight about the scratches that, along with Trethwell's bruises, now adorn Lord Halden's face. You've already suffered embarrassment enough. I'd not have you get caught up in the ugliness.'

'Then what do you mean to do afterwards?'

'Go to Entremer after I've said my piece.'

'You truly mean to bury yourself at Entremer? How will you ever find a husband there?'

Pru laughed. 'You forget, odd that I am, that alone among the family, I love Entremer. Riding out through the verdant pastures, up on to the ridges, down by the river where the cascades make ferns and frogs flourish… I spent some of my happiest childhood days there, Temper and I trailing after Chris and Gregory and generally making nuisances of ourselves. In any event, after this spectacle in Bath, I expect I shall end up just as notorious as Mama. It's time to admit my naïve dream of finding a husband and family is unattainable. Unless I truly were ready to marry a man more interested in my dowry than my person.'

Lady Stoneway shook her head, tears glittering on her lashes. 'Well, it's not right. I so hoped our sojourn here would end with you engaged, looking forward to having a husband, home and family of your own!'

'Oh, the result may not be so bad. Just think, I'll no longer have to kowtow to ill-intentioned matrons who smile at my face and whisper calumnies behind my back. I shall find something else useful to become. Something where I can be who I truly am, without having to rigidly control every thought and action.'

Lady Stoneway nodded. 'I would like to see you free of artificial fetters, able to be the lovely woman you are.'

Warmed by her aunt's support, Prudence gave her hand a squeeze. 'Shall we return now? You can get your maid started on that packing.'

They walked, once again in silence, back across the garden towards the town house. Pru still felt a weight of sadness at letting go of the dream that had guided every thought and action since she'd first realised what the implications her mother's notoriety would mean for her own future. But the tiny tendril of hope she'd felt earlier had grown and strengthened.

No more struggling to force herself to be someone she was not. With the death of her dream came a quiet acceptance of her fate and that sweet whisper of freedom.

As they reached the town house stairs, Lady Stoneway stopped Pru with a hand on her arm. 'I haven't yet given up all hope of seeing you settled. Surely, somewhere in Bath or England, lives a man who can see past the superficial to the true and beautiful heart of you.'

Pru felt a pang, remembering the man who'd recently told her almost the same thing. 'A lovely thought. Perhaps it will turn out to be true. I think I shall read for a while. Will you go up and begin your packing?'

'What, abandon you because of that scheming weasel? Never. I'd rather like to spit in his face myself! If he does tell his tale and make you infamous, then so be it. I shall stand by you.'

Torn between gratitude and humility at her aunt's support and a desire to spare her any further indignities, Pru said, 'Are you sure? If he does take that step, and I'm almost certain he will, what happens next has to reflect badly upon you.'

Lady Stoneway shrugged. 'Temper insists she will go her own way, my sons are all successfully married and I have no daughters with reputations to protect. What do I care if society spurns me? I know my true friends will not and their company is all that matters to me. Besides,' she added with a chuckle, 'why should your mama have all the fun? It might be quite energising to be thought scandalous—if it induces some charming rogue like Lieutenant Trethwell into pursuing me!'

Trying to imagine her proper aunt slipping off to an assignation with some dashing military gentleman, Pru had to laugh, too. 'I hope it does.'

They walked back inside, but before they could hand their cloaks over to the butler, he held a note out to Pru.

'A footman from Lady Isabelle's brought this for you. From Lord Halden.'

Shooting a look to her aunt, Pru took the missive, unfolded and quickly scanned it.

'Will there be a reply, Miss Lattimar? The footman said he would return after doing another errand for her ladyship.'

'Yes, I'll pen one immediately. Thank you, Soames.'

'It's what I expected,' Pru told her aunt as they mounted the stairs to their respective chambers. 'Ambiguously worded, neither admitting nor threatening anything for which he could be taken to account should anyone other than me chance to read it, but with the meaning quite clear. Accept his offer immediately, or he will see to my ruination.'

Lady Stoneway's lips tightened, her expression turning almost militant. 'Then let the battle lines be drawn. Did you want to go out tonight?'

Pru sighed. 'I think I must—before his story circulates so widely that all doors are closed to me.'

'If you wish to discover immediately whether or not he's made good on his threat, I would suggest attending Lady Arbuthnot's reception rather than the Assembly Ball. She's the most influential—and malicious— gossip in Bath. If he intends to spread a story that will ruin you, he will most likely start with her.'

'Very well. I have a few words to say to that lady anyway. I'll go and write that reply.'

Lady Stoneway reached over to grasp her chin and tilt it up. 'Courage, my dear.'

Prudence laughed, filled with the first genuine amusement she'd felt since the incident this morning that had spun her world out of control. 'No courage needed, Aunt Gussie. Tonight I'm going to shock society and I intend to enjoy every minute of it!'

After pulling out pen and paper in the privacy of her chamber, Pru scanned again Lord Halden's request to call on her that afternoon 'to receive her positive reply to a previously posed question', which, if she were to deny him, 'would have the results we already discussed'.

What a lover-like note, she thought scornfully. Dashing off a reply informing him there was no reason for him to call, as she would not change her answer to that 'previously posed question, whatever the consequences', she summoned her maid to deliver the note for Soames to hand over when Lady Isabelle's footman returned.

Seated at her desk by the window, she watched the maid walk out, knowing with a sense of finality that its receipt would set irreversible events into motion. A moment later, gazing out of the window, she saw Lady Isabelle's footman knock at the town house door, then emerge again, heading back towards the Royal Crescent.

As he paced off, with a sigh, she bid farewell to the sweet image that had energised her for the last month: playing with her children in a flower-filled vicarage garden, her husband watching them indulgently from the garden bench where he was working on his next Sunday's sermon.

Absently she rubbed at the mark on her neck, nostalgia fading as her anger intensified and her intensions hardened. With nothing left to lose, she would inform society just what a scoundrel Lord Halden was before leaving for what, despite Aunt Gussie's fond hopes, was likely to be permanent, solitary exile at Entremer.

Pushing away the image of the contemptible Lord Halden, her thoughts shifted to the man who, though reputed to be a rogue, had shown himself the exact opposite. 'Surely there is in London a man who can see the gold of your worth through the dross of gossip surrounding you,' Johnnie had told her.

What a shame the only man who seemed to value her was a wandering soul whose free spirit would wither, should someone try to box it up in the confines of an English country manor. *If* she could manage to entice him to stay in the first place—by no means a sure thing, despite their attraction and the unexpected offer of marriage compassion had brought to his lips— an offer that seemed to shock him as much as it had her.

Oh, that more than *compassion* had prompted it! But she'd given him a clear opportunity to confess he'd fallen in love with her—and he'd been unable to take it. Much as it had hurt—enough that, to her shame, she'd actually slapped him—she could only be grateful for his honesty. If he *had* claimed to love her, she might have persuaded herself to believe it and succumbed to the temptation to accept the offer.

Which would have been worse than marrying Lord Halden. At some point, her fat dowry added to the amounts promised by his investors would allow him to finalise the details of setting up his trading venture. Probably sooner rather than later, the siren call to adventure would lure him from her side, leaving her alone in the countryside for months or years. Perhaps for ever.

She didn't know what would be worse. Having him

with her, trying to conceal his boredom and restlessness and desire to be elsewhere, or sending him off, not knowing whether some gale at sea or hostile native ashore would snuff out his life. Miring her in permanent anxiety, wondering for ever whether something had happened to him or whether he just wasn't yet ready to return to her. Wondering whether she would ever see him again.

Either prospect was unbearable. Not once she finally accepted the truth her heart had been whispering for some time. Despite cautioning herself to avoid it, she'd fallen in love with Johnnie Trethwell.

Living the rest of her life without him was going to be far more bitter than enduring social exile at Entremer.

Chapter Fifteen

Steeled to her purpose, early that evening, Pru descended to the morning room to find her aunt awaiting her, already dressed for their evening out. 'Are you sure you want to accompany me?' she asked, going over to give that lady a kiss on the cheek. 'I shall always be grateful for everything you've done for me. All your support and l-love,' she added, her voice breaking a little. 'My affection and gratitude will not diminish a jot if you choose to avoid the humiliation of tonight's spectacle.'

Giving her a little hug, Aunt Gussie laughed. 'I wouldn't miss it for the world! I can't wait to see what you've got planned.'

'You'd best brace yourself. Meek, mild, submissive Prudence Lattimar is gone for ever. A defiant, ill-behaved termagant has taken her place.'

'Well, then, my lovely termagant, let me have So-ames summon us chairs!'

Any faint hope that Lord Halden had not followed through on his threat evaporated the moment they entered Lady Arbuthnot's drawing room. Immediately after the butler announced them, every guest within hearing distance turned to stare. While the ladies' eyes registered shock and reproof, the gentlemen, their expressions curious and appraising, gave her the same sort of blatantly disrespectful scrutiny she'd experienced from the soldiers, looks that would have been an unpardonable insult, had they been directed towards any other gently born maiden.

Raising her eyebrows at Lady Stoneway, Pru murmured, 'I had better seek out our hostess immediately, before she learns of my arrival and has the butler toss me out.'

Spotting over the heads of the other guests the nodding plumes in the awful shade of puce Lady Arbuthnot seemed to favour, Pru set off in that direction. As she advanced, the other guests turned their backs on her—rather helpfully, she thought with gallows humour, since it enabled her to cross the room as swiftly as Moses parting the Red Sea. Reaching her hostess, she stood silently, waiting until the lady's conversational partner—or the sudden hush in the room—alerted her to Pru's presence.

Soon enough, the matron talking with Lady Arbuthnot stuttered into silence, her eyes going wide. Lady Arbuthnot turned, recognised her and stiffened.

Before that lady could decide whether to simply cut her, or order her to be ejected, Pru placed a hand on her arm.

Jerking it away, Lady Arbuthnot hissed, 'Hussy! I'm astonished you have the effrontery to enter my house!'

'You did invite me.'

'Well, yes, but that was before—'

'Before you heard Lord Halden's salacious story?

From Lady Isabelle, I would imagine, for he himself hasn't shown his face, has he? Probably because he does not wish to appear until the scratches I left there when I fought him off have faded. But I am not ashamed to appear before you, bearing the mark *he* left upon me,' she said, drawing aside the fichu covering her neck.

As those nearby gasped, she continued, 'Perhaps society will forgive his unprovoked attack on a lady whose only fault was refusing to marry him and give him access to the dowry he badly needs. Funds that will allow him to continue his nightly visits to the fleshpots of Corn Street and pay off enough of the debts he's run up to every tailor, bootmaker, haberdasher and wine shop in London, Bath and Oxford that he doesn't have to fear outrunning the magistrate. Didn't his family, no longer wishing to support his dissolute habits, send him here to Lady Isabelle so she might find him a rich bride? Alas, I had no wish to spend my life—and my fortune—on a man who consorts with harlots and throws away thousands on the turn of a card. For that grievous fault, he attacked me, warning that if I didn't relent and marry him, he would see me ruined. Although I suspect that a man so deficient in character cheats at cards as well, at least in this instance, he told the truth.'

'That…that is a monstrous accusation!' Lady Arbuthnot exclaimed when Prudence stopped for breath.

'But true, for all that it is monstrous. In making me his target, he ran little risk, did he not? After all, what other prospects did I have? What true gentleman would risk marrying the scandalous daughter of a scandalous lady? Who, rumour says, was once pursued by your own late husband.'

Her face turning almost as purple as her headdress, before the indignant Lady Arbuthnot could sputter out a response, Pru continued, 'You are probably quite wise to cut me. It's so unpleasant to listen to truths society doesn't wish to acknowledge! Such as the fact that I was certain Lady Isabelle would spread the rumour first to you, since everyone knows you possess the most acid tongue in Bath. I am leaving now, so you needn't summon the butler. Oh, before I go—you really should try gowns and bonnets in a different colour. That puce hue you seem to favour doesn't compliment your complexion at all. Good evening, Lady Arbuthnot.'

After giving the furious woman a graceful curtsy, Pru turned and crossed the silent room to where Lady Stoneway awaited her. Together, heads held high, they walked out as the shocked hush erupted into cacophony.

'A magnificent speech, my dear, and so very effective! I wager I'm not the only person who's wanted for years to confront Lady Arbuthnot—but lacked the courage. No need to drop by any other entertainments—that verbal salvo shall be the talk of the town within the hour!'

Prudence chuckled. 'I'm sure it will. We'd better get back to the Circus before even the chairmen refuse to serve us. You can spend the rest of the evening packing.'

'Not quite yet,' Lady Stoneway replied, her expression merry. 'I shall remain a few more days, visiting my closest friends and hearing all the delicious gossip that is sure to follow.'

'I wish one of the results would be society cutting Lord Halden, but I'm not naïve enough to believe that will happen.'

Her aunt nodded. 'Some will believe you, though even those who do are unlikely to challenge him. At the very least, perhaps the truth may warn off rich widows and the mothers of eligible heiresses he might otherwise have managed to charm.' Lady Stoneway laughed. 'Mentioning the possibility that he cheats at cards was a master stroke! Men might discount your claim that he attacked you—females bring such things upon themselves, they believe—but they absolutely disdain a cheat!'

'Perhaps I maligned him,' Pru retorted. 'If so, I'm not sorry. Let *him* try living with infamy for a change.'

Having reached the side entrance where the chairmen waited, conversation ended as they climbed into the sedan chairs that would bear them back home.

How much longer should she stay in Bath before leaving for Entremer? Pru asked herself as the chairmen set off.

As her aunt noted, she thought her message had been effective. Having followed that lady's good advice by delivering it first to the most notorious gossip in Bath, she could be sure the news would spread swiftly enough that she need not repeat it anywhere else. With no true friends in the city save her aunt in whose company she might wait to assess the results, she had no need to linger.

Only one true friend, she amended. Apparently, Lord Halden had been cognizant enough of the danger to his continued health and safety of trying to extend his revenge to include Trethwell, he'd not implicated the Lieutenant in the affair, for which she was grateful. Since Johnnie's name had not been tarnished by association with the debacle, would he follow the wise path and avoid her? No doubt his aunt would strongly urge such a course.

Perhaps she wouldn't even have a chance to bid him goodbye.

Biting her lip to stave off the tears sparked by that melancholy thought, she resolved to remain two more days in Bath. She'd ride out each morning, hoping to see him. If he hadn't tried to approach her by then, she would know he had chosen to be prudent and bid him a one-sided goodbye while riding the trail where she'd spent such happy hours in his company...falling in love with him.

Which might, after all, be a better outcome. How was she to bid goodbye for ever to the man who held her heart without breaking down and confessing her love to him?

Which, because he was kind and felt some fondness for her, would only distress him and make him uncomfortable that he was not able to vow his love in return. Not to mention curdling her sweet memories of their rides together by giving them an unpleasant and awkward finale.

Unless... If he did appear, perhaps she could defer the heartbreak by luring him into a coming together that would render her recollection of their parting bittersweet but joyful for all the years to come.

Several streets away at the Assembly Rooms, Johnnie was biding his time impatiently, exerting his famous charm conversing with the most influential society matrons present and alert for any hint that Lord Halden had unleashed the whispering campaign he'd threatened against Miss Lattimar. He was also hoping the lady herself would appear, so he could offer her his support and protection, should some ugly confrontation develop.

By the time the hour had advanced to nearly midnight, when the dancing would end, she had still not arrived, nor had he heard any rumours. Encouraged, he was beginning to hope that perhaps Lord Halden had heeded his dire warning after all. Until, returning to his aunt after dancing with the latest dowager, he noticed a stir of excitement in the ballroom, newcomers plucking friends by the sleeve and leaning close to whisper in their ears.

Which was exactly what Lady Woodlings did as he reached her side. 'Walk with me to the tea room,' she murmured, her face sober as she took his arm.

'What is it? What has happened?' he asked…even as, with a sinking heart, he had a very strong suspicion what news she was about to impart.

'It's about your Miss Lattimar. Apparently she's proved all the sceptics true and gone and ruined herself. She even had the effrontery to confirm it to Lady Arbuthnot's face, confronting that lady in her own drawing room!'

'When? How?'

'Tonight, about an hour ago! Apparently, Lord Halden's cousin, Lady Isabelle, paid a call on Lady Arbuthnot this afternoon, telling her she must banish Miss Lattimar from her company forthwith. Lord Halden had just confided in her—in strictest confidence, of course—that Miss Lattimar had invited him to ride with her, then dismissed her groom and lured him into taking liberties with her person! Such liberties, he became sadly convinced that, though he had hoped the rumours about her character were unfounded, so abandoned did she reveal herself, he had no choice but to regretfully decide he must withdraw his suit. For what gentleman would wish to risk marrying a woman who'd proved herself as dissipated as her mother?'

'"Lured" him into taking liberties, did she?' Johnnie said sarcastically.

'Oh, really, Johnnie! What healthy young buck would have the will to refuse the advances of a woman that beautiful?'

'A gentleman of honour?' he suggested. 'Who then would not "confide" in a woman guaranteed to spread the news as quickly as possible to all the world?'

'I know you have…a fondness for her. But you can hardly continue to defend her character after she has already publicly admitted the lapse!'

'Did she? Just how did *she* describe the incident?'

Lady Woodlings coloured a little. 'Well, she alleged that Lord Halden had attacked *her*, in order to compromise her into marrying him, so he might have access to her dowry, supposedly to settle a large number of debts and to…to support his visits to houses of ill repute. Claiming he told her if she refused to wed him, he would see her ruined.'

'And so he has, hasn't he?' Johnnie said, the slow burn of fury rising up.

'Surely you can't believe her version of events! Not after she defied every principle governing the behaviour of a gently raised young lady! Bad enough to have admitted such a shocking interlude, were she persistently questioned about it. But to go out in public and *proclaim* it to the world? Had such an attack actually happened, a truly virtuous maiden would have been prostrate on her couch with distress and mortification, and done everything in her power to suppress any knowledge of it!'

'Perhaps. But I happen to know her account is true. Because I was there.'

'What?' his aunt gasped. '*You* were present? But— how? Why?'

'I was riding the Lansdown Hill road this morning and heard Miss Lattimar crying out, somewhere in the fog. I galloped up to find her struggling to escape Lord Halden and came to her rescue. Before he could truly ravish her, as he'd threatened.'

Anxious foreboding coloured her expression. 'You... you didn't strike him, did you?

'How well you know me, Aunt. He'll bear the mark of my fists for some time. As well as the marks from the fingernails she used on him, trying to free herself. That is, if he lives long enough. I warned him if he tried to ruin her, I would make him pay for it.'

Seeming to sense the rage in him, she clutched his arm. 'Johnnie, you mustn't do any such thing! Don't you know what would happen, were you arrested for assaulting the son of a duke? At the very least, you'd be imprisoned, if not transported!'

'In truth, I'd rather kill him than assault him, but I suppose ruination isn't a capital offence. Even if it does destroy the life of the woman he maligned.'

'Oh, that you ever insisted on forcing an acquaintance with that woman!' Lady Woodlings cried. 'I was afraid the witch might be the ruin of you!'

'Witch? I'd rather call her courageous and principled. And you probably don't have to worry about having the magistrate invade Queen Square to put me under irons. Miss Lattimar was sure, if Lord Halden did disregard my warning and spread his lies, that he would quit Bath and go into hiding before I found out about it—the cowardly cur. Which I fully expect I'll discover to be the case when I go to Lady Isabelle's town house, after I summon a chair to take you home.'

His aunt took a deep breath of relief. 'I hope to Heaven he has fled! Are you so sure he will have, Johnnie?'

'Nearly certain. If he meant to punish me for attacking him, I'd have already been taken up by the law. He would also have concocted a way to work my assaulting him into his tawdry little tale. Of course, he would then have to admit he'd been beaten—without landing a finger on me. And he would have known for sure that, sooner or later, I'd come after him. This way, I imagine he's hoping I'll be relieved enough not to have been implicated in this sordid little scene that I will forget about retribution. Either that, or he plans on remaining in hiding until I'm away from England again.'

'Well, I, for one, can only be happy he was too much a coward to involve you.'

'Yes,' Johnnie said bitterly. 'He's only brave enough to involve a *woman*. Whom he can destroy with no more deadly a weapon than false testimony.'

His aunt sighed. 'Sadly, you're correct. Unfair it might be, but Miss Lattimar is thoroughly ruined, whether or not Lord Halden's tale is true.'

With a wry smile, Johnnie shook his head. 'Don't you see how brave she is? Any other woman would have caved in and married the reprobate rather than risk censure and ruin. Or if she could not stomach that, fled the city before the scandal broke over her head. But not intrepid Prudence Lattimar. Not only did she defy Lord Halden, she walked into the house of the most ferocious dragon in all of Bath and boldly told her side of the story—in front of a roomful of guests. What a woman!'

To his surprise, a reluctant smile twitched the corner of his aunt's lips. 'I suppose she *is* brave. Not only did she affirm what any other lady would have died rather than admit, apparently she took Lady Arbuthnot to task for her acid tongue and her wretched taste in gowns.'

Johnnie threw back his head and laughed, warmth and a fierce pride in Prudence Lattimar filling him. What a soldier and comrade she would have made!

'Devil a bit! I only wish we had witnessed the spectacle. Shall we get you that chair? After all, there will be nothing else happening tonight save heated conjecture over whether or not what she alleged is true. And you know me. If dragged into such a conversation, I might not be able to restrain myself from setting the record straight by giving a personal account.'

Looking thoroughly alarmed, Lady Woodlings seized his arm. 'Let us depart immediately, then. All you would accomplish by revealing your part in it would be to sully your own reputation! There's nothing you can do to salvage hers.'

If only society were a man he could pummel, as he had Lord Halden, Johnnie thought as he let his aunt lead him away. Much as it drove him mad with frustration, Aunt Pen was correct. There was no way he could beat gossip and innuendo into submission.

Rather than elevate the truth, making public his witness of the events would probably further submerge it. News that a second gentleman had been involved would likely lead to colourful additions to the story— speculation about a love triangle, the salacious hint that the assignation had been a *ménage-à-trois*. Scandalous embellishments that would only increase the tale's interest and prolong its life.

It would do nothing to clear Miss Lattimar's name.

Where was she now? he suddenly wondered. 'Did Miss Lattimar leave the reception immediately after her confrontation with Lady Arbuthnot?' he asked his aunt as he assisted her into a chair.

'So I understand. If she knows what's good for her, she'll be out of Bath by tomorrow.' Lady Woodlings sighed. 'The wolves are going to be merciless.'

With the hour approaching midnight, it was too late now to call on her at Lady Stoneway's. He could only hope she would ride tomorrow morning. So he might assure her of his support and ask what he might do to help her.

But first, he needed to see his aunt home. And check on the whereabouts of Lord Halden Fitzroy-Price.

Chapter Sixteen

Early the next morning, her mood bittersweet, Prudence urged the grey mare up Lansdown Road to the heights above the city on what might well be her last morning in Bath. If the rumours had reached even the hired groom, who wavered over refusing to accept money to accompany her, it was probably time to leave.

'Don't know as I should do this any more, miss,' he'd said, looking torn between offending her and distaste at what he'd obviously heard about her behaviour. 'Might get me turned off, if'n the owner finds out I bin letting ladies go on ren-day-voos.'

'Indeed? If you are taken to task for it, tell him it is more likely to *increase* his business, as every lady in Bath who desires a "ren-day-voo" will hasten to this livery. But don't worry. Should you lose your position, I will compensate you handsomely and make sure you obtain another, better one.'

'Still not sure I want to take yer money,' he replied, daring to raise an insolent gaze to her face. But when she fixed on him the same cold, unflinching stare she'd used on Lady Arbuthnot, he dropped his eyes, colouring, and gave her a little bow, obviously recalling that despite her infamy, she was still a lady and he a hired servant.

She'd probably need to use that expression for the rest of her days. But, fiercely pleased with the effects it had produced in these first two instances, she preferred it to the mask of serenity she'd hidden behind for so long.

Pulling up the restive mare—she had no heart for a gallop this morning—Prudence gazed off to the east, towards the city. Would Johnnie ride out to meet her?

The view over Bath, its dewy rooftops and church spires sparkling in the light of the just-risen sun, was spectacular. She wasn't sure whether it was sympathy with her sadness or mockery at the destruction of her hopes that the morning had dawned so bright, clear and beautiful. Just as she wasn't sure whether she should be relieved or heartbroken if Johnnie did not appear and she left Bath without seeing him again.

It wasn't until after the incident yesterday, when she'd realised she would have to quit the city, that she'd seriously considered what her life would be like in future—and realised how deeply Johnnie Trethwell had penetrated into her heart and mind. What a leap of joy she felt, just seeing his rangy form and winning smile from across the room! How amused and energised she became, listening to colourful tales that gave her a glimpse into the wider world of his travels and experiences, events that had moulded him into the remarkable man he was. How much more invigorated and alive she was when conversing with him, able to freely express her thoughts and reactions.

Despite how small and cold and lonely her own

world would seem without his luminous presence, she would always be grateful for having had him explode into her life like a shooting star. Brief but brilliant, the light he cast had illumined her world and shown her how to free herself from the hopeless role of Perfect Young Lady. He'd demonstrated that, for at least one man, she could be valued for who she truly was.

Whatever friends and associates she made in future would also have to accept her that way.

'I love you, Johnnie Trethwell,' she whispered to the glorious morning. 'I shall pray every day for your safety and happiness as you continue your life of adventure.'

As if her wistful prayer had conjured him, as soon as she'd finished voicing it, she heard the welcome sound of approaching hoofbeats. As her heart gave that now-familiar little leap of joy, Johnnie rode up on his black hack and reined in beside her.

Her emotions still raw and volatile, she'd been afraid she might blurt out her love for him. Instead, she simply gazed at him, mute and humbled and strangely shy. Now that he had made an appearance, would she have the courage to follow through on her tentative plans?

He was staring at her, too, in that intense, completely focused way he had, that sent prickling sensations all over her body and made her feel so intensely alive. The power of their attraction sizzled and sparked in the air between them.

'So, you decided not to abandon me, like the rest of Bath,' she said, at last finding her tongue as she urged her mare to a walk.

'I'd much rather embrace you,' he replied with a laugh, signalling his mount to match the pace of hers.

'What a scene you directed at Lady Arbuthnot's last night! I only wish I had been present to witness it. Although it's probably best that I was not. I wouldn't have been able to keep myself from adding corroborating testimony which, as Aunt Pen pointed out, would probably have only made things worse by adding another fillip of intrigue to titillate the gossips.'

'Yes—well—probably wise,' she stuttered, having difficulty concentrating on his words after he'd said he'd like to embrace her. *Would you truly, Johnnie?* she thought. *We shall soon discover how strong that desire is—if I don't lose my nerve.*

'You were right, by the way,' he continued, recalling her attention.

'R-right? About what?'

'Lord Halden. The cowardly cur must have bolted as soon as he'd whispered his poison into Lady Isabelle's ear. Expecting you and Lady Stoneway would attend the Assembly Ball last night, I'd been biding my time there, tooling various dowagers about the floor, when the news of the contretemps at Lady Arbuthnot's reception reached the hall, probably an hour or so after you'd fired your cannonade. By then, I felt it was probably too late to call at the Circus. But after seeing my aunt into a chair, I did nip up to the Royal Crescent to check on the whereabouts of the intrepid Lord Halden.'

Diverted despite herself, she said, 'What did you do? Bang on the front door and demand to see him?'

'What, and have the servants claim he was "indisposed" or "not at home to visitors"? A waste of time at best, and at worst, the inconvenience of milling down several innocent bystanders before I could reach my real quarry. No, I got in via the mews.'

What a storyteller he was, stringing her along detail by detail! 'And so you entered by through the kitchen?'

'No need to disturb good folk who'd already put in a long and arduous day,' he replied, grinning at her, enjoying as much as she was the game of reveal. 'I took the...*vertical* route.'

That puzzled her for a moment before enlightenment dawned. 'You climbed up the back wall of the town house? But his rooms would have been on the second floor—threatening you with a drop of thirty feet or more, if you lost your grip!'

He made a sweeping motion down his side. 'My dear, you see before you a man who has trekked across bazaars in native dress. Scaled fortress walls and fought off attack by natives brandishing deadly-sharp *talwars*. What to me is a paltry two storeys' worth of smooth Bath stone?'

'Rogue!' she said, laughing. 'What next? Did you break in through an upstairs window?'

'No need to break something that, with a little persuasion, one can open.'

'So you strolled in and...what? Terrified a housemaid by suddenly appearing and asking which was his room?'

'No, no, the household was all asleep by then. It was simple enough to tiptoe through the different bedchambers and discover one—still in quite a state of disarray—that must have been his. Half-emptied drawers standing open, some mismatched gloves and unpolished boots lying about, as if his valet was forced to pack in haste. I knew then he'd left Bath for good.'

'I don't recall the moonlight being bright enough for you to have seen all that in a bedchamber.'

'No need for moonlight. I lit a taper. You can't think I'd stumble around in the dark. Much too clumsy! If one must housebreak, one should do so with efficiency and grace.'

Beyond amusing her, he'd been trying to distract her from the grim and permanent consequences of yesterday's events. Ruin and exile.

Unfortunately, his clever tale couldn't make her forget for long.

Or mask the fact settling like hot agony in her chest that they would soon part and, most likely, she'd never see him again.

'Thank you for that one last story,' she said. 'I am glad that you did not reveal your part in the events. Not that I worry about an additional layer of scandal being plastered over my already tarnished image, but I would hate to have some of the dirt rub off on yours. Which might…might impede your chances of wedding that rich widow Lady Woodlings hopes to find for you.'

He recoiled, an expression of distaste on his face. 'That might be Aunt Pen's ambition, but as you should know, it has never been mine!'

'Do your…intentions remain the same as they were when you mentioned them at the warehouse? To become a broker for collectors?' she asked softly, her fingers tightening on the reins, trying not to hold her breath as she resisted the faint hope that the traumatic events of yesterday might have led him to the same sort of dramatic revelation about his feelings it had for her.

He was silent a moment before saying, 'I expect so. It's time I turned my efforts to moving on.'

You didn't really expect him to suddenly declare his love, did you? Suffocating what had been only a feeble hope at best, resolutely Pru focused back on her plan. She had one last card to play before this game ended and it would require all her concentration to do it correctly.

And they had almost reached the spot for her to play it—if she didn't lose her nerve.

'How soon do you intend to inform your aunt of your plans?'

'How soon do you expect to leave Bath?'

Only by keeping in mind her intent was she able to ward off a misery that threatened tears. 'As soon as I can make ready. Tomorrow, probably.'

He nodded. 'I'll speak to Aunt Pen today, then.' He chuckled, though the amusement sounded forced. 'Although she might well disown me when she hears what I intend. The horror of it! A Trethwell, becoming virtually a *shopkeeper*! My family would probably prefer I seduce the wives of every man in the Cabinet and die over my ears in debt, surrounded by a bevy of demi-mondaines.'

'You'll be an explorer and adventurer,' she corrected. 'You'll have clerks to handle the actual transactions.'

He smiled. 'A fine distinction. Perhaps it will be enough to mollify Aunt Pen and the family.'

Her heartbeat accelerating as the moment drew near, Pru tried to keep her tone light and teasing. 'Didn't you once tell me that you could deny me nothing?'

The sudden fire in his eyes told her he remembered the conversation exactly.

'I did...within reason.'

They'd reached the little copse by the road where she'd lost her hat—oh, how long ago now it seemed!

But it had sheltered her that day. She hoped it would serve that purpose this morning.

Turning the mare into the entrance, she beckoned him to follow. Once she'd reached the deepest recesses, she dismounted, tethering the mare's reins to a bush where a break at the far side gave on to the meadow behind, full of lush spring grass that would tempt the animal to graze.

Following her lead, Johnnie jumped down from the saddle and tethered his own horse.

Though she made herself step over to him and boldly placed her hands on his shoulders, she had to clear her throat twice to get the words out.

'Remember how you told me that there were ways to experience passion that would not risk my conceiving a child?'

'I never told you that,' he said shortly.

Beneath her fingers, she could sense the tension in his body, almost feel the coiled strength of him, poised to resist—or succumb. Could she persuade him to the latter?

'True. I inferred that...but you didn't deny it. Is that a more correct account?'

'It is,' he admitted, his voice sounding thick.

'Then, Johnnie...won't you please show me? One last gift, before I go into exile at Entremer and you set off on your adventures.'

'I hate it that Lord Halden's infamy has reduced you to exile...and there's nothing I can do to prevent it!'

She shrugged. 'That's past regretting, and perhaps for the best.' She laughed ruefully. 'I probably would have made a wretched vicar's wife. Allowing our chil-

dren to play in public fountains. Telling off the offi-
cious wives of wealthy parishioners.'

Smiling, he shook his head. 'No, you'd be brilliant.
At whatever you decided to do.'

'Perhaps. But there's only one thing I want to do
now. To fully experience what drives men and women
so wild with longing, a man will seduce a woman he
cannot keep and a woman will take lovers she cannot hold.'

'Here—where riders pass by not ten yards away?'
he asked, a tinge of desperation in his voice.

'You've never taken a woman in a woodland copse?'
When he hesitated, she laughed. 'I thought so.
Then…love me, Johnnie Trethwell. Make me forget I'll
be infamous for ever, never winning the settled home
and husband I've dreamed of. Give me one brief, beautiful, glorious moment of pleasure to warm all the days
and nights ahead without you.' Gazing into his blazing
eyes, she traced his lips with one gentle finger. 'Please,
Johnnie,' she whispered. 'Give us both that gift.'

His breath coming short, he stared at her, the heat
emanating from his body firing hope and wild anticipation.

Finally, with a growl, he pulled her closer and tilted
her chin up. 'It will be glorious,' he promised roughly.
'But it will not be brief.'

And then he kissed her.

Maybe he shouldn't have given in and granted her
request. But as soon as Pru's lips touched his, he knew
they had both been made for this. Though he burned to
give her *everything*, every last drop of the fulfilment
she desired, he would at least give her a taste of the

passion she craved—without ruining her for the husband who would surely find her some day, whatever backwater she retreated to.

Not every man in England could be blind and stupid.

That was his last rational thought, before instinct and sensation took over from intellect. Her hands were already plucking open the buttons of his jacket, dragging loose the knot of his cravat and pushing it aside as she insinuated her fingers beneath his shirt to rub at the bare skin of his chest. His hands clenching on her shoulders, he shuddered as her touch set his skin aflame.

'Does that please you?' she murmured against his mouth.

'Yes.'

'And this?' She slid her free hand down his chest to cup his erection. Which surged under her fingers, giving its own answer.

He placed his hand over hers, helping her stroke him. 'More of this later, *chahna*, but not yet.'

'*Chahna?*' she murmured, caressing him.

'It means love. Light. You are both.' Taking her mouth again for another deep kiss, he struggled out of his uniform jacket and tossed it to the ground. Still kissing, he let her finish unknotting his cravat, then pulled it free and dropped it, too. He leaned his head back to let her kiss his neck, down the V of skin exposed by neckline, before she realised there was a better way to bare his chest and began pulling the shirt out of his trousers.

He let her push the fabric up as she slid her hands under, rubbing over the rise of his chest, her fingertips massaging the flat of his nipples, then dipping down to trace the concave abdomen below the rise of his ribs. Before she could descend further and drive him completely beyond control, he seized her hands and kissed them.

'Let me touch you!' she protested, looking up at him, her mouth deliciously kiss-reddened, her eyes heavy-lidded with desire.

'So you shall, my angel. But let me touch you first.'

Placing hands on her shoulders, he urged her down on to the makeshift blanket of his jacket. Easing her back, he kissed her again as he undid the fastenings of her pelisse and tossed the two sides back, then unbuttoned the blouse beneath to expose her undergarments. Working his hands underneath her back, he deftly loosened her stays—she wore only short jumps, thank heaven—and slid them down her torso, below her breasts.

He couldn't free her from the chemise, trapped as it was under the layers of stays and skirt, but was able to push it down enough that his exploring fingers could slide under and reach the dusky, peaked nipples visible beneath the fine linen. As she gasped, he took her mouth again, his tongue teasing and fencing with hers in rhythm with his stroking fingers.

But then he just had to taste her. Releasing her lips, he kissed his way over her chin and down her throat, licking and sucking at the delicate skin in the hollow. He tantalised her, nipping at her collarbones, skimming his lips over the swell of her breasts, his pace slowing as his tongue crept closer to the rigid nipples his thumbs were caressing.

She arched her back, thrusting her breasts up at him, and he drew the cloth-covered buds into his mouth.

As the wetted fabric thinned and softened, becoming a barely perceptible barrier, he suckled harder, exulting as her breathing grew shorter and her movements more frantic.

He slid his hand over her riding boot and up under her skirts, his member leaping as his hand left leather for the touch of soft, sweet skin before his fingers met the ankle-length bottom of her drawers. He caressed her linen-clad calves, the skin behind her knee, the long expanse of thigh, nudging her legs wider as he progressed.

Finally he reached the prize he longed for. Finding the slit in her drawers, he pushed his hand within and cupped her mound, as she had cupped him.

She gasped again and bucked. He paused, letting her accustom herself to that intimate invasion. Once she stilled, he began to caress her in time to the long, suckling pulls of his mouth on her nipples. She grew ever more agitated, panting and twisting her torso against him, swinging an arm up to anchor his head against her breasts. As her hips started to thrust upwards, he slid a finger into her cleft—which was as hot and wet as he'd dreamed it would be.

Taking her mouth again, he exulted as she opened herself to him, giving him access to her buried pearl. He rubbed it with his thumb, then moved another finger to penetrate her passage.

She broke the kiss, gasping, her bent arms going rigid as she arched into the pressure of his fingers and thumb. Moments later, he felt the rich moisture as her climax swept through her.

He leaned over her limp, spent torso to gently kiss her lips. Despite the thickness of the copse, this woodland glen was too near the road for him to risk prolonging the interlude as long as he'd have liked. But once she recovered, he was determined to show her at least one more variation on the road to pleasure before he let her go.

He leaned on his elbow by her side, smiling as he silently watched her. How completely she abandoned herself to passion! She seized pleasure freely and without inhibitions, just as she conversed. No subterfuge, no holding back, no concern with doing the right or conventional thing.

Hell's bells, she was a magnificent lover!

A few moments later, she stirred and opened her eyes. 'That was…wonderful,' she whispered, awe in her gaze as she smiled up at him. 'But…not so wonderful for you,' she murmured, reaching over to stroke his still-rigid member.

He groaned, drinking in the feel of her fingers on him. 'It will be,' he promised, leaning over to kiss her fingertips. 'Just not yet.'

'But I want to pleasure you, too,' she protested, giving him a sultry pout. 'At least, let me touch you.'

Though he wasn't sure how long he'd last if he permitted it, he didn't have the will to refuse her. When he didn't stay her hand, she popped open the buttons on his straining trouser flap—slowly, one by one, as teasingly as he'd uncovered her.

She waited until she'd loosed the last button, drawing a groan from him as cold air hit his overheated flesh, before pulling his mouth down for another kiss. Loving her boldness and enthusiasm, this time he let her take the lead, enjoying her growing expertise as she explored his lips, her tongue touching, testing, tasting…while her fingers explored his erection.

First, she trailed one tentative finger along his length…then used her whole hand to grasp and stroke. Then moved her thumb to massage his moist velvet tip, nearly driving him over the edge.

Knowing his time was short, he broke the kiss and moved away from her exploring fingers. After muting her inarticulate protest with another quick kiss, he tossed back her skirt, petticoats and shift and moved his mouth where his fingers had explored.

This time, he skipped over the drawers to nibble at the hard turn of a hipbone under skin, then kissed and caressed the velvet of her abdomen up to her ribs, as high as he could manage before the stays and chemise blocked his path.

And then he went downwards again, licking and kissing over the sweet rise of her mound until at last, parting the drawers, he slid his tongue to her little bud, revelling in the texture and scent he'd dreamt about and yearned to taste for so long.

She cried out as he sampled her, writhed and gasped and thrust up her hips when he delved his tongue into the honey of her passage. Moving his mouth back to suckle her little pearl, he slid his fingers deep inside, stroking its length until she shattered around him a second time.

She sagged back on to his coat, limp and boneless. Tenderness curled around his heart as he gently smoothed a tendril of hair back from her flushed forehead. When she opened her eyes and smiled up at him, despite the aching need of his unsatisfied member, he had to lean down and kiss her again.

'Now I know why that figurine in the warehouse

was smiling.' She ran a finger across his lips when he released her. 'What else can you show me?'

'Greedy girl!' he teased. 'There's so much more, but we dare not risk remaining here much longer.'

'Surely we can remain long enough for…this,' she murmured, reaching through his open trouser flap to stroke him.

He jumped, as needy and sensitive as his member. 'That's not wise, my siren,' he said with a strained laugh. 'Proceeding down that path leads to childbed.'

'Not if I do for you what you just did for me, would it? So won't you…show me? Teach me what you like.'

Once again, temptation paralysed him. He couldn't get his tongue around the words to deny her, or make himself move away from her hand resting on him. Her eyes watching him intently, she stroked his whole length once, twice.

Then, as if she possessed all the knowledge of Venus, she bent her head and licked him. 'You like this?'

He ought to stop her, but he didn't seem to be able to make his mouth work. Arms corded with the effort of holding himself immobile—so that he wouldn't lose his last tentative grip on sanity, push her beneath him, and plunge his aching shaft into the sweet depths of her— he watched as, with a naughty temptress's slowness, she used both hands to explore his shaft. And then— he almost reached completion that instant—took the rigid tip of him into her mouth.

He groaned as she ran her tongue over him. 'Like this?' she asked, licking and releasing him. 'Or more? With me, you went…deeper.'

Following some instinct as primal as it was unerring, she enveloped him. He gasped, then cried out as she took him deeper…and started suckling.

He stood it as long as he could—probably only a few seconds—before he pushed her away, slammed his mouth against hers and hugged her close as a powerful climax roared through him.

Afterward, they lay tangled together on his rumpled coat for some time before he could summon enough energy to lift his head. As he did so, he heard hoofbeats and the murmured voices of a group of riders trotting past.

'We must dress ourselves and return, *chahna*,' he said, giving her a regretful kiss. 'The later the hour grows, the more riders who'll pass this hideaway. All that's needed is for one of our horses to whinny a greeting and we could be discovered.'

He sat up, then chuckled as he looked at her. 'It's a good thing you're already ruined. I don't know how we're going to put you back to rights.'

'We shall do well enough.' Sitting up, she turned to let him slide her stays into place and tighten them, then fasten her blouse and spencer. Readjusting her skirt, she walked over to her mare and extricated some items from the saddlebag. 'I brought these, just in case.'

'So you planned this?'

'I hoped for it,' she admitted. 'After making myself *persona non grata* at Lady Arbuthnot's last night, I… I wasn't sure you'd ride out to meet me again. I imagine your aunt would not be happy you did, if she knew about it.'

Declining to confirm that all-too-accurate observation, he said instead, 'How very prepared you were. I think you'd have made an excellent campaigner.'

She sighed. 'I hope at least to become a proficient breeder of horses.'

She brought the small packet over, opening it to hand him some moistened rags. Using those and the comb she'd included, they were able to make each other presentable enough that a casual observer would never suspect a passionate encounter had taken place within a stone's throw of the roadway.

After returning her supplies to the saddlebag, she stood by the mare's side and looked over at him. 'If you would give me a leg up, we can be on our way back.'

A strange but intense sense of foreboding unlike anything he'd ever before experienced tightened his chest. What was wrong with him? He prided himself on finishing an amorous episode with humour and grace, leaving both partners smiling.

For some reason, he was reluctant to send Prudence Lattimar back to town—to pack up and move out of his life. But what else was he to do? Sweet and intensely pleasurable as his dealings with her had been, he'd known from the beginning that their…friendship, liaison, passion, whatever one wanted to call it, would only be temporary.

Though he hadn't expected it to be terminated so abruptly, he'd never before had any trouble ending transitory attachments.

Trying to shake off the feeling, he found himself saying, 'Shall I accompany you back to the Circus?'

She hesitated a moment, staring at him, her gaze mirroring the longing he knew must be in his own. Although, except for last time, after she'd been attacked, they'd always discreetly parted before returning to her aunt's house, she said, 'Yes, I'd like that.'

He chastised himself as an idiot for the request on the ride back, for conversation was desultory—she asking where in India he would go to look for artefacts, him answering—but the sparkle had gone from their interaction, leaving an awkward melancholy that had never before been present.

They returned horses and groom to the livery, after which Johnnie walked Pru back to her aunt's house on the Circus. Having reached the address, they both halted.

'It would be better if…if I get started with my preparations, so I won't ask you in,' Prudence said. Her eyes shadowed, her face expressionless, she looked up at him.

'I don't expect I'll see you again, so let me say goodbye, Lieutenant Trethwell. I can't begin to express how much you have enriched my life. I wish you a future full of adventure, excitement and success.'

Feeling strangely bereft, he nodded. 'Goodbye, Miss Lattimar. I wish that you may find a country gentleman worthy of you, who will love you with all the passion and devotion you deserve.'

She gave a sad little shake of her head, as if dismissing such a wish as hopeless. Then, squaring her shoulders, she walked up the stairs and into the town house.

She didn't look back.

Chapter Seventeen

Prudence listlessly mounted the stairs to her chamber, each footstep sounding like the death knell of the happy future she'd come to Bath to find. Entering the room, she glanced at herself in the glass and shuddered. Their attempts at repairing her clothing had been marginally successful, but her coiffure was a disaster.

Sitting at the dressing table, she removed her riding hat and started pulling the pins from her hair, letting the heavy mass fall down her shoulders. After combing it out of her face with her fingers, she picked up her hairbrush, but couldn't summon enough energy or interest to drag it through the tangles.

Staring dully at the hand holding the brush, she told herself she should ring for her maid to help her out of her habit and into a morning gown, so she might go down to breakfast with Aunt Gussie. But she didn't think, in her current turbulent emotional state, that she could endure making polite conversation.

She should begin the tedious process of packing, then. It would be simple; there was no need to take to Entremer the number of morning, afternoon, walking, carriage and evening gowns her aunt had considered necessary for Bath society. She'd pack a few carriage gowns, for when she went into the village for supplies, one or two of the oldest morning and afternoon gowns for when neighbours called, this riding habit—which the maid would definitely need to sponge out before she wore it again—and that would be sufficient.

The other gowns could go back to London for Temper, her twin being able to wear whichever ones appealed to her. She'd have her sister send her other riding habits to Entremer. With the older gowns she'd left in the country and several pairs of Gregory's cast-off trousers she'd secreted away for forbidden gallops riding astride, she would have all she needed.

She mustn't be so glum, she tried to tell herself. The doors to the past would close today and there was nothing she could do about it. She should square her shoulders, start planning her future and make a list of what she must do upon arriving at Entremer so she might move forward as quickly as possible with her goal of beginning a formal breeding operation.

Only by filling her days with so much activity that she fell into bed each night exhausted would she be able to tolerate the anguish of losing Johnnie Trethwell.

Leaving him, she amended sadly. He'd never been hers to lose.

She thought she'd managed her feelings. She thought that, even while admitting she'd fallen in love with him, by knowing all along how slim was the possibility of his falling in love with her, she had armoured herself against the day when she would say goodbye for ever.

She'd been wrong.

The pain that seared her chest was worse than the

outrage and humiliation of being ruined by that toad Lord Halden, worse than relinquishing her dream of living a simple, respectable life as a vicar's wife in a small country town. Which probably would not, as Johnnie had predicted, have made her happy.

You would have.

It had taken every bit of will not to try to use the sensual power she now realised she possessed to lure him into fully consummating their union, thereby forcing him into making a declaration. Not even the rogue Johnnie Trethwell would deflower a well-born virgin and then refuse to marry her.

It had then taken every last bit of courage to bid him goodbye before Aunt Gussie's front door, rather than asking him inside. Where, giving up any pretence of pride, she would have broken down and confessed her love, begging him to come with her to Entremer, at least for a while, in whatever guise he preferred— friend, companion, lover.

She knew he cared about her—hadn't he even proposed, when she was in such despair about him leaving her with nothing? Of course, if she hadn't been practical enough to refuse him, when they were both calmer, he would probably have retracted that offer.

He did care for her…just not enough to give up his wandering ways. Nor was there any reason he should. His free-spirited, restless zest for exploration was at the heart of him, what made him uniquely Johnnie. She wouldn't change him if she could.

Even if she had managed to coax him into visiting Entremer, he wouldn't have stayed long. A man who'd known the dark-eyed temptresses of the East, *nautch* dancers, naughty English matrons and females of every stripe in between, wouldn't long be satisfied by a naïve, simple country girl who had only beauty to offer a man who'd tasted so many more exotic dishes at the feminine banquet.

Though, she thought wistfully, a reminiscent heat almost rivalling the pain, the passion they shared had been marvellous. Intense even for him, she was pretty sure, though as inexperienced as she was, she could well be mistaken.

Since she had held herself back and let him go, better to isolate herself at Entremer and stay there. Should she return in the near future to London, every time she went around a Mayfair corner or rode early in the park and saw the flash of a red coat, her spirits would charge upwards on a jolt of excitement and anticipation. Then, an instant later, realising the soldier was not Johnnie, she'd be flayed again by a sabre's slash of loss. Leaving her battered and bleeding, a dull ache of hopelessness thudding in her chest.

Temper had been wiser than she knew when she'd warned Pru to be careful what she wished for. Instead of finding the right gentleman to love her, she'd fallen hopelessly in love with the wrong one.

Dropping the hairbrush, she lay her head on her arms and wept.

For a long time after Prudence Lattimar walked inside her aunt's town house, Johnnie remained frozen to the spot, staring at the door, feeling as if he'd been gut-punched. Finally, his head told his body to stop staring like a looby and get moving. Turning, he headed back towards Queen Square, trying to master the uncomfortable sensations.

His interlude with Prudence had to end some time and, abrupt and unexpected as it had been, now was as good a time as any. He was healed enough that he couldn't justify hanging about much longer, enjoying Aunt Pen's bounty. It was time he focused his efforts on moving towards the future. A future which would lead him and Pru down different paths.

Of course, he regretted that it had happened this soon. He'd admired Pru's beauty and desired her on sight, had his fighting spirits roused by discovering she'd been unfairly tainted by the sins of her family. Coming to value her wit and intelligence, he'd found a kindred spirit in her honest observations and unconventional zest for life. And a perfect partner in passion.

He'd promised himself as an honourable friend he would resist her, but after her pleading—and a temptation impossible to deny—had made him break that promise this morning, he now conceded she'd been right. He was a better friend for giving her a sample of the joy passion could bring her.

And him. What a fiery brilliance burned in her! His first sampling hardly put a dent in the desire she inspired. Ah, to bury himself deep and feel her convulsions all around him! Just the thought of it made him harden again. But he was proud he'd managed to control himself and keep his most important vow, leaving her intact for a bridegroom.

He'd held his emotions in check, too—slipping up only once, when, seeing her so hurt and desolate when she'd accused him of leaving her with nothing, he'd rashly offered marriage. And been justly chided for proposing, though it hadn't been pity that motivated him. More like rage, frustration and pain at witnessing her anguish over the loss of her dream.

Once again, she'd shown herself to be a singular woman. Despite her distress, she'd remained sensible enough to realise that pledging her hand to a wandering adventurer wouldn't gain her what she truly wanted: a respected position in society beside a husband who was a pillar of his local community, who offered her a settled home in the country where she could live in peace with her family and her horses, far away from censorious society.

But then—she hadn't mentioned any of those reasons when she slapped him. Only that she'd not give herself to a man who could not offer her loyalty, devotion and love. Defiantly, she'd dared him to pledge that.

Loyalty would be easy. But shocked, and having never examined his feelings, he hadn't been able to honestly offer love.

Normally, a relationship grew and then withered naturally, without him ever having to consider the nature of his attachment to a lady. This one had been abruptly and prematurely terminated. So what, exactly, *did* he feel for Prudence Lattimar?

He'd admired women before, lusted after them certainly, enjoyed their company. But he'd never felt this... desolate and bereft after ending an attachment. Though he'd always enjoyed a liaison while it lasted, usually he was eager to kiss the current lady goodbye and move on to the next.

Which was what he preferred. After witnessing the agony that had racked Tom Alcorn after he lost Daya, he'd been convinced he never wanted to feel anything stronger for any woman than mild affection.

Still, he was not eager to kiss Prudence goodbye. Was it because their relationship had never reached the ultimate peak of becoming lovers?

He didn't think so. Novel as it had been to dance attendance on a woman whom he knew from the beginning he could not have, the charm of her person had held frustration at bay and urged him to get to know her better, each interaction sweetened by a delicious undercurrent of desire.

Rather than being impatient to move on to the next adventure, the thought of never seeing her again produced a strange, shockingly deep ache in his chest.

He was going to miss her lovely face and the constant state of pleasant sensual alertness she kept him in. He would miss riding with her, miss hearing her candid thoughts and intelligent observations delivered with no regard to the conventional behaviour expected of a lady. In her zest for life, she appreciated her familiar England, but also, most unusually, the foreign places he described to her. Even for one who'd preferred to explore alone, she'd make a marvellous travelling partner.

When he did finally set off to explore new territories or acquire exotic objects, somehow he *knew* that as he saw them, he would be thinking about how she might respond to those people and places and objects…and regret that she was not with him to share it.

Did that mean…he *loved* her? He had so little experience of the emotion, the only real love from a female he'd received in his life coming from Aunt Pen. What he felt for Prudence was both more, and different.

The love that poets celebrated seemed to require being overcome with a euphoria that took one out of oneself and made one do extraordinary things. He didn't feel like dancing down the middle of Milsom Street or turning cartwheels in the Assembly Rooms or turning up under her bedchamber window to recite bad verse written in her honour.

But he knew what he felt went beyond the physical or superficial. In some way he couldn't describe even to himself, she made him feel more...complete and infinitely happier. As if he were contently trotting his horse along a fine carriage trail through a beautiful woodland in a mist...and she appeared, bringing the sun with her, making what had been merely enjoyable into a sparkling delight.

And in this moment, with his chest feeling like a dacoit's curved dagger had just carved a hole in it, he realised that whatever name he put to what he felt for her, the emotion was far deeper and more intense than he'd ever suspected.

Maybe...maybe despite his intention not to become involved, he had somehow stumbled into love with her. All he knew was he could almost keen with agony at the idea of never seeing her again.

But what could he do to prevent that?

There was no guarantee, intrepid though she was and as enthusiastic as she'd been listening to his adventures, that Pru had any interest whatsoever in leaving her beloved English countryside to embrace the far-more-uncertain future of roaming about the world with him.

As glorious as that possibility appeared to him.

By her own admission, she would have to love and cherish *him* even to consider it. He knew she liked him, that he inspired desire in her...but love?

What did *he* really know about love? He might be completely misreading his feelings, to say nothing of hers.

Putting a hand to that annoying ache in his chest, he tried to convince himself that he felt this pain because their relationship had been cut short, rather than allowed to grow and then atrophy naturally. Or because, although he'd done all he could to help her take her rightful place, it hadn't been enough and he hated to lose a fight. Maybe it was his simmering anger and frustration over that failure that was fuelling these unusually strong feelings of melancholy and loss.

Instinctively, though, he knew it was something far more profound. Something that probably did deserve the name 'love'. Which was why, deep in his gut, it felt so wrong to stand aside and let Prudence leave Bath.

Maybe he should go back to her aunt's town house and demand to see her. Confess how much he'd come to realise he needed her and plead with her to accompany him on his future travels.

As his *wife*. The very word rattled him—a man who'd never before considered the possibility of marriage. But he couldn't contemplate offering Prudence any less than his heart *and* his hand.

If he truly meant to offer marriage, though, he needed to hie off to London and finalise the backing that would move his venture from proposition to reality. To ask her to wed him before he could present himself as the proprietor of a well-funded trading concern would make him appear just as much a fortune hunter as the despicable Lord Halden.

Before he dashed to London, he must break the news of his intentions to Aunt Pen. And then get himself to

London and back before Prudence immured herself in the depths of the country.

What if she couldn't be charmed into loving him, or wouldn't consent to travel with him?

His initial excitement cooled as the unwelcome demon in his chest took another bite.

Could he endure a future without her? Of course he *could*. Loneliness had been his best friend since childhood. But he knew without her, loneliness would take on a darker, more bitter hue…because, for one shining moment in his life, he'd known what it was to be with someone who lit up his heart and touched his soul.

It would be foolish to let go of that without fighting for her—and Johnnie Trethwell had never walked away from a fight, no matter how slim his chances of prevailing. Forging all his tempestuous emotions into determination, Johnnie set off to find his aunt.

Chapter Eighteen

Fortunately for his impatience, Aunt Pen was in the morning room drinking coffee when he returned. After filling a cup for himself and dropping a kiss on her forehead, he took a seat at the table beside her.

'Riding early, Johnnie?' she asked. 'You look a bit… windblown.'

Happily, he never blushed, so she'd not be able to tell from his countenance just how tempestuous that ride had turned out to be. 'Yes, I went riding. I ended up by deciding it was time to start preparing for my future.' Which was true, even if it did rather drastically edit the events of the morning.

'Ah, yes, your future. You do seem to be managing that leg better now.'

'It's healed, or nearly so. Which makes it time to visit London and start lining up the financing to launch my enterprise. So you see, despite what the gossips say, I don't intend to live on your bounty for ever,' he offered with a grin, trying to soften what he knew would be her disappointment at his announcement.

She sipped her coffee and regarded him thoughtfully. 'Would you remain in England if I settled money on you?'

'Darling Aunt Pen, if I were ready to be roped, saddled and corralled, I could have bedazzled one of those wealthy females you kept wanting to throw at me. Even to please you, I can't see myself remaining in England.'

Sighing, she shook her head. 'My dear Johnnie, you do try the heart of a fond aunt. So I can't talk you out of pursuing that trading venture?'

'I'm truly sorry to disappoint you, but I'm afraid not. I'll start with the arms and armour of the east with which I am familiar, and for which I have known sources, with the intention of moving on to acquire other objects my clients might desire. Silks from China, tapestry and textiles and brass work from India, spices from further east. Calculating the profit the dealer who sold to James's friends must have made, within a few voyages I can probably make enough to purchase my own ship and sail wherever I wish, no longer having to barter for hired transport.'

'If you had additional funds, you would be able to arrange for those things from the start, wouldn't you?'

Surprised, for she had always seemed to oppose this idea so vehemently, he said, 'That would advance the business much faster, yes. You aren't hinting that you might like to become an investor yourself, are you? It's just as risky a venture as you've always warned, Aunt Pen. I could make a great profit—or lose your entire stake, should a ship sink or a cargo be captured by pirates.'

'My dear boy, when have you ever been interested in doing a sure thing? Haven't I gambled on you since you were a child? Taking you in when your family said you were unmanageable? Funding your commission when I was warned you were so ungovernable, you would end up cashiered? And you have always rewarded those gambles. Much more important, you have returned the love I invested with love and loyalty tenfold.'

Johnnie swallowed hard, swamped by a wave of gratitude and love for her. 'Thank you, Aunt Pen. For everything you've done. I promise you, as one of the initial investors, you will stand to profit most if—when—this venture is successful.'

'Oh, *I* don't plan to invest in it.'

He wrinkled his brow, confused. 'But I thought… You said you would gamble—'

'It won't be *me* who gambles. With my own boys settled, nothing is more important to me than your happiness. And if adventuring far from the shores of your native land is the only way to secure that, so be it. I didn't think you should have to wait until I stick my spoon in the wall to take advantage of having a rich aunt who dotes on you.'

'No, Aunt Pen, you don't need to *give* me money!'

'Johnnie Trethwell, since when have I needed to consult you about what I wish to do with my own blunt? Wait right here.' Waving an admonishing finger at him, his aunt rose and walked from the room.

Curious, humbled, impatient, he made himself sit and wait for her, his mind afire with speculation. Had she truly settled money on him? Would it be enough to start his venture immediately, even before he secured backing from his other investors?

She returned a few minutes later, dropping a small book on the table in front of him. 'As you'll see when you look within, I've established an account for you at my bank in London, with funds already transferred into it. Those belong to you and you alone. Go ahead, open it.'

He did as she bid—and then caught his breath, shocked at how large the total was. Jumping up, he came over to wrap her in a hug. 'Thank you, Aunt Pen, for once again believing in my dream.'

Hugging him back, she said tartly, 'All I ask, my dear, is that you write your old aunt—from whatever undiscovered backwater you are adventuring in! But there's one other thing, Johnnie.'

Returning to his seat, he said, 'What's that, Aunt Pen?'

'With wealth of your own, you won't have to wait to finalise arrangements with your potential trading partners in London. You now have sufficient funds of your own to support a wife.'

He stopped short and looked back at her. 'A…a *wife*?'

'Come now, Johnnie, I'm old, but I'm not blind! I've seen how you look at Prudence Lattimar. How a smile lights up your face when she walks into a room. How your whole body nearly hums with excitement and anticipation when she draws near. I know your parents' marriage was a disaster, but don't be a fool and ignore what your heart is trying to tell you. Not all unions are unhappy. Surely you remember how content I was with Woodlings.'

She'd defied her family to marry an obscure baron, given him three boys and lived very happily with him until his death. 'Yes, I remember.'

'I know you've always gone adventuring alone, so you have no experience of what joy it can be to share your life with someone who thinks as you think, appreciates the things you appreciate, who shares your tastes and your interests.' She lifted her brows. 'And your desires.'

Once again, he was glad he didn't blush. Sometimes Aunt Pen was a little *too* knowing. 'I admit, I've only lately come to realise it—' *this very morning 'lately'* '—but I do…understand what you're talking about. I think… I think I've been foolish enough to fall in love with Prudence Lattimar.'

'Well, don't show yourself even more foolish by believing you shouldn't approach her because you can't offer her the usual inducements of a title, an estate to manage and a high position in society. Those things are important to most women—but Prudence Lattimar isn't "most women", is she? If she were, she would have saved face by marrying that scoundrel Lord Halden.'

'Do you think she might consider…adventuring with me?'

'You'll never know unless you ask.' Reading the mix of excitement, joy and trepidation on his face, his aunt laughed. 'Johnnie Trethwell, when have you ever been shy about approaching a woman?'

'I've never been in love before!' he shot back, realising all at once the truth of it. And, now that he had the backing to make his venture possible, he didn't need to go to London first before asking for her hand.

That little demon in his chest took another bite, reminding him how very crucial to his future it was for him to persuade her to accept him and love him back.

His aunt softened. 'Loving her does make a difference, doesn't it? Suddenly, attraction is no longer just a pleasant game, delightful if you win, dismissed with a shrug if you don't. Suddenly, there is nothing more important than being able to spend your life beside the one person in the world who means everything to you.'

'So I woo her with your blessing?'

'You do. I admit, I was wary of your Miss Lattimar at first. But a woman who would turn down a duke's son, face ruin and tell off the most powerful woman in Bath? Who else would make a more splendid match for my unconventional Johnnie?'

Coming around to give her another hug, he said, 'I just hope she agrees with you.'

'Just be your charming self—how could she resist? Now, why are you still hanging about Queen Square, conversing with your old aunt? Off with you! You have adventures to plan—and a lady to win.'

Filled with doubt, wild hope and desperate purpose, Johnnie nearly rushed off to Lady Stoneway's town house that minute. But checking his impatience, he decided that if he meant to bedazzle a lady into being foolish enough to abandon the safety of England and accompany him on his wanderings, he would probably have better luck bathed, dressed in his best coat and not smelling of horse.

How far he'd come in a single day! From unprecedented and troubling distress over the thought of never seeing Prudence again, to allowing himself to consider what she truly meant to him...to being ready to offer marriage.

By the time he'd finished talking with his aunt, the truth of loving her was resonating so deeply within him that he was no longer sure he could exist without her. Somehow, he must win Prudence's hand.

Even if he was lucky enough to have gained her

love, it was by no means certain she'd agree to marry him—and trade the safety of England for the wilds of wherever. It was her sister, she'd told him, who wanted to explore beyond her native land. The only fervent desire Pru had ever expressed was to have a conventional husband and a settled home in the English countryside.

She'd been enchanted by his stories…but that didn't mean she'd be equally enchanted at the prospect of living them.

As he tied his cravat and shrugged into his jacket, he let himself consider for the first time what he would do if she could not be persuaded to leave England.

Could he go, without her?

The pain that possibility produced made him realise that, through all his adventuring, he'd been searching for something more, not really knowing what it was. As if he'd put into place nearly all the pieces that made up the puzzle of his life and needed to find just one more to make the picture whole.

Prudence Lattimar was that piece. Without her, he would never be whole or complete.

All he'd ever wanted was to explore new places, new people, new experiences. Could he continue to do that, if Prudence wouldn't go with him?

Could he truly be content remaining in England, breeding horses, if that was the only way he could share his life with hers?

For a long time he sat, gazing into the distance, remembering the joy he'd felt rambling around Aunt Pen's Woodhaven with his cousins, knowing in this one place, with these particular people, he was loved and accepted. He'd never found that anywhere else. He'd always been an outsider, not just with his own family, but at school and in the army.

With Prudence, he would be home again—wherever that home might be. What was more important than that?

To marry Daya, Tom Alcott had been ready to give up his native country and his profession. For the first time, Johnnie fully understood why spending his life with the woman he loved had been more important to Tom than any other tie, any other loyalty. Why claiming that joy had been worth every risk, even the devastation Tom had suffered after losing her.

Johnnie might not have looked to love someone with that sort of all-encompassing tenacity, but now he did. Thinking of how he felt about Pru, the brilliance that life became when he was with her, he was fiercely glad he had fallen for her—whatever happened.

Tom had been right. Claiming such joy *was* worth the risk.

All Johnnie needed to sacrifice to avoid losing the woman he loved was a few journeys for the trading company which, in any event, he could direct from England.

He'd still use all his charm to persuade Pru to travel with him. But if it came down to it, more important than any future explorations would be having Prudence Lattimar beside him for ever.

Decision made, he gave himself one more inspection in the glass and set off.

By early afternoon, Pru had put herself back together, rung for her maid to change her into a plain day dress and given instructions about beginning the packing. Still too battered emotionally to want to face Aunt Gussie or anyone else, she'd asked Soames to inform any callers that she was not at home to visitors and taken refuge in the library. Hunting up her aunt's copy of *Debrett's*, she flipped through, looking for the addresses of several peers she knew who had horses that might make suitable breeding stock for her father's herd and who might be interested in beginning such a project.

She'd completed two letters and was starting a third when Soames's knock at the door interrupted her. 'Lieutenant Trethwell to see you, miss,' he informed her from the doorway. 'I told him you were occupied and not receiving, but he said the matter was most urgent. Knowing that he has been a…particular friend, I thought I should check with you before—'

Johnnie was here? Excitement and trepidation flashed through her. Why would he come, when they'd already said their goodbyes, unless… 'Thank you, Soames,' she interrupted. 'It was good of you not to send him away.'

The normally impassive butler gave her slight smile. 'I rather think that, had I attempted to, he would have simply barged right past me and gone in search of you. I've shown him to the blue parlour. Shall I notify your aunt and send refreshments?'

'Um…yes, that would be good. Thank you, Soames. Tell him I'll be in directly.'

'I expect it will take Lady Stoneway a few minutes to make herself presentable, if you wish to wait for her. Or not.' Giving her a wink, the butler bowed and withdrew.

My goodness! Soames, playing accomplice to an assignation!

Her amusement swallowed by nervousness, Pru jumped up and flew to stand before the mirror over the sideboard. Heavens, why had she chosen to wear this old rag of a gown? She'd told the maid not to bother with her hair, merely brushing it out and plaiting into a long braid that she'd wrapped and pinned around her head. She looked like a down-on-her-luck governess!

No matter. She was far too eager to see Johnnie and discover why he'd sought her out to waste the time it would take to change into a more attractive gown or repair her coiffure.

Feeling like a migrating flock of birds had taken up residence in her stomach, swooping and soaring and beating their wings, she swallowed hard and walked to the blue parlour. Praying his unexpected visit meant what she hoped it did. Knowing she would be so desperately disappointed if he'd merely brought her some book or trifling thing to take with her to Entremer, she might have to flee the room to avoid blurting out her unrequited love and desperate need for him.

She stopped outside the door, taking a deep breath. *Whatever happens, you can bear it*, she told herself. And walked in.

Oh, what a liar she was! Seeing his dear face, smiling at her, it was all she could do not to run over and throw herself in his arms. Wherever the ship carrying him from England went, she was likely to stow aboard. With any luck they'd be halfway to India before he discovered her.

'Miss Lattimar,' he said, rising to his full height as she entered. Recalling how—was it really just this morning?—they had lain together on his coat in the copse beside the Lansdown Road, pleasuring each other, the strict formality of last names and bows and curtsies exchanged seemed ludicrous.

He came to her eagerly, his grey-green eyes ablaze as he handed her a bouquet of flowers. 'Beauties for the beautiful.'

Hope made her heart knock so hard against her ribs she had trouble getting the words out. 'To wish me on my way?'

'In a manner of speaking. May...may we sit?'

Goodness, he seemed so...nervous and uncertain! Nothing like the easy, confident Johnnie she knew.

Suddenly she recalled the butler's words. 'Soames said the matter was urgent. Nothing has happened, has it? No injury to your aunt?'

'No, no, Aunt Pen is fine. She...ah...sends her compliments, by the way.'

'Does she, now? You must be interpreting her words rather loosely! I don't think she's ever approved of me.'

'On the contrary! She thinks very highly of you, I assure you. In fact, it was her regard for...for both of us that propelled me to come.'

He was still so nervous, her hope hadn't died yet, but she was getting more and more confused. 'Your visit has something to do with your aunt?'

'Yes,' he said, looking relieved, as if she understood his purpose—which she did not at all. 'You see, after we parted this morning, I talked with Aunt Pen about the new trading enterprise I want to begin. She not only approved it, she'd already set up a fund for me to begin the venture, even before I secure the additional sponsors in London.'

'Congratulations!' she said, truly happy for him. 'That's wonderful news. When will you depart?'

'That depends. On something else that's even more important.' He paused and looked away, clasping and unclasping his fists.

Pru gazed at him in exasperation. Goodness, her chest might explode from the pressure of ferocious hope and overstrained nerves before she dragged everything out of him!

'It depends upon…what?' she prompted impatiently.

'Well—on you.'

Joy welled up, but she wanted to make sure she wasn't misinterpreting.

'On me? My plans to leave for Entremer?' she probed. 'Which will happen shortly, tomorrow if the packing is complete.'

'But that's just it. I don't want you to go to Entremer. I want you to come with me!'

Joy leapt up and did a few backflips—startling all those birds in her stomach into flight again. 'Johnnie Trethwell…are you asking me to *marry* you?'

'What do you think I've been trying to do?' he cried, his voice rife with exasperation. 'And making just as much a hash of it as I did the first time! My famous address seems to desert me when the matter is vital.'

Everything within her wanted to throw herself at him, shouting 'yes', but this was so important—her very life's heart depended on it—she had to know he was asking her for the right reasons. Not just because he'd decided he'd like a companion on his travels and the passion they shared was incomparable.

'Do you remember my answer the first time you asked?'

'Well, first you slapped me.'

She smiled. 'I'll omit the physical assault this time.'

He smiled back. 'I'd appreciate that. But if you are asking if I remember your conditions, I do. I've discovered a declaration must contain much more than a simple request that you do me the honour of granting me your hand. I know now that I must promise you my loyalty, devotion and love.'

Her heart beat faster. 'And you can now offer that?'

'I can, and so much more. I admit, I hadn't really much considered how I felt about you until today, when I suddenly faced the prospect of never seeing you again. The thought was...unbearable. So in the course of admittedly very few hours, I've come to realise that, not only do I love you, I cannot tolerate the thought of living without you. Yes, I still wish to travel and have adventures, but they will be so much more satisfying and meaningful, if I can share them with you. Will you let me?'

'Oh, Johnnie,' she whispered, almost not able to speak, so full was her heart.

'Don't give me your answer yet!' he said hastily. 'It's true that I have never wanted anything but to travel and explore. But...but if you think you can't bear leaving England, I think... I know I can give that up, to stay here with you. Thanks to Aunt Pen, I already have the funds necessary to begin my venture, enough to hire agents to carry out the explorations I meant to undertake myself. Enough funds to purchase some property here in England, where we could breed the horses you love, if that would make you happy. I just know that *I* won't be happy, wherever I am...unless you are with me.'

'You would give up adventuring for me?'

'I will. You mean that much to me, *chahna*.'

'Oh, Johnnie,' she whispered again and this time she did fling herself into his arms. 'Of course I will marry you! I've wanted nothing but you for ages!'

'Ages? Until a few days ago, you wanted Lord Halden.'

'That was before I knew his true intentions. But I'm so glad he turned out to be just a fortune hunter! Had he actually been set on entering the clergy, I might never have listened to my heart and discovered what I truly want. The man who led me to discover who I truly *am*. Who loves and values me as I am. Splashing in fountains, insulting dowagers...and sharing passion in a grove ten yards from the Lansdown Road.'

Naturally, after such a declaration, he had to kiss her. When they both stopped to breathe, she said, 'You don't need to give up your life for me. I... I admit, travelling beyond England was always Temper's dream, not mine. I used to think all I wanted was respectability, a home in the English countryside. But the stories you've told have awakened me to how wide, varied and wonderful the world is beyond the borders of our land. I would be thrilled to explore more of it with you.'

His molten gaze sizzled. 'You truly would? It would mean becoming worse than scandalous, you know. In the eyes of many, you'd be nothing more than the wife of a *tradesman*.'

She shook her head. 'I prefer adventurer.'

'I don't care what you call me, as long as we're together.'

'Which is exactly what I want.'

He leaned down to kiss her again. She met him eagerly, revelling in the taste and touch of him, the dance of tongue with tongue. Oh, how she wanted more of him, everything!

Johnnie pushed her away, making her whimper in protest until she heard what he must have—a deep masculine voice clearing its throat loudly. Looking up, she saw Soames standing on the threshold, the tea tray in his hands, smiling at them, before he quickly hid the smile behind his normal impassive countenance.

'Should I assume congratulations are in order?'

'You should!' Johnnie said, laughing. 'Miss Lattimar has just done me the honour of agreeing to become my wife.'

'Excellent! Shall I try to speed up Lady Stoneway and fetch some champagne?'

'Please do,' Pru said—waiting only until the butler had withdrawn before seizing Johnnie by the neck for another deep, passionate kiss.

'So no breeding of horses,' she said a few minutes later. 'What about the raising of children?'

'I think I can promise to follow through on that part,' he assured her, nuzzling her nose.

'Excellent. Might I have an advance on the child-making part…during our ride tomorrow?'

'Certainly not,' he said with mock-seriousness. 'No more trysts, until after we're wed. Besides, I must go to London to secure your father's permission and he might well refuse me.'

'First, I'm of age, so we can wed regardless. Second, he'll be so happy to see me married, he would probably have accepted the loathsome Lord Halden. So don't fear to lose my dowry.'

'We don't need it. Aunt Pen was generous.'

'We can leave it for the children, then. And get some practice at getting them…tomorrow? After all, I have so much more to learn.'

'I shall love teaching you. *After* the wedding,' he said primly.

Pru sighed with exasperation. 'For a former rake and adventurer, you've turned shockingly moral.'

'It must be your previous persona rubbing off on me. But, *chahna*, when I make you completely mine, I want to have a bed and soft sheets and all the time in the world to love you. Not have to worry over some horse's whinny giving us away and being discovered *in flagrante delicto* beside the Lansdown Road.'

'I shall have to wait, I suppose,' she said regretfully, though that disappointment hardly cast a shadow over the radiance of the happiness filling her. 'Although it might be thrilling to be discovered by the Lansdown Road.'

Laughing, he kissed her forehead. 'Hussy! I think I've loved you since that day in Sidney Gardens. So, you will go adventuring far from home with me, my love?

'With all my heart. Home is where you are—wherever in the world that might be.'

Smiling tenderly, he kissed her nose. 'Then we shall be home, together, my love.'

Throwing her arms around his neck, she laughed, so filled with joy, hope and exuberance she felt she might float off the ground. 'We may end up becoming more infamous than Mama!'

* * * * *

If you enjoyed this story
be sure to check out
the Hadley's Hellions miniseries
by Julia Justiss

Forbidden Night with the Viscount
Stolen Encounters with the Duchess
Convenient Proposal to the Lady
Secret Lessons with the Rake

And look for the next book in the
Sisters of Scandal duet,
coming soon!

COMING NEXT MONTH FROM

⊕ HARLEQUIN®

ℋISTORICAL

Available October 16, 2018

All available in print and ebook via Reader Service and online

CONVENIENT CHRISTMAS BRIDES (Regency)
by Carla Kelly, Louise Allen and Laurie Benson
Delve into three convenient Regency arrangements with a captain, a viscount and a lord, all in one festive volume.

A TEXAS CHRISTMAS REUNION (Western)
by Carol Arens
Bad boy Trea Culverson returns, bringing excitement back into widow Juliette Lindor's life. With the town against him, can Juliette show them *and* Trea that love is as powerful as any Christmas gift?

A HEALER FOR THE HIGHLANDER (Medieval)
A Highland Feuding • by Terri Brisbin
Famed healer Anna Mackenzie is moved by Davidh of Clan Cameron's request to help his ailing son. But Anna has a secret that could jeopardize the growing heated passion between them...

A LORD FOR THE WALLFLOWER WIDOW (Regency)
The Widows of Westram • by Ann Lethbridge
When widow Lady Carrie musters the courage to request that charming gadabout Lord Avery Gilmore show her the wifely pleasures she's never had, he takes the challenge *very* seriously!

BEAUTY AND THE BROODING LORD (Regency)
Saved from Disgrace • by Sarah Mallory
Lord Quinn has sworn off romance, but when he happens upon an innocent lady being assaulted, he marries her to protect her reputation. Quinn must help Serena fight her demons, and defeat his own...

THE VISCOUNT'S RUNAWAY WIFE (Regency)
by Laura Martin
After many years, Lord Oliver Sedgewick finally finds his runaway wife, Lucy. The spark between them burns more intensely than ever, but does their marriage have a chance of a happy future?

HOME on the RANCH

YES! Please send me the **Home on the Ranch Collection** in Larger Print. This collection begins with 3 FREE books and 2 FREE gifts in the first shipment. Along with my 3 free books, I'll also get the next 4 books from the Home on the Ranch Collection, in LARGER PRINT, which I may either return and owe nothing, or keep for the low price of $5.24 U.S./ $5.89 CDN each plus $2.99 for shipping and handling per shipment*. If I decide to continue, about once a month for 8 months I will get 6 or 7 more books, but will only need to pay for 4. That means 2 or 3 books in every shipment will be FREE! If I decide to keep the entire collection, I'll have paid for only 32 books because 19 books are FREE! I understand that accepting the 3 free books and gifts places me under no obligation to buy anything. I can always return a shipment and cancel at any time. My free books and gifts are mine to keep no matter what I decide.

268 HCN 3760 468 HCN 3760

Name _____ (PLEASE PRINT) _____

Address _____ Apt. # _____

City _____ State/Prov. _____ Zip/Postal Code _____

Signature (if under 18, a parent or guardian must sign)

Mail to the **Reader Service:**
IN U.S.A.: P.O. Box 1341, Buffalo, New York 14240-8531
IN CANADA: P.O. Box 603, Fort Erie, Ontario L2A 5X3

Get 4 **FREE REWARDS!**

We'll send you 2 FREE Books
plus 2 FREE Mystery Gifts.

SPECIAL EDITION

A Kiss, a Dance & a Diamond

Helen Lacey

SPECIAL EDITION

Her Man on Three Rivers Ranch

Stella Bagwell

Harlequin® Special Edition
books feature heroines
finding the balance
between their work life
and personal life on the
way to finding true love.

FREE
Value Over
$20

YES! Please send me 2 FREE Harlequin® Special Edition novels and my 2 FREE gifts (gifts are worth about $10 retail). After receiving them, if I don't wish to receive any more books, I can return the shipping statement marked "cancel." If I don't cancel, I will receive 6 brand-new novels every month and be billed just $4.99 per book in the U.S. or $5.74 per book in Canada. That's a savings of at least 12% off the cover price! It's quite a bargain! Shipping and handling is just 50¢ per book in the U.S. and 75¢ per book in Canada*. I understand that accepting the 2 free books and gifts places me under no obligation to buy anything. I can always return a shipment and cancel at any time. The free books and gifts are mine to keep no matter what I decide.

235/335 HDN GMY2

Name (please print)

Address   Apt. #

City   State/Province   Zip/Postal Code

> Mail to the **Reader Service:**
> **IN U.S.A.:** P.O. Box 1341, Buffalo, NY 14240-8531
> **IN CANADA:** P.O. Box 603, Fort Erie, Ontario L2A 5X3

Want to try two free books from another series? Call 1-800-873-8635 or visit www.ReaderService.com.

Get 4 FREE REWARDS!

We'll send you 2 FREE Books <u>plus</u> 2 FREE Mystery Gifts.

Presents.
USA TODAY BESTSELLING AUTHOR
Dani Collins
Consequence of His Revenge

Presents.
USA TODAY BESTSELLING AUTHOR
Melanie Milburne
Blackmailed into the Marriage Bed!

Harlequin Presents® books feature a sensational and sophisticated world of international romance where sinfully tempting heroes ignite passion.

FREE
Value Over
$20

YES! Please send me 2 FREE Harlequin Presents® novels and my 2 FREE gifts (gifts are worth about $10 retail). After receiving them, if I don't wish to receive any more books, I can return the shipping statement marked "cancel." If I don't cancel, I will receive 6 brand-new novels every month and be billed just $4.55 each for the regular-print edition or $5.55 each for the larger-print edition in the U.S., or $5.49 each for the regular-print edition or $5.99 each for the larger-print edition in Canada. That's a savings of at least 11% off the cover price! It's quite a bargain! Shipping and handling is just 50¢ per book in the U.S. and 75¢ per book in Canada*. I understand that accepting the 2 free books and gifts places me under no obligation to buy anything. I can always return a shipment and cancel at any time. The free books and gifts are mine to keep no matter what I decide.

Choose one: ☐ **Harlequin Presents®**
Regular-Print
(106/306 HDN GMYX)

☐ **Harlequin Presents®**
Larger-Print
(176/376 HDN GMYX)

Name (please print)

Address   Apt. #

City   State/Province   Zip/Postal Code

Mail to the **Reader Service:**
IN U.S.A.: P.O. Box 1341, Buffalo, NY 14240-8531
IN CANADA: P.O. Box 603, Fort Erie, Ontario L2A 5X3

Want to try two free books from another series? Call 1-800-873-8635 or visit www.ReaderService.com.

Get 4 FREE REWARDS!

We'll send you 2 FREE Books
plus 2 FREE Mystery Gifts.

Harlequin® Desire books feature heroes who have it all: wealth, status, incredible good looks... everything but the right woman.

FREE
Value Over
$20

YES! Please send me 2 FREE Harlequin® Desire novels and my 2 FREE gifts (gifts are worth about $10 retail). After receiving them, if I don't wish to receive any more books, I can return the shipping statement marked "cancel." If I don't cancel, I will receive 6 brand-new novels every month and be billed just $4.55 per book in the U.S. or $5.24 per book in Canada. That's a savings of at least 13% off the cover price! It's quite a bargain! Shipping and handling is just 50¢ per book in the U.S. and 75¢ per book in Canada*. I understand that accepting the 2 free books and gifts places me under no obligation to buy anything. I can always return a shipment and cancel at any time. The free books and gifts are mine to keep no matter what I decide.

225/326 HDN GMYU

Name (please print)

Address   Apt. #

City   State/Province   Zip/Postal Code

Mail to the **Reader Service:**
IN U.S.A.: P.O. Box 1341, Buffalo, NY 14240-8531
IN CANADA: P.O. Box 603, Fort Erie, Ontario L2A 5X3

Want to try two free books from another series! Call 1-800-873-8635 or visit www.ReaderService.com.

---

*Terms and prices subject to change without notice. Prices do not include applicable taxes. Sales tax applicable in N.Y. Canadian residents will be charged applicable taxes. Offer not valid in Quebec. This offer is limited to one order per household. Books received may not be as shown. Not valid for current subscribers to Harlequin Desire books. All orders subject to approval. Credit or debit balances in a customer's account(s) may be offset by any other outstanding balance owed by or to the customer. Please allow 4 to 6 weeks for delivery. Offer available while quantities last.

Your Privacy—The Reader Service is committed to protecting your privacy. Our Privacy Policy is available online at www.ReaderService.com or upon request from the Reader Service. We make a portion of our mailing list available to reputable third parties that offer products we believe may interest you. If you prefer that we not exchange your name with third parties, or if you wish to clarify or modify your communication preferences, please visit us at www.ReaderService.com/consumerschoice or write to us at Reader Service Preference Service, P.O. Box 9062, Buffalo, NY 14240-9062. Include your complete name and address.

HDI8